LADY COURTNEY'S SECOND CHANCE

THE SEASON OF SECRETS
BOOK 3

BRONWEN EVANS

Dragonblade Publishing, Inc. is an imprint of Kathryn Le Veque Novels, Inc.
P.O. Box 23
Moreno Valley, CA 92556
ceo@dragonbladepublishing.com

Produced in the United States of America

First Edition January 2026
Trade Paperback Edition

ARE YOU SIGNED UP FOR DRAGONBLADE'S BLOG?

You'll get the latest news and information on exclusive giveaways, exclusive excerpts, coming releases, sales, free books, cover reveals and more.

Check out our complete list of authors, too!

No spam, no junk. That's a promise!

Sign Up Here

www.dragonbladepublishing.com

Dearest Reader;

Thank you for your support of a small press. At Dragonblade Publishing, we strive to bring you the highest quality Historical Romance from some of the best authors in the business. Without your support, there is no 'us', so we sincerely hope you adore these stories and find some new favorite authors along the way.

Happy Reading!

CEO, Dragonblade Publishing

ADDITIONAL DRAGONBLADE BOOKS BY AUTHOR BRONWEN EVANS

The Season of Secrets
Miss Tiffany Has A Secret (Book 1)
Lady Farah Creates a Scandal (Book 2)
Lady Courtney's Second Chance (Book 3)

PROLOGUE

LORD ROCKWELL WARE sat in the leather-worn carriage, hoping this wasn't a wasted trip. He was traveling to a small village called Malahide outside of Dublin, Ireland, in very temperamental weather. He glanced at his companion and prayed the weather would hold. He closed his eyes and memories of a previous trip filled his thoughts, when he'd sat in a dingy tavern in Dublin a few weeks ago, sure he was seeing a ghost.

The man had been seated in shadows, his back to the room, but something about the set of his shoulders, the angle of his head as he bent over his ale, had sent ice through Rockwell's veins. When the stranger had turned slightly, offering a profile view, Rockwell had nearly choked on his drink. The beard was fuller, the face more weathered, and a vicious scar ran from forehead to cheek, but those features…

Lucien.

His best friend since childhood. His brother in all but blood. The man who had vanished into the chaos of the Irish Rebellion five years ago and never returned. The man they had buried in an empty grave at Danvers Parish Church while his father, the Earl of Danvers, had wept, and his sisters had worn widow's weeds for their lost brother.

He shook the images away. He'd arrived in Ireland again a few days ago to look for the man he'd seen in that tavern on his previous visit. He had to know if it had been Lucien and if his friend was alive. He'd made good progress. After a few days in

Ireland, he'd managed to learn from a market trader and brothel madam, the name of a man who could be Lucien.

"Aye, that'd be John Collins. Lives up near Malahide. Good man, John. Keeps to himself mostly, but he's helped many a neighbor with their crops."

John Collins. The name had tasted like ash in Rockwell's mouth.

And so here he was, in a carriage driving toward Malahide with Lady Farah Perrin at his side—another impossible complication in his increasingly complicated life. She had been injured while hiding in his trunk, and she'd found herself shanghaied on his ship bound for Ireland to find Lucien, another long story.

On top of looking for a friend everyone thought was dead, he now had to contend with figuring out how he would sneak Lady Farah back into London without anyone being aware of her absence. Otherwise, she'd be completely compromised, and he'd find himself married to her. Currently, Farah was pretending to be his sister, Ashley.

Unfortunately, Farah was as invested in this mad journey as he was. Perhaps more so, given her tender heart and romantic notions about lost loves and second chances.

"There," Farah said softly, pointing toward a collection of cottages. "That must be Malahide."

Rockwell squinted against the sun, making out the cluster of whitewashed cottages that dotted the coastline like scattered shells. Somewhere among them lived the man who might be Lucien, Viscount Furoe, and heir to an earldom, living as a simple Irish farmer named John Collins.

The impossibility of it all struck him anew. How could Lucien—brilliant, educated, aristocratic Lucien—have survived all this time in such circumstances? How could he have simply vanished from his former life without a trace? And why had he never returned home or even let anyone know he was alive? Why John Collins? It just couldn't be him. Could it?

"What if we're wrong?" Farah asked, as if reading his

thoughts. "What if this John Collins is simply a man who resembles your friend?"

"Then we will have taken a very tedious journey and risked your reputation for nothing," Rockwell replied, though his gut told him otherwise. That glimpse in the tavern, brief as it had been, had ignited a certainty in him that defied logic. "But I don't think we're wrong."

As their carriage approached the village store, Rockwell's mind raced through the implications. If Lucien was indeed alive, what had happened to him? Why had he stayed in Ireland, living under an assumed name? And what of his family—his father and sisters who had mourned him these five years? What of Lady Courtney, who had worn black for a full year and still, four years later, remained unmarried, claiming no man could compare to her lost love?

The questions multiplied with each shuddering wheel turn, but Rockwell forced himself to focus on the immediate task. First, they had to find this John Collins. Then they had to determine if he was truly Lucien. Only then could they begin to unravel the mystery of what had happened during those missing years.

The village was quiet in the early afternoon, with only a few fishing boats preparing for work on the shoreline. Rockwell helped Farah from the carriage and then stood for a moment, taking in the peaceful scene. It was so different from the London they had left behind—the frantic pace, the constant noise, the weight of social obligation that pressed down on every interaction. Here, the air smelled of salt and seaweed and growing things. Gulls cried overhead, and somewhere in the distance, he could hear the lowing of cattle.

If Lucien had indeed been living here for five years, Rockwell could understand why he might have found contentment. There was something deeply appealing about the simplicity of it all, the connection to land and sea that was absent from their London lives.

"Where do we begin?" Farah asked, adjusting her simple

traveling cloak. They had both dressed as plainly as possible, hoping to blend in among the locals rather than announce themselves as English nobility.

Rockwell, scanning the coastline, replied, "We'll start walking and ask as we go."

"Let's split up. I'll find the vicarage. Surely the local vicar will know everyone."

"Good idea. I'll ask in the village."

Unfortunately, his clothes could not hide his accent and he got very little information from the suspicious and anti-English villagers. So he made his way up the hill toward the graveyard and vicarage to meet Farah. He pushed open the rusty gate and began to walk through the gravestones when he heard Farah talking. As he rounded the corner he saw her—and then—oh, my God—Lucien.

The next minute, Rockwell found himself barreling toward his friend. But Farah caught him, pulling hard on his coat and pulling him away from Lucien. "He doesn't know who you are, let alone who he is. He's got amnesia."

Rockwell stumbled backward, shock and then relief on his face.

"Lucien," Rockwell breathed.

As if hearing his name spoken, the man straightened and looked him in the eye. Rockwell's knees nearly gave way. The beard was fuller than it had been in the tavern, and that scar was even more prominent in the daylight—a jagged reminder of whatever violence had befallen him. But the eyes, the shape of the face, the way he held himself...

There was no doubt. This was Lucien, Viscount Furoe, lost heir to the Earl of Danvers. Alive.

Before Rockwell could speak, a small figure pulled on his coat—a little girl with dark curls bouncing as she moved. She launched herself at Lucien's legs, and he swept her up with the ease of long practice, his face transforming with a smile that was achingly familiar.

"Daid!" The child's voice carried on the morning air. "Look what I found!"

She held up something small in her hand—a shell or perhaps a pretty stone—and the man examined it with the grave attention that such treasures deserved. The domestic scene was so peaceful, so complete, that Rockwell hesitated. What right did he have to shatter this contentment? What right did any of them have to drag Lucien back to a world he no longer remembered, to duties he couldn't recall accepting?

But then he thought of the Earl of Danvers, and the family that was about to lose everything. The earl already thought he'd lost his heir. He thought of Lauren and Madeline, who still wore lockets with their brother's miniature. Of Lady Courtney, who had turned down three proposals in the past year alone because no man could measure up to her lost love.

And he thought of Lucien himself—the brilliant, passionate man who had once argued politics until dawn and written poetry by candlelight. Who had been destined for great things, who had responsibilities and a legacy that stretched back generations. Did that man not deserve the chance to choose his own fate, rather than having it chosen for him by circumstance?

"Daid, this is my new friend, Farah. But I don't know this man," the little girl said, pointing at them.

The man—John, Lucien, whoever he was now—looked at him and Rockwell saw only polite curiosity there. No recognition. No spark of memory. This man looked at his oldest friend and saw a stranger.

"Stay calm," Farah whispered. "We must be careful not to shock him."

Rockwell could see the changes five years had wrought. Lucien's hands were callused from farm work, his skin weathered by sun and sea air. He moved with the easy confidence of a man comfortable in his skin, but there was something watchful in his eyes, the wariness of someone who had learned not to trust too easily.

"I don't know him either," Lucien said, his accent purely Irish now, with no trace of the cultured English tones Rockwell remembered. "Who are you?"

Rockwell watched the girl cradled in Lucien's arms. The child was undeniably Lucien's daughter—she had his dark hair, his intelligent eyes, even his stubborn chin. But her manner of speaking, her accent, spoke of an upbringing far different from the formal education a viscount's daughter would have received.

Farah recovered first. "I'm here in Malahide looking for someone."

"Oh, you're English," Lucien said, shifting the little girl to the side. "I'm John Collins. This is my daughter, Ava-Marie."

John Collins. The name felt like a knife twist in Rockwell's chest. His friend, his brother, reduced to this fiction. Who had done this to him? How had Lucien become this humble farmer with no memory of his past?

"Yes, she introduced herself to me," Farah said, and Rockwell could hear the strain in her voice as she struggled to maintain the pretense. "Have you always lived here in Malahide?"

A frown crossed Lucien's face, and he touched his scar unconsciously. "No. I think I lived in England before coming home, because I got injured in France, I believe. Or so my wife used to tell me. I can't remember anything from before five years ago. A head wound took my memories."

France. Rockwell nearly laughed at the bitter irony. Someone had told Lucien he'd been wounded in France, probably to explain his injuries and his presence in Ireland. But Lucien had never fought in France—he had been in Ireland, fighting in the rebellion that had nearly torn the country apart.

Someone had lied to him. Someone had taken advantage of his injured state and stolen his entire identity.

The rage that filled Rockwell was so intense it nearly overwhelmed him. His friend—brilliant, trusting Lucien—had been deceived in the cruelest possible way. Robbed not just of his memories but of his very self, his family, his future. Someone had committed a theft so profound, it beggared belief.

"Mr. Collins," Farah said carefully, "this is my friend, Lord Rockwell Ware, and he has been looking for you for a long time. He's simply overjoyed at finding you. Is there somewhere we could go talk?"

Lucien looked between them, confusion and wariness warring in his expression. "Looking for me? But how could you be looking for me when you don't even know me?"

The simple logic of the question was heartbreaking. How could they explain that they were looking for someone he used to be? Someone he couldn't remember being?

"Perhaps we could sit down," Rockwell said, finding his voice at last. "What we have to tell you… It will be difficult to believe."

The truth, Rockwell reflected grimly, was indeed more complicated than any lie. But he'd found his friend and now he was determined to take him home, ensure he took his place in society and with his family, and help him restore the Danvers good name and finances.

CHAPTER ONE

LUCIEN FUROE STARED up at the imposing façade of Danvers House, his throat tight with an emotion he couldn't name. The grand Georgian mansion loomed before him, its weathered stone and tall windows holding no hint of familiarity. According to Lord Rockwell Ware, who stood beside him radiating quiet concern, this had been his home for the first three and twenty years of his life. He was now eight and twenty and had not stepped foot in this house for the past five years.

Home. The word felt hollow, meaningless. His home was a modest cottage in Malahide, Ireland, with worn wooden floors and a leaky roof that had driven him mad every spring. But that home, like so much else in his life, had proven to be built on lies.

"Are you ready?" Lord Wolfarth—Wolf, as he preferred— asked from his other side. Both brothers had become unexpected allies, though Lucien was still working out their motives for bringing him back to England. Rockwell professed it was because they were best friends in his past life, and that this family needed him because his father had gambled away the family's finances, to the point that they were looking at debtors' prison.

Rockwell cleared his throat again. "Are you ready?"

"As I'll ever be." Lucien straightened his cravat, a nervous gesture he'd developed since donning these foreign gentleman's clothes. The fine wool coat felt confining after years of simple linen shirts and sturdy working clothes. But he was a viscount now, or so they told him. Viscount Furoe, heir to the Earl of

Danvers.

The grand entrance door swung open before they could knock, and an elderly butler appeared, his eyes widening at the sight of Lucien.

"My lord," the man whispered, his lined face paling. "It cannot be…"

"Hello, Phillips," Rockwell said smoothly. "Might we come in? We have news for the family."

Phillips stepped back, his rheumy eyes never leaving Lucien's face. "Of course, my lord. The family is at home. I shall announce—"

"No need," Wolf cut in. "Better we handle this…delicately."

Lucien followed them into a vast entrance hall that stretched up two stories, dominated by a sweeping marble staircase. Strong June sunlight filtered through tall windows, catching on gilt-framed portraits and crystal chandeliers. The faded opulence made his head spin. This was supposedly his birthright, yet he felt like an imposter in a play he hadn't rehearsed.

A soft gasp drew his attention to the staircase. A young woman stood frozen on the stairs, her knuckles white against the banister. She was perhaps twenty years of age, with dark hair like his own and eyes the color of storm clouds.

"Lucien, you're alive!" she breathed, and the naked hope in her voice made his chest ache. "Where have you been?" She came tearing down the stairs and threw herself into his arms.

The impact of her embrace sent shock through his system. His body went rigid, every muscle tensing as unfamiliar arms wrapped around him with desperate familiarity. She hugged him hard and long as her tears fell, yet he could only stand frozen, his own arms hanging uselessly at his sides.

As she hugged him, he felt helpless in her grief. "How could you stay away?"

He wanted to respond, to say something—anything—but his throat had closed. This woman—this stranger—was crying tears of joy over him, and he felt nothing but the hollow ache of absence where recognition should have been. The guilt was immediate and crushing.

She stepped away, and he saw her face crumple as she took in his stiff posture, his vacant expression. Her joy flickered and died like a candle in wind.

"Lucien?" The uncertainty in her voice was worse than her tears.

He turned toward her, searching her features desperately for any spark of recognition. The shape of her nose, the curve of her mouth, even the way she tilted her head—it all seemed significant, like a language he should understand but couldn't read. He recognized his features but not her. Nothing. Just as with the house, the gardens, the butler—she was a stranger wearing the face of family.

Wolf said quietly, "Your brother has no memories of who he is or who you are. He received a head injury in the Irish Rebellion and cannot remember anything from before that day. He has been living in Ireland, believing his name to be Mr. John Collins."

Lucien was surprised that this sister didn't crumple to the ground. Isn't that what ladies of quality did when faced with dreadful news?

She looked at him closely. "I'm just so thankful you're not dead. Father… He'll be, he'll be so *relieved.*"

"Lady Lauren," Rockwell said gently, "might I present Lord Lucien, Viscount Furoe." The formal introduction hung awkward in the air between them. "Lucien, this is your sister, Lady Lauren Cavanaugh."

"My sister." He tested the words, finding them strange on his tongue. He executed the bow he vaguely remembered from a dark recessed area of his brain, and Rockwell had also refreshed the social graces he wasn't quite sure of. "My lady."

Lauren's grey eyes swam with unshed tears; her face paled with barely contained emotions. She was dressed in a morning dress of soft blue muslin that spoke of better times. He could see patches on the sleeve. Behind him, Wolf shifted restlessly, and

Lucien caught the significant look that passed between him and Lauren. There was history there, he realized. Yet another story he should know but didn't.

"Welcome home," Lauren said, her voice trembling slightly. "Madeline will be beside herself. She's at a friend's house, but I think it would be best if I spoke to her first. It will be quite a shock. And as for Father—"

"Another sister?" The information Rockwell and Wolf had given him on the journey tumbled through his mind. Everything was so new, and he struggled to keep it all in order.

"Yes." Lauren swallowed hard. "Your younger sister. She was twelve when you…when you died—that is when you left."

Left. Such a gentle word for whatever violence had stolen his memories and sent him stumbling, half-dead, into a new life in Ireland. Into Ava's life.

Ava. His chest tightened at the thought of her. Beautiful, mercurial Ava who had nursed him back to health, who had spun pretty lies about a marriage that had never happened, who had given him their daughter—

No. He couldn't think about Ava-Marie now. His little girl was safe at Rockwell's London townhouse with her cousin Caitria, and no one here need ever know the truth of her birth. The story Rockwell and Lady Farah crafted on the journey back was simple enough: a hasty marriage to a local Irish girl, now deceased. It was close enough to the truth to sit easy on his conscience, and it protected his daughter's future.

Now it also protected his sisters and family name.

Lauren stood wringing her hands. "Is nothing familiar? Would you…would you like to see through the house, or perhaps our mother's portrait?"

He didn't have the heart to tell her nothing would bring the memories back. But he would humor her, given what a shock this must be. Besides, it put off the main reason for being here—to learn how precarious the family financial situation was. Rockwell had hinted it was very dire, and the shabbiness and lack of servants indicated he was right. Anger at the father he didn't remember grew.

He nodded, following her up the sweeping staircase and into a long gallery lined with stern-faced ancestors he should recognize but didn't. She stopped before a large portrait of a striking woman in her early forties. Dark hair like his own was arranged in elegant curves around a heart-shaped face, and something in her slight smile tugged at the edges of his mind.

"She's lovely," he said softly, meaning it.

"She died two years ago." Lauren's voice cracked. "I wish she could be here to see that her son is alive and the heir is not lost…" She trailed off, watching his face with desperate hope.

The twist of grief in his chest surprised him. He mourned not the mother he couldn't remember, but the fact that he couldn't remember her. That he'd been alive and well in Ireland, working his small piece of land, while this woman died, believing her son lost.

A crash from above made them all start. Heavy footsteps stumbled across the upper floor, and Lauren's face tightened with something like resignation.

"Father," she whispered, just as a man appeared at the top of the stairs.

The Earl of Danvers was a wreck of a man, his clothes fine but rumpled, his face flushed with what could only be strong drink despite the early hour. He swayed slightly as he stared down at their group.

"My boy? Are you a ghost come back to haunt me?" The words came out slurred.

He half-stumbled down the stairs, and Lucien tensed, fighting the urge to step back. The earl reached the bottom and lurched forward; his arms outstretched. This time Lucien did pull back, an instinctive retreat that made the older man's face crumple.

"Of course you are a figment of my imagination. My son is long dead, and I have no heir. God is punishing me… I'm sorry, so sorry." The earl's hands fell to his sides. "Lauren, forgive me…" Then he turned to go back upstairs.

"Father," he said, clearing his throat. "I'm not a ghost. It's me. Lucien."

His father slowly turned and then slid to the floor. "Lucien?"

"Perhaps we should move to your library, Lord Danvers," Rockwell suggested smoothly, stepping forward. "There's much to discuss."

The men helped his father stand but his lordship brushed them away and swayed his way to the Danvers library. Then he collapsed into a worn leather chair, while Lucien remained standing, his body humming with the need to move, to run, to escape back to his simple life in Ireland.

But that life had been built on lies, he reminded himself harshly. Ava's lies. Ava had stolen his true identity, and he was here to claim it back.

The once-grand library of Lord Danvers bore silent witness to the family's declining fortunes. Tall Georgian windows, their paint peeling and wood frames warped, still managed to cast long rectangles of summer light across what remained of the Turkish carpet. The room stretched two stories high, its upper gallery accessed by a curved mahogany staircase.

Empty spaces between books told their own story—precious volumes likely sold off, one by one, to keep the family afloat. The remaining collection stood in uneven rows, their leather bindings dry and cracked, some sprouting tufts of green mold along their spines. A musty sweetness pervaded the air, mingled with the sharp tang of wood rot from the sagging shelves.

The ceiling's ornate plasterwork, once cream and gold, had yellowed to the color of old teeth. Water stains mapped continents across its surface where the roof leaked, though strategically placed copper pails caught the worst of the drips. Their dull surfaces matched the tarnished oil lamps that hadn't been polished in some time.

"Please excuse the…" Lauren stuttered to a halt.

Lucien was beginning to see the extent of the fiasco he'd

come home to. He suddenly understood why, on the journey home from Ireland, Rockwell had urged him to make marriage for a large dowry a priority.

He walked further into the room, his dismay barely able to be hidden. A massive marble fireplace dominated one wall; its mantel cluttered with miniature portraits in gilt frames too precious to sell. The armchairs grouped nearby—once plush crimson velvet—all faded to a tired rose, their stuffing visible through worn patches and frayed seams. Yet he sensed there was still a certain dignity to them.

Near the window stood Lord Danvers' desk, its leather top cracked and dry as autumn leaves. Stacks of unpaid bills and increasing other correspondence weighed down one corner, while a half-empty decanter suggested how his lordship often chose to face them.

A single footman entered to tend the meager fire, carefully rationing the coal and wood. Through the windows, the untended wilderness of what was once a formal garden spoke volumes about the current state of the Danvers town house.

Lucien couldn't bring himself to wonder about the state of their country estate—or was it estates? He didn't even remember. He sank into another chair, staring at the man who was his father. He ignored his sister and his friends.

"The debts," the earl said suddenly, his voice thick with shame. "I thought you dead, boy. Dead like your mother. The cards...the dice...they helped me forget, just for a while."

Lucien's jaw tightened. "How bad?"

"Bad enough to lose it all, if something isn't done soon," Wolf said bluntly, ignoring Rockwell's warning look. "He should know the truth of what he's coming home to."

"We need a moment with Lady Lauren," Rockwell said quietly. "If you'll excuse us?"

They withdrew to the corridor, leaving Lucien alone with his father. The silence stretched between them, heavy with five years of absence.

"Ten thousand pounds," the earl said finally, staring into his empty glass. "At least. The money lenders are circling like vultures. I've mortgaged what I could, but I can't touch the entailed estates. Still, they too are almost ruined…" He looked up, his bloodshot eyes desperate. "I never thought to saddle you with this burden. When you disappeared after the rebellion…when months passed with no word…I lost myself in grief and guilt. If I hadn't picked that stupid argument with you about taking that trip with Rockwell—"

"I don't remember any of it," Lucien cut in, his voice harsher than he'd intended. "Not the rebellion, not my reasons for being there, none of it." He ran a hand through his hair, a gesture that felt familiar though he couldn't say why. "My life began five years ago in a village near Dublin, with a head wound and no memory of who I was."

The earl flinched. "The physicians Lord Rockwell consulted… Do they think your memory might return?"

"I didn't consult with anyone. I don't need to." Lucien moved to stare out the window at the gardens below. This was all so different from his humble vegetable patch in Ireland, where Ava-Marie had toddled after him, helping to plant carrots with her tiny hands. "The man you knew, your son…he is gone forever."

"You're here now," the earl said softly. "That's what matters."

Lucien's laugh held no humor. "Yes, just in time to save the family from ruin, it seems. For you had no concern that your daughters could be thrown on the streets." The bitterness in his voice surprised even him. He turned back to face his father as Lauren and the men returned. He didn't know what they told her, but Lauren's eyes were red-rimmed, even though she managed a tremulous smile.

"Madeline will be home soon. Shall I have Phillips prepare your old rooms?"

The thought of sleeping in a stranger's chambers—even if that stranger was his former self—made his skin crawl. "Thank you. I'll need other rooms prepared too." At Lauren's confused expression, he added, "My daughter and my wife's cousin are to join me."

"Your daughter?" The earl sat up straighter, suddenly more alert than he'd appeared all morning. "You're married?"

"No. My—wife—died two years ago of the lung disease." His father's relief was obvious and at that moment, he hated the man. He was counting on his son marrying well.

Lucien kept his voice carefully neutral. "Lucien's daughter, Ava-Marie, is four." *And illegitimate*, his mind supplied treacherously. But they would never know that. As far as England was concerned, he'd married Ava in a small village church, and their daughter was as legitimate as any peer's child. The lie sat bitter on his tongue, but he would tell it a thousand times to protect his little girl.

"My son returns, and I have a grandchild," the earl breathed, wonder replacing some of the worry in his face. "I never thought… That is, when we believed you dead…"

"She's all I have of her mother," Lucien said quietly, the half-truth easier to speak than the full lie. In truth, Ava-Marie was all he had of his life in Ireland, the only pure thing to come from Ava's deception. "I would appreciate it if we could delay any…formal announcements of my return until she's settled."

"Of course," Lauren said quickly. "Whatever you need." She hesitated, then asked, "Will you at least stay for tea? There's so much to tell you, about the family, about…" She trailed off, biting her lip.

About his life before, he knew she meant. About the man he'd been, the brother she'd lost. About the fiancée no one had mentioned yet, though he knew from Rockwell that she existed. Lady Courtney Montague, the woman he'd supposedly loved enough to pledge his life to, yet couldn't summon even a shadow of memory for.

"Tea would be pleasant," he said finally, because he couldn't bear to disappoint them further. Not when they looked at him with such desperate hope, searching his face for glimpses of a man who might as well be dead.

As Phillips wheeled in the tea cart, Lucien caught his reflection in a gilt-framed mirror. A stranger stared back at him, wrapped in fine wool and starched linen, playing at being a viscount. Somewhere in Ireland, a humble farmer called John Collins had died, leaving only this hollow shell of a lord in his place.

He accepted a cup of tea from Lauren, noting how her hands trembled slightly as she passed it to him. His sister. The word still felt foreign, though something in her grey eyes tugged at him, like a half-remembered dream. Perhaps that was a start.

He leaned forward and spoke about the elephant in the room. "I had a fiancée, I believe. She is still unmarried?" When Lauren looked swiftly between Rockwell and Wolf, he added, "Tell me about her."

Lauren's smile was like the sun breaking through clouds. As she began to speak, Lucien settled back in his chair, letting her words wash over him. He couldn't be the brother she remembered, but perhaps he could become someone new, someone worthy of the hope in her eyes. Someone who could protect his daughter's future and save his family from ruin, even if he never remembered being part of it.

But that may rely on another woman he could not remember—Lady Courtney. He dreaded meeting her. He'd have to see if Lauren had any etchings of her.

But it was a beginning, of sorts. Easing back into society would have to be enough for now.

CHAPTER TWO

L UCIEN STOOD IN Lord Lorne's drawing room waiting to meet the Marquess's daughter, Lady Courtney—a woman he'd once been engaged to. The urge to tug at his cravat was overpowering. The emerald silk had been Lauren's choice. "You always favored green," she'd said with that tremulous hope he'd grown to dread. He'd worn it to please her, though the color felt wrong somehow. In Ireland, he'd favored simple linen in earthen tones, clothes that wouldn't show the dirt from working his land or make him stand out at the local pub.

The opulent room made him acutely aware of the vast gulf between his old life and his new reality. Where his father's house showed the shabby remnants of former glory, Lord Lorne's drawing room fairly gleamed with wealth. Gilt-framed mirrors reflected the afternoon light, multiplying the sparkle of the crystal chandelier. The Turkish carpet beneath his boots—he'd had to buy new boots, his old ones were deemed too rough for London society—was thick and unworn, its colors still vibrant. Fresh flowers scented the air from delicate porcelain vases; unlike the wildflowers Ava would gather for their rough wooden table in Ireland.

He wandered to the fireplace, noting the fine marble mantelpiece with its elegant ormolu clock. No copper pots caught drips here, no water stains marred the elaborate ceiling roses. Even the furniture spoke of careful maintenance—the silk damask upholstery pristine, the mahogany tables gleaming with fresh polish. This was the world he'd apparently been born to, yet he felt more out of place here than he ever had in his humble cottage.

What would the lady of this house make of his rough manners? Despite Rockwell's careful coaching, he knew he still moved more like a farmer than a viscount. His hands, though clean and newly manicured, still bore the calluses of manual labor. Would Lady Courtney recoil from those hands? Would she see past the fine clothes to the country bumpkin beneath?

The sound of approaching footsteps made him stiffen. He'd insisted on coming alone, despite Rockwell's protests. This meeting needed to happen without an audience, without the weight of everyone's expectations pressing down on him. He squared his shoulders, trying to project a confidence he didn't feel. Time to see if his former fiancée could stomach the rough-hewn man who'd replaced her cultured viscount.

The door opened.

A massive grey blur shot past Lady Courtney's skirts before she could catch the leather collar, and Lucien found himself nearly knocked backward by an enthusiastic mass of shaggy fur. A towering Irish wolfhound, greying around the muzzle but still strong enough to plant both paws on his chest, whined joyfully in his face. The dog's tail wagged with such force, its entire body shook, and it tried desperately to nuzzle his chin, its rough coat brushing against his face.

"Freya, down!" Lady Courtney's voice cracked with emotion. "I'm so sorry, she's usually better behaved, it's just—" She broke off, pressing trembling fingers to her lips. "You gave her to me, the day we became engaged. She…she remembers you."

Lucien steadied himself, gently lowering the dog's paws to the ground. The creature immediately pressed against his legs, whining softly, tail still wagging. He felt a strange tightness in his chest as he looked down at the hopeful brown eyes gazing up at him. Another piece of his past he couldn't recall, another relationship severed by his memory loss.

He turned his attention to the hound's owner. Lady Courtney Montague was exactly as described, yet nothing like he'd imagined. Tall and willowy, she seemed to float into the room, her auburn-rich hair arranged in elaborate curls that caught the afternoon light streaming through the windows. She moved with the innate grace of the aristocracy he still struggled to emulate, each step measured and precise, though he noticed her fingers trembling slightly at her sides. Her face held a delicate beauty that spoke of good breeding and gentle living—so different from the sun-weathered features he'd grown used to in Ireland.

But it was her eyes that caught and held him: a striking amber brown, like whiskey held up to candlelight, and filled with such naked longing that he had to force himself not to look away. Those eyes went wide at the sight of him, and for a moment, her careful composure cracked. He saw the flash of joy, quickly followed by uncertainty, and beneath it all, a grief so profound it made his chest ache in response.

"Lucien," she breathed, and the raw emotion in that single word made him want to flee. "Forgive me, I mean Lord Furoe." Instead, he executed a perfect bow, just as Rockwell had coached him.

"Lady Courtney." The formal address seemed to pain her. She took an instinctive step forward, then caught herself, smoothing trembling hands over her pale blue muslin skirts.

"They told me you were alive, but I…" She trailed off, studying his face with an intensity that made him want to turn away. "You truly don't remember me?"

"I remember nothing before waking in Ireland." The words came out harsh and it piled the guilt on. He softened his tone. "I'm sorry."

"It's not your fault." A flash of something—grief, perhaps, or pity—crossed her face before she mastered it. "Please, sit. Would you care for tea?" Freya curled up on the floor at Courtney's feet.

The social niceties felt surreal. Here he sat, taking tea with the woman he'd supposedly loved enough to pledge his life to, and he felt nothing but discomfort and a gnawing sense of guilt.

"How are you finding your return to London?" Courtney's voice was soft as she poured the tea with practiced grace. "It must be…overwhelming."

Lucien accepted the delicate porcelain cup, acutely aware of his calloused hands against the fine China. "Everything is strange," he admitted. "Like walking through someone else's life."

"Your family must be overjoyed to have you home. As am I." She paused, then added more gently, "Lauren talks with me often. She's my very good friend. Her support after you were believed killed…. We consoled each other. She's been…worried about your father and the family financials."

"The situation at home is far from ideal." The bitterness in his voice spilled out like the tea drops over the rim of his cup, no matter how he tried he couldn't contain it. He took a sip of tea to cover his discomfort.

"I know it cannot be easy," Courtney said, her amber eyes studying him with unexpected understanding. "To return to a life you don't remember, to responsibilities you never asked for." She set her cup down with a faint clink. "If there's anything I can do to help—with society, with…anything—you need only ask."

Including marrying me? He wanted to ask but feared her reply. What if she said yes? What if she said no?

The genuine warmth of her offer caught him off guard. He'd expected reproach, or at least the awkward pressure of expectations, not this quiet compassion. "That's…very kind."

"We were friends long before we were anything else, Lucien." A shadow crossed her face. "At least, I believe we were. I hope we might be again."

He nodded, not trusting himself to speak. The woman before him showed the same desperate hope he'd seen in his sister's eyes, and the barely concealed disappointment in his father's. But she offered simple acceptance of who he was now. She hadn't raised the subject of their previous engagement. Perhaps she no longer wanted him. How arrogant he was to think she'd simply welcome him back. A stranger. A shell of his former self.

"Your sister tells me you have a daughter." Her voice remained carefully controlled, though he caught the flush rising on her neck as she refreshed his tea.

"Yes. Ava-Marie." His throat tightened at thoughts of his little girl, who was currently exploring her new home with wide-eyed wonder. "She's four."

"Named for her mother?" The question held no judgment, but Lucien tensed anyway.

"Yes." He set the untouched tea aside. "Lady Courtney, I should apologize—"

"For falling in love with another while you had no memory of me? For building a life without me?" She shook her head, a sad smile playing at her lips. "You were dead, Lucien. For five years, I mourned you. I visited your empty grave. I wrote you letters I could never send."

The mention of letters made him sit straighter. "Letters?"

"Yes, I still have all of yours. Perhaps somewhere in your study are my letters too." She rose and crossed to a small escritoire, withdrawing a ribbon-bound bundle. "Perhaps...perhaps they might help? They span our entire courtship, from when we first met at Lady Ashworth's ball to..." She swallowed hard. "To the week you disappeared."

Lucien stared at the packet she held out. His own words, written in a hand he no longer recognized, chronicling a love he couldn't remember. The thought made his head spin.

"I can't accept these." But even as he spoke, his hand reached for them.

"They're yours," she said simply. "As much a part of your past as your house, this life." She hesitated, then added softly, "As I was."

He studied her properly then, trying to see what his past self had loved about her. She was beautiful, certainly, in that refined way of the *ton*. So different from Ava's wild beauty, with her untamed copper curls and fierce green eyes. Where Ava had been all passion and impulse, Lady Courtney radiated quiet strength and careful control.

She said they'd been friends first. Perhaps his previous self had grown to love her, for while she was an attractive lady, verging on beautiful even, he felt no spark, no fire in his belly to have her. Not like his reaction to Lady Farah. When Lady Farah had found him in Ireland and told him the truth about who he was, she'd been like a safety beacon calling him home. And the guilt returned, making his stomach clench.

"I'm not him anymore," he said finally. "The man who wrote these letters...he died in Ireland."

"I know." Her voice caught. "But you're still Lord Lucien Furoe. Still the man who taught my brother to fish, who argued philosophy with my father, who danced with me at Almack's and made me laugh even when I was trying to be proper. Still the man I gave my heart to." She smoothed her skirts again, a nervous gesture. "I don't expect you to love me. I don't even expect you to like me. But I would very much like the chance to know who you are now."

The simple honesty of her words struck him. No demands, no expectations of recovered memories or rekindled love. Just an offer of...friendship? Understanding? He wasn't sure.

"I should warn you," he said, fingering the ribbon-bound letters, "I'm not very good company these days."

"Neither am I." That sad smile again. "Five years of mourning dulls one's social graces."

Despite himself, Lucien felt his lips twitch in response. "Then perhaps we can be poor company together."

Her eyes lit with something that might have been hope. "I'd like that." She smiled. "Please tell me about Ireland," Courtney said softly, her hands clasped tightly in her lap. "Were you...were you happy there?"

Lucien studied her face, searching for any hint of the connection they'd supposedly shared. She was beautiful, with an elegant grace that spoke of her aristocratic upbringing.

"I was content," he said carefully. "We had a small cottage near the sea in Malahide. I worked the land, grew vegetables, raised some sheep. It was a simple life but satisfying."

"And your wife?" The word seemed to catch in her throat.

"Ava." He looked away, memories of her deception churning in his gut, though he kept his voice steady. "She nursed me back to health after my injury. We married in the local church." The lie came easier now, practiced. "She was kind, made me feel safe when I had nothing—no memories, no past, not even my own name."

"It must have been very different from the life you'd known here," Courtney observed, her voice free of judgment.

"So I'm told. I cannot remember what my life here was like, so I could hardly miss it," he replied with a slight smile. "Though apparently, I took well to farming. The local grain merchant said I had a natural gift for it."

"Your mother was Irish," Courtney offered. "You used to spend summers at your grandmother's estate in County Cork. You loved it there."

The information hit him like a physical blow. Another piece of himself he couldn't remember. "That explains why the language came so naturally to me, even with no memories."

"What about your daughter? Will you tell me about her?"

His face softened genuinely. "Ava-Marie. She's four now, full of life and mischief. She has my coloring but her mother's spirit." He smiled fondly. "She loved to play hide and seek in the village graveyard of all places."

"It must have been difficult, losing her mother so young."

"Thankfully we have Caitria, Ava's cousin. She's been like a second mother to Ava-Marie since Ava fell ill." He studied Courtney's face. "I know this must be…difficult for you to hear."

"No more difficult than it is for you to have to tell me, I imagine," she replied with surprising gentleness. "To come back to a life you don't remember."

"I don't know who I am anymore," he admitted. "Lord Furoe feels like a costume I'm wearing."

"Perhaps," Courtney suggested softly, "you don't have to be who you were. Perhaps you can be someone new. Or a mix of old and new. Someone who builds a future rather than trying to recapture the past."

Their eyes met, and for a moment Lucien glimpsed what his past self might have seen in her. Not just her beauty, but compassion, wisdom and understanding.

Courtney watched Lucien as he spoke, her heart aching at the familiar yet foreign way he moved, the ghost of remembered gestures haunting his unfamiliar mannerisms. He still looked like her Lucien except for the scar down the side of his face. Still so handsome, it was a struggle to breathe.

The way he ran his hand through his hair when troubled, that was pure Lucien. But the careful way he held himself, the slight Irish lilt that crept into his speech when he talked about his life in Malahide, his guarded smile—those belonged to a stranger. The old Lucien was full of life and spirit. This Lucien was battered and bruised. His eyes held no mischievous sparkle.

It had taken all of a few seconds upon walking into the room, for her to realize the Lucien she had loved and pined for was gone and he was never coming back. This Lucien, this stranger, was not the love of her life.

But still her heart clenched with longing. A familiar looking stranger, that made her want to pull him into her arms and kiss him senseless. She wanted to feel that it truly was him. But she couldn't.

Because he didn't remember her. The pain in her chest would not ease.

She'd once been his heart's desire. He couldn't keep his hands off her. Always finding ways to sneak a kiss and when they'd shared their secret night together… Her fingers rose to trace her lips, but she caught his raised eyebrow.

She wanted to ask so many questions. Did he still love poetry? Did he still argue philosophy with the same passion that had first drawn her to him at Lady Ashworth's ball? Did he still have that deep laugh that used to make her heart skip? But those questions would only highlight what he'd lost, remind him of a man he couldn't remember being.

Instead, she found herself asking about his farm, his life in Ireland. She watched his face light up when he spoke of his daughter, and there…there was the tenderness she remembered, the capacity for deep love that had made her fall for him all those years ago.

"You always wanted children," she found herself saying, then immediately regretted it when his expression shuttered.

"Did I?" He shifted uncomfortably. "I'm sorry, I don't…"

"No, I'm sorry," she said quickly. "I shouldn't make comparisons. It's not fair to either of us."

But it was hard not to. Hard not to notice how his eyes still crinkled at the corners when he smiled, even if the smile itself was different, more reserved, weighted with experiences she knew nothing about. Hard not to hear echoes of his old wit in his occasional dry observations.

He was like a familiar painting viewed through rippled glass. The basic shapes were there, but everything was subtly distorted, changed. The aristocratic education and manners were camouflaged, perhaps mixed with a farmer's practical wisdom. The carefree young lord who'd stolen her heart had been transformed by amnesia and hard work into someone both more and less than he'd been.

Yet there was something compelling about this new version of him. She could see why the Irish woman—Ava—had loved him. Even without his memories or title, he radiated a quiet strength, an innate nobility that had nothing to do with his birth.

And he was so extraordinarily handsome, other men paled in comparison.

That was why, all those years ago, she'd been so surprised when he'd singled her out for his attention. She wasn't a great beauty, not like Valora or even Farah. She'd thought it was too good to be true, but he'd courted her and made her love him and then he'd gone to war… At the time, she'd not understood it would be dangerous. Lucien told her he was going to ensure fighting didn't break out. He believed the Irish fighters would talk with him, given that he was Irish on his grandmother's side and he could speak the language.

When she learned he'd been killed, she had been so angry at him, but the anger dissolved and turned to profound grief when she realized she'd never see him again. Never have his strong arms around her. Never know a love that filled her soul.

She was just alone.

Now he was back with no memory of her. Would she be as lucky a second time around? She also wasn't a young debutante anymore. She was four and twenty.

"Will you tell me about our engagement?" he asked suddenly, startling her from her thoughts. "Rockwell mentioned it, but…"

She hesitated. How could she explain their courtship without making him feel guilty for not remembering? How could she describe their love without making him feel pressured to recapture something that might be lost forever?

"We were friends first," she said finally. "That was the foundation of everything. We could talk for hours about books, art, music. You made me laugh. You challenged me to think differently about things. You didn't try to shelter me, as if women could not possibly be equal to men." She smiled at the memory. "You courted me for nearly a year before proposing. The letters will tell you more." She looked out the window at the sunny day, but the room still felt gray. "We were so in love." She turned to look at him. "I'm not saying that to hurt or raise expectations, but to explain why this is very difficult for me. I have never really gotten over you and now here you are, alive. But you're not the man I fell in love with. And I know what Lauren and Rockwell are hoping for, that I'm to be your savior."

"I feel the same. We have that in common." His voice was gentle. "What *do* you want from me now?"

The question hung between them, heavy with implications. Courtney met his gaze squarely, seeing both the man she'd lost and the stranger he'd become.

"I want to know you," she said honestly. "Not the man you were, but the man you are. If you'll let me."

Something flickered in his eye, relief, perhaps, or gratitude. "I think I'd like that," he said softly. "To be friends again. To see if..."

He didn't finish the thought, but he didn't need to. They both knew there could be no promises, no guarantees. Only the possibility of something new growing from the ashes of what was lost. She had to remind herself that he might need her more than she needed him.

To start at the beginning would have to be enough.

But she was also conscious that Lucien didn't have much time. The sisterhood investment group was well aware of how precarious the Danvers' finances were. The money Tiffany earned from their investments had been helping Lauren keep the creditors from the door. Lucien needed to marry and marry well.

The afternoon ended far too soon. Freya followed Lucien as he took his leave, and she had to call her back. "We'll see him again soon, my girl," she said as she stroked her hound's head. Perhaps she should be like Freya and simply accept him for who he was now, not caring what had happened or that he'd been gone for so long.

But people were not dogs. Still, their first meeting gave her hope.

CHAPTER THREE

L ATER THAT DAY, Lucien stood at the window of the drawing room at Danvers House, watching night fall over London. The room felt alien despite everyone's assurances that he'd spent his youth here. Like everything else since returning from Ireland, it was a constant reminder of what Ava's deception had cost him.

Ava had been working as a prostitute in a high-class brothel and had found him injured in the streets of Dublin. She'd taken him in and, learning he had amnesia, told him he was her husband, and he had believed her. He'd had no reason not to. He spoke Gaelic and was in Ireland. She'd seen a way out of a life she hated and took it. He found it hard to blame her.

She was a great beauty, and he hadn't been able to resist her Irish free spirit. But she'd kept him from his true family and responsibilities. But then he had Ava-Marie.... What if he'd come home five years earlier?

He held one of his love letters to Courtney in his hand.

My dearest Courtney,

I find myself once again at my desk in the midnight hours, unable to sleep for thoughts of you. The moon hangs full outside my window, and I am reminded of that night at Lady Ashworth's ball when we discussed Keats' "Bright Star." You argued that the narrator wished not for immortality, but for the steadfastness to remain forever in a moment of perfect love. I wonder now if you knew even then what was growing between us.

Do you recall how we debated for hours in your father's library about whether pure reason could exist without emotion? You were so passionate in your defense of sentiment, your eyes bright with conviction, while I stubbornly clung to logic. How fitting that you should prove your point so thoroughly by making me fall in love with you, destroying all my carefully constructed rational arguments about marriage and duty.

I went riding today through the northern fields of our estate, where the wildflowers bloom in such profusion. I found myself collecting them as I once saw you do, choosing each blossom with care. Bright cornflowers, blue as your favorite ribbons, delicate Queen Anne's lace like the lace at your wrists, bold poppies red as your lips when you smile. I pressed one of each between the pages of this letter, though I fear they are poor substitutes for your beauty.

Father continues to press me about taking more control of the estate, but all I can think of is how empty my days would feel without being able to discuss issues with you afterward. Your mind challenges me, your wit delights me, and your heart... oh, your heart humbles me with its capacity for both fierce intelligence and tender emotion.

I find myself counting the days until I see you again at the Michaelmas ball. Will you save me the first waltz? And perhaps we might slip away to the library afterward to continue our discussion about Voltaire? Though I confess, these days I find myself far more interested in stealing kisses than winning arguments.

Tell me, my love, do you still read poetry in the garden at sunset? Do you still defend Shakespeare's comedies with such charming vehemence? Do you still believe, as you once told me, that true love must be built on friendship first? Because if so, then surely what we have must be the truest love of all.

I send this letter with a thousand wishes—that it finds you well, that it brings a smile to your lovely face, that it carries to you even a fraction of the love that fills my heart. Until we meet again, I remain

Forever yours,
Lucien

P.S. I realize I have filled this entire letter with questions and not left you room to answer. How like me, you would say, to monopolize the conversation! Write back and tell me everything! Your thoughts, your days, your dreams. Each word from you is precious to me.

His hands clenched into fists at his sides, crumbling the note. Five years. Ava had stolen five years of his life with her lies. Five years that could have changed everything. But then he'd experienced love. He'd loved Ava with all his heart, only to learn that she'd stolen another love from him.

And now he couldn't remember her.

The door creaked open, and Caitria slipped in. "Ava-Marie is finally asleep. She keeps asking when we can go home."

Home. That humble cottage in Malahide that had never really been his. Another of Ava's carefully constructed lies.

"She's had a lot of change. Is she thinking Lord Wolfarth's house is home or is it Ireland? I wonder if she knows. Thank you, Caitria." He turned to face her, noting the shadows under her eyes. "You should rest too. It's been a long journey."

She hesitated. "Are you well? You seem…troubled."

A harsh laugh escaped him. "Troubled? I suppose that's one word for it." He ran a hand through his hair, pacing the length of the room. "Do you know what I learned today? Five years ago, when Ava found me, my father still had most of the family fortune intact. The estate was prosperous. My sisters had their Seasons to look forward to. And I was engaged to marry a woman who apparently loved me enough to remain faithful to my memory all these years."

"My lord…" Caitria began, but he cut her off with a sharp gesture.

"If Ava had told me the truth, if she'd helped me find my way home instead of spinning her web of lies, everything would be different. I would still have helped her escape that life she hated and never wanted. My father might not have lost himself in grief and gambling. My sisters wouldn't be wearing patched gowns and living in a crumbling house. And while I would still not have remembered Lady Courtney…she might have been able to move on, or we could have had the time to learn if…"

He broke off, the weight of possibility crushing his chest. He'd seen Courtney today, beautiful and poised, her eyes full of a love he couldn't remember deserving. What might have grown between them if he'd returned five years ago? Even without his memories, they could have built something new. Instead, she'd spent those years mourning while he played at being a farmer, believing himself married to a woman who'd stolen him like a magpie stealing something shiny.

"Courtney loved me," he said quietly. "In all those letters she shared with me—preserved with such care—I can see how much we loved each other. We could have had a life together, children of our own. Instead…"

"Instead, you have Ava-Marie," Caitria said softly. "Would you trade her? Even now?"

The question hit him like a physical blow. "No," he admitted. "Never. She's the only pure thing to come from all of Ava's lies." He pressed his forehead against the cool glass of the window. "But I'm so angry, Caitria. Every day I discover new consequences of Ava's choices. New ways her deception destroyed lives."

"She loved you," Caitria offered hesitantly. "In her way."

"Did she?" He turned, his voice bitter. "Or did she just see an opportunity? A gentleman with no memory, ready to be molded into the husband she wanted? Even on her deathbed, she didn't tell me the truth. She let me believe…"

A sharp knock interrupted his dark thoughts. Both turned to see Phillips. "Viscount Milburn, my lord," he announced. Courtney's brother, Tarquin, stood in the doorway, his expression grim.

"Forgive the late intrusion," Tarquin said, stepping into the room. "But I thought you should know. Your father was seen entering Crockford's gaming hell an hour ago."

Lucien's chest tightened. After all their discussions today about the family's precarious finances, after all his father's tearful promises to change…

"Excuse me, Caitria," he said tightly. "It seems I have urgent business to attend to."

"Be careful," she warned. "You don't know London anymore."

But he was already striding from the room, the viscount falling into step beside him.

"I'll be with him," Tarquin called over his shoulder.

The unfamiliar weight of his new responsibilities settled around his shoulders like a sodden cloak. This was his life now. Trying to salvage what remained of his family's fortune while a little voice whispered that none of this would be necessary if Ava had simply told him the truth.

"Your father's been like this since your 'death'," Tarquin explained as they descended the stairs. "The grief broke something in him. He gambles to forget, drinks to numb the pain. It's gotten worse since your mother passed."

"And no one thought to stop him?" Lucien demanded.

Tarquin's expression hardened. "Many tried. Your sisters. Your friends. Your father's friends…. But a man determined to destroy himself will usually find a way."

"But I'm home now. He has no excuse, and I won't tolerate this behavior. I'll lock him away if I have to."

They emerged into the cool night air, and Lucien tried to get his strangled emotions under control.

"If only you'd come home sooner. Thank God Rockwell found you when he did," Tarquin said as they entered his carriage waiting outside. "That bloody woman… Courtney told me what happened," Tarquin was referring to Ava and her lies, and while his heart had loved her, he could not defend her actions to Tarquin.

"I loved her," he said suddenly, surprising himself. "Even knowing what she did, I still love her. We built a life together, raised our daughter…" He broke off, the familiar guilt twisting in his gut at perpetuating Ava's lie about Ava-Marie's legitimacy. They could find no record of his marriage to Ava. She'd told him they were married when in fact they never were.

"She helped you when you were alone. I'm not surprised you loved her. She was all you had. But now?" Tarquin asked quietly.

"Now I don't know if any of it was real. Did she truly love me, or was that just another manipulation? Did she die knowing she'd succeeded in keeping me from my real life? Or did she regret it at the end?"

Lucien caught a glimpse of his reflection in the carriage window. A stranger stared back at him, caught between two lives— the simple farmer he'd been and the lord he was supposed to be.

"I should have been here," he said as the carriage lurched into motion. "Five years ago, I should have been here to stop all this."

"You can't change the past," Tarquin replied. "You can only decide what to do with the present."

Lucien nodded grimly. First, he would drag his father from the gaming hell before he could lose what little remained of their fortune. Then…then he would have to figure out how to be Lord Furoe, how to save his family from ruin, how to build a future from the wreckage of his past.

A future he could stomach. A future he wanted. He deserved to be happy. He just didn't know how to make that happen.

And somewhere in all of that, he would have to decide what to do about Lady Courtney. The woman who had loved him enough to wait five years, only to have a stranger return, wearing her fiancé's face. The woman who might have been his wife, might have borne his children, might have shared his life if not for Ava's selfish choice. He couldn't ask her to honor their engagement because his marriage to Ava would have voided it. And he certainly didn't want anyone to know he was never married. Only Rockwell and Farah knew that secret. That would make

Ava-Marie illegitimate and could destroy any chance of her making a good marriage later.

He glanced at Courtney's older brother. What were his thoughts on his sister marrying a man returned from the dead? A man who needed her money more than he needed her.

It was now obvious Lucien had run out of time to find a wealthy wife. Could he marry Courtney? He'd loved her once. And Lauren let slip that she had apparently turned down offers of marriage.

The carriage clattered through London's darkened streets, carrying him toward the first of many battles to come. But as the city passed in a blur outside the window, Lucien couldn't help wondering what his life might have been if Rockwell had never found him. Would he have remained a happy man? Would he have been satisfied living a simple Irish peasant life?

The questions haunted him, even as he knew they were pointless. He couldn't change the past. He could only try to salvage what remained, to build something new from the ashes of what was lost.

But oh, how the weight of those lost years pressed down on him. And oh, how the anger burned—at Ava, at himself, at the cruel twist of fate that had stolen his memories and allowed her deception to succeed.

The carriage drew to a stop outside Crockford's, and Lucien straightened his shoulders. Time to be the son and heir his father needed, even if he couldn't remember being either.

Some lies, he was learning, had consequences that echoed far beyond the grave.

He was conscious of Tarquin by his side as they made their way into the seedy club. He was trusting a man he couldn't remember but he knew the man had his best interests at heart. How a man like Tarquin knew this sort of club was a story for another day.

The stench of stale spirits, sweat, and desperation hit Lucien as he entered Crockford's. Tarquin's steady presence at his side kept him grounded as they navigated the dimly lit gaming hell. Despite his memory loss, something about the atmosphere felt disturbingly familiar—perhaps his body remembered what his mind could not.

Raucous laughter and the clink of glasses mingled with the rustle of cards and the rolling of dice. Well-dressed gentlemen hunched over gaming tables, their faces transformed by greed or despair. Scantily clad women wove between the tables, offering drinks and themselves, and the forced smiles of the men who'd lost more than they could afford met his gaze.

"There," Tarquin murmured, nodding toward a corner table. "Your father's at cards with Baron Lockwood."

Lucien's jaw clenched at the sight. The Earl of Danvers sat slumped in his chair, his cravat askew and his eyes glazed. Across from him, a man Tarquin had called Baron Lockwood, sat with a shark-like smile which spoke volumes.

"The baron is known for seeking out vulnerable prey—men with more title than sense, men in their cups, desperate enough to bet what they couldn't afford to lose," Tarquin hissed. "It looks like he has your father in his sights."

"How much has he lost?" Lucien asked quietly.

Tarquin's expression darkened. "Difficult to say, but given the stack of vowels beside Lockwood, I'd wager it's significant."

Lucien started forward, but Tarquin caught his arm. "Careful. Lockwood's dangerous when crossed. He has a habit of calling out men who interfere with his…entertainment."

"I don't care if he calls me out," Lucien growled. "I won't let him bleed my family dry."

He approached the table, noting how his father's hands trembled as he reached for his cards. Baron Lockwood looked up, his pale eyes assessing Lucien with predatory interest.

"Well, well. If it isn't the prodigal son, risen from the dead." Lockwood's smile didn't reach his eyes. "Come to join our little game?"

"I've come to collect my father." Lucien kept his voice level, though rage burned in his chest. "This evening's entertainment is over."

The earl looked up, his bloodshot eyes widening. "Lucien? But you're in Ireland… Aren't you in Ireland?"

"No, Father. I'm here now." Lucien placed a hand on his father's shoulder, feeling the slight tremor beneath the fine wool coat. "It's time to go home."

"Can't leave yet," the earl slurred. "Got to win it back… Got to fix what I've done…"

Baron Lockwood's smile widened. "Your father's already five-hundred pounds in my debt tonight. But I'm feeling generous. One more hand—double or nothing. What do you say, Danvers?"

Five-hundred pounds. The sum hit Lucien like a physical blow. Even if they sold every remaining painting, they couldn't cover such a loss.

"The game is over," Lucien said firmly. "My father is in no condition to continue."

"The game ends when I say it ends." Lockwood's voice held a dangerous edge. "Unless you'd care to take his place? I'm told you were quite the card player before your…unfortunate demise."

He couldn't remember if he'd been good in his past but he'd been a very good card player in Dublin. Lucien felt Tarquin tense beside him, ready to intervene if needed. But something in Lockwood's smug expression made his blood boil. This man had been systematically destroying his family while Lucien worked his small farm in Ireland, believing himself a simple widower.

"Very well." Lucien shrugged off Tarquin's protest and took his father's seat. "But we play by my rules."

"And those would be?"

"If I win, you tear up every vowel my father signed tonight. If you win, I'll honor his debt—and add another five-hundred pounds of my own."

Tarquin bent and whispered in his ear, "He's known to cheat. I urge caution."

Lockwood's eyes gleamed. "Bold of you, considering you've

spent the last five years mucking out stables or whatever it is you've been doing in Ireland."

"Do we have a deal?" Lucien kept his voice ice-cold.

"Oh, most definitely." Lockwood gathered the cards, his movements deliberate. "The table is playing Faro. Is that to your taste?" When Lucien nodded, Lockwood merely added, "Faro, then. Your father always favors it. I have no idea why. He has no luck at it."

"Mine will be better." Lucien accepted the cards Lockwood dealt, aware of the crowd gathering to watch. His father had been led to a chair nearby, where Tarquin kept a steadying hand on his shoulder.

As Lucien studied his cards, instinct took over. He had played a lot in Ireland, against men who cheated more than this man. His hands knew how to handle the cards, how to arrange his suits, how to track what had been played. It felt like speaking a language he'd forgotten he knew.

The first few tricks went to Lockwood, who grew more confident with each winning card. But Lucien watched, waited, counting cards with a precision that surprised even him. When he finally played his carefully preserved ace of hearts, Lockwood's smile faltered.

"Perhaps your time in Ireland hasn't entirely dulled your skills," the baron said, his tone less certain.

"Perhaps not." Lucien won the next trick, then the next. "Though I did learn something valuable there—how to recognize when someone is taking advantage of another's weakness."

Lockwood's face darkened. "Careful, Furoe. You're dancing close to an insult."

"No dance at all." Lucien laid down another winning card. "I'm stating plainly that men like you, who prey on others' desperation, disgust me. You're no better than a common thief."

"How dare you—"

"No, how dare you?" Lucien's voice carried across the now-silent room. "You knew my father was in his cups, knew he couldn't think clearly, yet you encouraged him to keep playing. How many other men have you ruined this way? How many families have suffered because you exploit their loved ones' afflictions?"

"If you're trying to provoke me into calling you out—"

"I'm trying to provoke you into showing a shred of human decency." Lucien won another trick. "Though I suspect that's beyond your capabilities."

The final hand came down to a single card. Lucien played his last trump, and Lockwood's face went white.

"Impossible," the baron breathed. "You couldn't have—"

"I believe those vowels are mine." Lucien held out his hand, his expression unyielding.

For a moment, he thought Lockwood might refuse. But the baron's reputation would suffer more damage from denying a gambling debt than from losing to a recently returned peer. With trembling fingers, Lockwood handed over the stack of papers.

Lucien stood, tucking the vowels into his coat pocket. "Trust me, you won't see my father at these tables again." He placed his hands on the table directly across from Lockwood. "But if you do, I advise you to refuse to play against him or there will be consequences."

"Are you barring me from playing with your father?" Lockwood's voice dripped with venom.

"No. I'm informing you that if you ever approach him again—here or anywhere else—I will ensure society knows exactly what kind of man you are. Try finding a wife or open doors within society with that reputation hanging over your head." Lucien's smile was cold. "I may have lost my memories, but I've gained something else: the ability to recognize predators wearing gentlemen's clothes."

He turned to his father, who stared at him with a mixture of shame and awe. "Come, Father. Let's go home."

The earl stumbled to his feet, leaning heavily on Tarquin's arm. As they made their way toward the exit, Lockwood called out, "This isn't over, Furoe."

Lucien didn't bother turning around. "Yes, it is. Because next time, I won't be so gentlemanly in expressing my displeasure."

Outside, the cool night air helped clear his father's head somewhat. The earl sagged against the carriage door; his face lined with misery.

"I'm sorry," he whispered. "So sorry. I thought...if I could just win enough...fix what I've done to our family..."

"Gambling more won't fix anything." Lucien's voice gentled slightly. "The damage is done, Father. Now we must focus on rebuilding."

"How can you even look at me?" The earl's voice cracked. "I've ruined everything. Your sisters' futures, the estate, your mother's legacy..."

"Yes, you have." Lucien helped his father into the carriage, then climbed in after him. "But I'm here now. And I won't let you destroy what little we have left."

Tarquin joined them, signaling the driver to move. As the carriage rolled through London's darkened streets, Lucien studied his father's broken figure. The anger that had sustained him inside Crockford's faded, leaving only a bone-deep weariness.

"Tomorrow," he said quietly, "we will discuss terms. You'll sign over control of all accounts to me. No more gambling, no more drinking yourself into oblivion. If you truly want to honor Mother's memory, you'll help me salvage what remains of our family's legacy. And perhaps a trip to our country estate will help."

The earl nodded miserably. "Whatever you say, my boy. Whatever you say."

Lucien leaned back, the vowels heavy in his pocket. One crisis averted, but how many more awaited? How much damage had been done in those five years while he'd lived his simple life in Ireland? And how much of it could he truly repair?

Tarquin caught his eye and gave a slight nod of approval. At least he had allies in this strange new world he'd been thrust into.

It felt strange to have to rely on Courtney's brother. He would need these strangers in the battles to come.

"Be careful. You made an enemy tonight. Lockwood is a nasty piece of work."

"I had little choice," he replied. As with most things in his life, there was no choice.

As London's grand houses gave way to the familiar stretch leading to Danvers House, Lucien found himself thinking of Courtney. If he married her immediately, this could all go away.

What would she make of this evening's display? Would she recognize anything of the man she'd loved in his cold confrontation with Lockwood? Would Tarquin approve of the match? He had nothing to offer her.

Lucien didn't know. But he was beginning to understand that he couldn't simply step back into his old life. He would have to forge a new path, combining the strength he'd found in Ireland with the responsibilities he'd inherited here.

And perhaps that was the real legacy of Ava's deception—not just what was lost, but what he'd gained. The ability to have experience in two worlds.

Courtney was right. He could build a new life, not like his life before his memory loss, or like his life in Ireland. Some combination of the two.

This time he'd build a world that he wanted. No more lies. No more making compromises. This would be on his terms.

He ran a weary hand over his face.

Damn it to hell. He just didn't know what those terms were.

Lucien ignored his father's loud snores.

"You could marry. I'm sure Courtney would look favorably on a marriage to you. She still loves you."

"And your family would welcome that?"

Tarquin shrugged. "I saw an honorable man I recognized tonight. Courtney could do much worse."

He closed his eyes, ashamed of what his family had become. "I know you mean well, Tarquin. However, I'd prefer to handle my affairs my way." The carriage arrived outside his home. "Thank you for coming to me tonight. I am in your debt." As he was indebted to everyone, it would seem.

As he helped his father inside, a thought sprung up in the back of his mind that Courtney could do much better than him.

And she probably knew it.

CHAPTER FOUR

COURTNEY HAD BARELY finished breaking her fast when a note from Farah arrived. She was inviting her to walk in the park with her and Caitria and Ava-Marie. They would call for her at midday. That was kind of her. Farah had traveled back from Ireland with Ava-Marie and the little girl knew her more than anyone other than Caitria. Farah's presence would help the little girl fit into her new life easier.

"Good morning, dearest," Tarquin said, striding into the breakfast room just as Courtney was finishing her tea. His cravat was slightly askew, and dark circles shadowed his eyes, suggesting he'd had a late night.

"You look exhausted," she observed, gesturing for him to join her. "I didn't hear you come in last night."

"I was with Lucien." He helped himself to coffee, watching his sister's face carefully. "At Crockford's."

Courtney's hand stilled on her teacup. "What happened?"

"His father was gambling again. With Lockwood." Tarquin's lip curled in disgust. "That vulture had already taken the earl for five hundred pounds by the time we arrived."

"Dear God." Courtney set down her cup, her appetite gone. "Was Lucien able to—"

"He won it all back." A hint of admiration crept into Tarquin's voice. "You should have seen him, Court. He's…different from before. Harder somehow. The way he handled Lockwood…" He shook his head. "The old Lucien was all charm and wit. This one has steel in his spine."

"Ireland changed him," Courtney said softly.

"Five years of working the land with his own hands would change any man." Tarquin studied his sister's face. "But there's something compelling about him now. He's lost that aristocratic polish but gained something else. A sort of…raw authenticity. He sees through society's masks more clearly than before."

Courtney's heart squeezed. "Did he seem…happy? When you knew him before, was he truly happy in our world?"

Tarquin considered this. "He played his part well—the charming heir, the devoted son. But looking back, I wonder if he ever felt truly at home in it all. Perhaps that's why he volunteered to go to Ireland—to fight. You never cared for society's superficial games either."

Courtney knew why he'd volunteered. Lucien had felt caught between his Irish and English heritage and had wanted to try and bring an end to the conflict.

"And now?"

"Now he moves through our world like a wolf among lap-dogs—aware of the rules but not bound by them. When he confronted Lockwood…" Tarquin smiled grimly. "He didn't threaten violence or call him out. He simply promised to tell society exactly what kind of man Lockwood is. The farmer's practicality combined with the peer's understanding of reputa-tion. Quite effective."

Courtney absorbed this, trying to reconcile her memories of the polished viscount with this new version her brother de-scribed. "Do you think he can save his family?"

"If anyone can, it's him." Tarquin's expression grew serious. "Court, I know you still love him—"

"Tarquin—"

"Let me finish. I know you love who he was. But this man…he might be better suited to you now than he was before. The old Lucien would never have confronted Lockwood so directly. He would have maneuvered within society's rules. This one…" He smiled slightly. "This one simply cut through the nonsense and called evil by its name. You'd always know where you stand with him."

"That's what I'm afraid of," Courtney murmured. "He might come to ask for my hand but tell me that he's not in love with me. And God help me, I might say yes, because I do still love him."

"Exactly." Tarquin reached across the table to squeeze her hand. "I'm not saying you should rush into anything. But don't dismiss the possibility that this version of him—the one shaped by hard work and simple living—might be a better match for your honest heart than the polished peer ever was."

Courtney felt tears prick her eyes. "I barely know him anymore."

"Then get to know him. As he is now, not as he was." Tarquin's voice gentled. "You've both changed in these five years. Perhaps those changes have brought you closer to who you truly are—and to each other—rather than further apart."

"He's so lost, Tarquin. Struggling to find his place between two worlds."

"Then be his compass, not his anchor to the past." Tarquin stood, pressing a kiss to her forehead. "Just…keep your heart open to the possibility that what you lost might be replaced by something even truer."

He straightened his cravat. "And now I must get some sleep. Being a good brother and keeping an eye on your former fiancé is exhausting work."

Courtney managed a watery laugh. "Thank you, Tarquin. For everything."

"What are brothers for?" He paused at the door. "Oh, and Court? His daughter takes after him. The real him—direct, honest, unbound by society's pretensions. You'll see when you meet her."

"What if she doesn't like me?"

Her brother smiled. "Who could ever not like you?"

With that, he left her alone with her thoughts, and the newly arrived note from Farah that would bring her face to face with the child who, in another life, might have been her own.

Walking up to her bedchamber to fetch her cape and gloves and hat, her nerves jumped like a grasshopper. She was going to meet Lucien's daughter. The daughter she thought she'd have with him.

She almost missed a step; the pain of loss was so great.

As she waited for the carriage to arrive, she pondered her brother's advice. It would be so easy to save Lucien and his family. She'd love to help Lauren and Madeline too, but the past five years had been lonely. She didn't want to be lonely—within, or outside of, a marriage.

She'd tried to fill her empty life with meaningful pursuits. She was patron to a few artists, worked to raise funds for several charities, but she'd made it very clear to society that she wasn't looking to marry. And last month, before she learned Lucien was alive, she'd just made up her mind that to spend the rest of her life alone—as a spinster—wasn't really what she wanted. She'd seen how happy Tiffany and Wolf were. She wanted that someone special too.

And they'd have to be someone special, because she'd have to confess that she wasn't a virgin.

She'd given herself to Lucien, neither of them expecting... She was just thankful no child had eventuated. That wasn't always how she felt. After he'd died, she wished she was carrying his child so she would have something of his.

Even though Lucien wasn't the man she remembered, her heart didn't care. It saw him and wanted him.

She heard the carriage approaching and went out to meet it. She could feel a headache coming on, her shoulders tight as a drawn bow. This meeting with Ava-Marie would tell her if she should consider letting Lucien back into her life. If Ava-Marie hated her, she'd have no choice but to walk away.

The carriage drew to a halt before Courtney's townhouse,

and she could barely hear the horses' hooves above her pounding heartbeat. Through the window, she could make out three figures: Farah's distinctive fair curls, a woman with dark hair who must be Caitria, and between them, a smaller figure with dark hair. Ava-Marie.

Courtney smoothed her skirts, grateful she'd chosen her blue walking dress—the color always helped calm her nerves. As she descended the steps, Farah alighted from the carriage, her warm smile doing little to ease the tension in Courtney's shoulders.

"Dearest Courtney." Farah embraced her, whispering in her ear, "She's absolutely lovely. Just breathe."

Courtney entered the carriage. And Farah introduced her to Caitria and Ava-Marie. Ava-Marie didn't give her a thought, chatting excitedly about the pond and the ducks.

Farah was talking about the trip to the opera tonight and Caitria sat quietly looking her over. She must have liked what she saw, for Caitria gave her a warm smile.

Soon they reached the park. She alighted and helped Farah down.

Caitria emerged next, offering a reassuring squeeze of Courtney's hand before turning to help the little girl down from the carriage. Ava-Marie landed with surprising grace for a child her age, her dark curls bouncing beneath a perfectly tied bonnet. She wore a dress of spring green that brought out the emerald sparks in her eyes—Lucien's eyes.

"Miss Ava-Marie," Farah said warmly, "Say hello to our guest. This is Lady Courtney Montague, a dear friend of ours."

The girl attempted a wobbly curtsy, then immediately tugged at her bonnet strings. "Do I have to wear this?"

"All the ladies do, so I'd say yes," Courtney said with a giggle.

"Papa says you're his friend and you're Lady Farah's friend too."

Courtney's breath caught. "Did he?" She managed to keep her voice steady, though her pulse thundered in her ears.

"Uh-huh." Ava-Marie nodded vigorously, making her curls

bounce. "He said you knew him from before. Long time ago."

"I did," Courtney murmured, unable to look away from this living reminder of what might have been. "Shall we walk? We might see some pretty flowers in the park."

"Can I pick some?" Ava-Marie asked eagerly, already starting to skip ahead before Caitria gently caught her hand.

"We'll see, dear," Farah said. "First, let's walk nicely together."

As they made their way through the park, Courtney found herself hanging back slightly, watching as Ava-Marie skipped between Farah and Caitria, occasionally tugging at their hands to hurry them along. Her movements were quick and restless, like a sparrow's, but there was something in her direct gaze that was purely Lucien.

As promised, they made their way to the Serpentine and spent some time helping Ava-Marie feed the ducks. Another little girl, Tessa, joined her at the water's edge, and they played and laughed.

When it was time to leave, Ava-Marie said out loud, "Tessa said I talked funny. She said she'd love to learn to talk like me." Courtney shared a worried look with Farah. But the little girl wasn't upset. She simply said, "I told her it was because I was born in Ireland."

"England is very different to Ireland, isn't it?" Caitria asked the child.

Ava-Marie nodded and smiled and waved at Tessa as she continued her walk with her nanny.

"It's all right to miss your old home," Courtney said softly.

"I miss my pony!" Ava-Marie declared. "And my kitty. Papa says we can't have a kitty here yet." She turned to Courtney suddenly. "Do you have a kitty?"

"No," Courtney said softly, memories washing over her of Lucien teasing her about her preference for dogs. "But I have an Irish Wolf Hound named Freya. You're welcome to come and play with her."

"What color is she? I love dogs too!" Ava-Marie's whole face lit up. "Papa says we might get a dog when—" She stopped abruptly, putting both hands over her mouth. "Oops. That's a secret."

Courtney couldn't help but smile at the child's poor attempt at discretion. The words 'when they could afford one' was probably going to come out of her mouth. They came to Cherry Tree Row, where spring had painted everything in soft pastels. Cherry blossoms drifted on the breeze like snow, and Ava-Marie gasped in delight.

"Look! Look! It's snowing flowers!" She spun in circles, trying to catch the petals, all attempts at proper behavior forgotten. "Lady Farah, why is it snowing flowers?"

"Those are cherry blossoms," Farah explained. "They fall from the trees in springtime."

"Can I keep them?" Ava-Marie was already gathering fallen petals in her small hands.

"They won't stay fresh for long," Caitria warned gently.

"But they're pretty now!" Ava-Marie insisted, then thrust her handful of petals toward Courtney. "Here! These are for you."

And just like that, she lost her heart to another Furoe.

Courtney accepted the slightly crushed blossoms, her throat tight. "Thank you, dear."

They walked on, Ava-Marie darting between them to collect more petals, occasionally stopping to point at dogs being walked or birds in the trees. Her chatter was constant but endearingly scattered, jumping from topic to topic with a child's lack of connection.

"It's nice in the sun, but I miss the nighttime and stars. My mama is a star, and I can see her every night. Papa reads me stories about stars," she announced suddenly, falling into step beside Courtney. "But he says he forgets some. Do you know stories?"

"I do," Courtney said carefully. "Would you like to hear one?"

"Yes! Is there a princess? I like princesses."

"Well, there was a queen named Cassiopeia—"

"Was she pretty? Did she have a crown?" Ava-Marie interrupted, twirling in place.

"She was very beautiful," Courtney began, but Ava-Marie's attention had already shifted to a butterfly fluttering past.

"Look! It's yellow! Papa showed me a yellow butterfly in Ireland. But it flew away." Her face fell slightly. "Everything in Ireland flew away."

The simple statement, delivered with a child's innocent sadness, struck Courtney's heart. She knelt down to Ava-Marie's level. "Sometimes things have to fly away for a little while. But that doesn't mean they're gone forever."

Ava-Marie considered her words, her small face serious. "Like Papa came back to London?"

"Yes, exactly like that."

The girl nodded, then suddenly threw her arms around Courtney's neck in an impulsive hug that smelled of cherry blossoms and sugar treats. "I like you. You're nice. And pretty."

Courtney hugged her back carefully, feeling tears prick at her eyes. Over Ava-Marie's shoulder, she saw Farah and Caitria tactfully looking away.

"Can we have tea sometime?" Ava-Marie asked as she pulled back. "Papa's teaching me how to draw but I'm not very good. The horses are my favorite 'cause they look funny."

"I would like that very much, if your papa agrees."

Courtney's heart stuttered at the mention of drawing, remembering the special picture she'd drawn for Lucien, of Lucien. It had been after their special night just before he'd left for Ireland. He was bare chested, with his lower half covered by a blanket. She wondered where he hid it. Had Lauren found it if they cleared out his room? She hadn't mentioned it.

"He will agree!" Ava-Marie said with a child's certainty. "He loves drawing and teaching me. He gave me his watercolor set that he found in his room."

The revelation that his family had kept her engagement gift to him left Courtney speechless. Before she could respond, Farah was calling that it was time to go.

"Just five more minutes?" Ava-Marie pleaded, but she was clearly tiring, her earlier boundless energy flagging.

"We should head back," Caitria said, noticing Ava-Marie's flagging energy. "It's nearly time for your afternoon rest, dear."

"Just five more minutes?" Ava-Marie pleaded, but a yawn betrayed her.

The walk back to the carriage was quieter, Ava-Marie's earlier exuberance softening into sleepy contentment. She held Farah's hand with her right and Courtney's with her left, occasionally swinging between them.

In the carriage, she curled up against Caitria's side, her eyes heavy. "Will you tell me more stories next time?" she asked Courtney drowsily. "About the stars and the pretty queen?"

"Of course," Courtney promised, watching as the child drifted off to sleep.

"She's absolutely taken with you," Caitria observed quietly.

"Courtney has that effect on people," Farah said, her fond smile holding years of friendship. "She's always seen straight to their hearts."

Courtney sighed. "She's going to face a formidable future. The daughter of an earl but with a common Irish farmer as a mother. There will be many in society who will scorn her pedigree." She thought it odd that Farah's face paled, and Caitria looked alarmed. "Is there more to this story?"

Farah recovered the quickest. "You're right. But I'm sure her accent will disappear over time, and Lucien would only let her marry a man who did not care about her past."

Courtney nodded. "Plus, she'll have all of us to look out for her."

They dropped Caitria and Ava-Marie at their home first, then continued on to Courtney's townhouse. As the carriage drew to a halt, Farah reached across to squeeze her friend's hand.

"Are you all right?" she asked softly.

"No," Courtney admitted. "But I think perhaps I might be, someday." She touched the crushed cherry blossoms in her lap, these simple tokens of a child's affection. "She's so much like him, Farah."

"She has his likeness and kindness," her friend observed quietly. "Did you see how she tried to share everything she found? The flowers, the stories, her excitement about drawing? I remember that Lucien was like that."

Courtney nodded, unable to speak past the lump in her throat. The afternoon's warmth was fading, but something else was warming her from within—not quite hope, not yet, but perhaps the possibility of it. Like a star emerging from behind storm clouds, distant but bright with promise.

She thought of Tarquin's words from this morning. *Be his compass, not his anchor to the past.* Looking down at her glove, where Ava-Marie's crushed cherry blossoms left traces of pink, Courtney wondered if perhaps she could be both—a bridge between who they had been and who they might become.

"He's collecting me for the opera tonight. Will you be there?"

Farah replied, "Rockwell is hosting us all in his box."

She caught the choke in her friend's voice. "Do you love Rockwell?" Courtney asked Farah. "What happened between you in Ireland? And don't tell me you're just friends. You're unhappy. Did he—did he do something?"

"Other than make me fall in love with him and then make it clear that even if he married me, he'd sail away?" Then Farah burst into tears. Courtney hugged her and let her sob.

"Aren't we a pair."

Farah sat up and wiped her eyes. "That's unfair. He didn't make me do anything. I let myself fall in love with him. And now I don't know what to do. I'm lying to everyone about being sick. If my brother found out I'd been in Ireland with Rockwell... He'd have me marching down the aisle next to him before I could blink."

"Would that be so bad?"

"Would you march down the aisle with Lucien?"

"Touche. Not this Lucien. Not yet anyway."

"And I wouldn't with Rockwell, either. He'd marry me and then sail the world." They both laughed, but the laughter died as the groom came to open the door for her.

Farah took both of her hands in hers. "Lucien is a good man. Give him a chance. You could make him happy. And he deserves that. You could help him heal and find contentment—and love."

She nodded. "I had already decided that, once I'd met Ava-Marie. I had to be sure she would accept me." The groom helped her alight. She leaned in the window and said to Farah, "but you forget one thing." At Farah's raised eyebrow she added, "Lucien has to want me."

Farah had nothing to say to that. In fact, she looked a tad guilty.

"I'll see you tonight." Then Courtney made her way inside, confusion and hope warring in equal measures. She ran up to her bedchamber, calling for her maid. Tonight, she would ensure she looked as good as she possibly could.

She wanted to attract Lucien's attention. She wanted the chance to see if he could love her again.

As she lay in the bath, one thought raced through her brain. She could simply tell him. She knew that as a gentleman, if he learned he'd taken her innocence he would do the right thing. She chewed on her bottom lip. Should she tell him?

Not until she was sure she wanted him.

CHAPTER FIVE

LUCIEN'S CARRIAGE PULLED up to Courtney's townhouse, his fingers drumming restlessly against his thigh. The constant, unspoken hope that something, anything, would trigger his memories was almost driving him insane. He took a deep breath, straightened his cravat, and descended from the carriage.

The butler recognized him immediately, of course. Everyone seemed to treat him as if he were sick and helpless, and many couldn't understand why he just couldn't remember. They all seemed to have expectations of his memories suddenly returning like a lost cat. "Lady Courtney will be down shortly, my lord," the man said with a bow that felt unnatural.

Lucien waited in the familiar-yet-strange drawing room, surrounded by paintings and furnishings that should mean something to him but didn't. His eyes caught on a portrait of himself with Courtney—younger, happier, his arm wrapped possessively around her waist. The man in the painting was a stranger wearing his face. That hadn't been on the wall when he was here yesterday. It was as if Courtney had put it there to help him remember.

But he wouldn't.

The churning in his gut started as guilt cloaked him again.

The soft rustle of silk announced her arrival. Lucien turned, and for a moment, his breath caught in his throat. Courtney stood at the top of the stairs, resplendent in a gown of deep burgundy that made her pale skin glow. Her dark hair was elegantly arranged, adorned with matching garnets that caught the candlelight. He'd been wrong. She was, without question, a beautiful woman.

Something stirred in his chest. Not a memory, exactly, but a ghost of feeling, an echo of what the man in that portrait must have felt. His body seemed to recognize her even if his mind didn't, responding to her presence with an inexplicable pull.

He waited until she descended and stood before him. "You look stunning," he said, and meant it. But even as the words left his mouth, he felt the weight of her hopeful gaze, saw the way she searched his face for any sign of recognition.

"Thank you," she replied softly, her smile genuine but tinged with that ever-present sadness. "You look very handsome yourself."

He offered his arm, and as they walked to the carriage, he found himself thinking of Farah. The thought brought both relief and guilt. While Courtney's every look and gesture seemed laden with five years of shared history he couldn't remember, Farah's presence was refreshingly uncomplicated. She had known him before, yes, but him losing his memory held no consequences for her. She saw him only as he was now, lost, confused, trying to piece together a life he couldn't recall.

As he handed Courtney into the carriage, he caught another whiff of her perfume, rose and something else, presumably a scent he had once known well. It should mean something to him. The man in that portrait would have known exactly what it was, would have bought it for her perhaps. But he wasn't that man anymore.

They settled into the carriage, and Lucien found himself looking forward to reaching the opera, because Farah would be there. With her, he didn't have to pretend or try to remember. She accepted him as he was, never pushing or hoping for miraculous recollections. She understood what it was to be adrift, to be trying to find one's place in a world that had already assigned you a role you weren't sure you could play.

"It is nice of Lord Rockwell to help welcome you back into society," Courtney ventured, her tone carefully casual.

"Yes. Lady Farah has been attentive too. Then again, she is also friends with my sisters," he replied, perhaps too quickly. "She's been very kind, helping me adjust."

He saw the flash of pain in Courtney's eyes and hated himself for causing it. This beautiful woman beside him deserved better than an ex-fiancé who couldn't remember loving her, who found himself increasingly drawn to another woman simply because she didn't carry the weight of their shared past.

As they approached the opera, he resolved to try harder with Courtney tonight. She deserved that much at least. But he couldn't quite suppress the leap of anticipation in his chest at the thought of seeing Farah. She was familiar. She'd found him in Ireland and her compassion was one of the reasons he'd decided to come back to England. Farah knew all his secrets and still accepted him and Ava-Marie. Just as he knew hers—that she'd been traveling unescorted in Ireland with Lord Rockwell. If that came out, she'd be ruined.

She was the safe option. Daughter of a duke, with a large dowry. If he didn't think Farah was in love with Rockwell, she'd be the sensible choice. But if she did love Rockwell, why did she not want to marry him?

Lucien had even made Farah a promise on the return to England. If society learned of her scandalous trip to Ireland with Rockwell to find him, and she really didn't want to marry Rockwell, he would offer for her to save her reputation. So, until Farah and Rockwell's situation was sorted, he himself was trapped. He couldn't offer for another until he knew he wouldn't have to save Farah.

Looking at Courtney's profile in the flickering light of the passing streetlamps, he wondered if it was possible to fall in love with the same woman twice, and what it meant that his head seemed to be pulling him in two different directions.

COURTNEY SAT LIKE a statue in the Wolfarth box at the Royal Opera House, every muscle tense as she watched Lucien as he sat beside her. The familiar curve of his neck, the way his dark hair curled slightly at the collar... It was all achingly familiar and yet belonged to a stranger. The candlelight caught the gilt edges of the box, casting dancing shadows that matched her tumultuous thoughts.

"Can you remember attending the opera?" Wolf's gentle question broke through her reverie. She winced, knowing what would come next.

"I wish everyone would stop asking me if I remember anything. Because I don't," Lucien snapped, his harsh tone making Courtney's heart constrict. The silence that followed felt like a physical weight. When he sighed and offered his apology, she managed to smile at him, though her chest ached with the effort of holding back tears.

Wolf's kind response about living in hope only seemed to agitate Lucien further. "I suggest everyone forgo the idea of a miraculous remembrance. I can't and won't remember."

The words struck Courtney like physical blows. She blinked rapidly, fighting back tears as she felt Farah's sympathetic gaze. Drawing on every ounce of her strength, she placed her hand on Lucien's arm, trying to bridge the vast distance between them with that simple touch. She took the victory when he didn't shake it off.

The opera began, but Courtney barely registered the music. Instead, she found herself watching Lucien, noting every shift in his posture, every subtle movement. Her stomach twisted as she noticed his gaze repeatedly drifting to Farah. The way he leaned forward slightly when she spoke, the intensity in his eyes when he looked at her—it was painfully familiar. He used to look at her that way, before...

When Lucien leaned forward to whisper to Farah during Madame Butterfly's aria, Courtney thought she might shatter. His warm murmur about beauty, clearly meant for Farah's ears, drove Courtney to action. She couldn't sit there anymore, watching the man she loved shower attention on her dearest friend.

"Farah," she called out as soon as the intermission began, her voice unnaturally bright even to her own ears. "Would you accompany me to the ladies' retiring room?"

In the privacy of the retiring room, Courtney's carefully maintained composure crumbled. The questions poured out of her about Lucien, about Farah, about what she was supposed to do with this man who wore her fiancé's face but looked at her like a stranger. Each word felt like glass in her throat, but she had to know.

Farah's fierce loyalty and honest answers both comforted and wounded her. Yes, Lucien might be developing feelings for Farah. No, Farah didn't return them. Yes, there was still hope for Courtney and Lucien to build something new.

As they fixed their hair and returned to the box, Courtney felt simultaneously stronger and more fragile. Farah's promise that no man would come between them warmed her heart but couldn't completely ease the ache of watching Lucien—her Lucien—navigate this new world without the memory of their love.

She settled back into her seat for the second act, the tragic notes of Puccini's opera washing over her. How fitting that they should be watching Madame Butterfly, she thought, a story of love and loss and waiting. But unlike Cio-Cio San, Courtney wouldn't let her hope destroy her. She would be patient, would give Lucien the time and space he needed, would trust in Farah's friendship and her own resilience.

Still, as she watched the opera unfold, she couldn't help but wonder. Was it harder to lose someone to death, as she had thought she had for five years, or to have them sitting right beside you, looking through you as if you were a stranger? How long was she supposed to be hurt by this? How much of a chance could or should she give him?

Farah's ball to welcome Lucien back to society was in a few days and if things hadn't improved by then… If she didn't feel as if Lucien was trying to get to know her, she would… What? What could she do?

Just then, she looked up and across the theatre, and she saw a pair of opera glasses looking their way. Not surprising, really, because everyone was fascinated by Lucien's return. But her heart gave a leap in her chest. That was Viscount Vale's box, and if she wasn't mistaken, that was his younger brother, Mr. Axton Fancourt pointing his glasses this way. She wondered what was holding his attention.

She liked Axton. He was handsome and charming. He came from a good family and most of all, he wasn't after a wealthy wife. He'd flirted outrageously with her at Lady Skye's ball last week and she'd enjoyed it. He was the man who made her reconsider her vow to remain a spinster.

Her spine straightened and she sat tall in her seat. If Lucien didn't want her, she'd find a man who did.

LATER THAT NIGHT, no sooner had Lucien stepped inside his home, having escorted Courtney home, than Lauren glided onto the landing above him wrapped in a dressing gown.

"Have you been waiting up for me?"

She gave a weak smile. "I wanted to know how the night with Courtney went?"

He trudged up the stairs to where she stood. "It was a nice night."

"Nice?"

He rounded on her. "What do you expect from me? I cannot

turn my feelings on and off at will."

He hated seeing the tears well in her eyes. "We need…we need you to marry. One of Father's debtors came by tonight and threatened me. Threatened to call in the debts and put us in the poor house. I'm—we're running out of time." He pulled her in for a hug. "I'm sorry, Lucien. I'm just so worried and I had hoped you'd like Courtney, find her acceptable, because you'd loved her once before."

He didn't say a word.

Lauren continued. "I know how much she loves you. So, I thought it would be easy. You'd simply ask for her hand because you loved her so much too. But I didn't realize that wasn't fair to you. How can I expect you to marry a stranger just to save the family you no longer know, when I have been putting off doing just that?"

"Please don't worry. If anyone else calls, ask them to call back when I am at home. Lord Rockwell has agreed to loan me funds to pay off any of the debtors that will not wait for me to sort out our situation." In other words, most debtors were waiting for him to marry and marry well.

What he didn't add was that, because he couldn't remember being a lord, he had no qualms in accepting the help. He felt no shame at having to borrow from Rockwell. This was a situation not of his making. Rockwell understood his need to have time to sort out his life and his family's financial situation. That was the reason why, after watching Farah and Rockwell at the opera tonight, he'd decided to help Rockwell marry Farah before the man lost her. Deep inside, Lucien could see that Rockwell loved Farah, but for some reason, he was fighting it.

Lauren stepped out of his hold. "Oh, that is nice of Rockwell. And it's such a relief. You must be relieved too. It gives you time to find someone who might make you happy."

"Have you found anyone who might make you happy?" he countered, forcing the conversation away from him and Courtney.

Her face flushed with color. "That is a tad difficult when everyone knows I have no dowry." He looked, really looked at his sister. She was a beauty. Surely there must be men interested in the daughter of an earl, one with such grace and beauty even without a dowry.

"It would seem English gentlemen are idiots."

She laughed at that. "Most of them are."

"Most?" he teased. Was there someone? The muscles in his jaw tightened.

"I really haven't had time to think of courting."

She was lying. Since his return, he'd noticed his sister's lips always twitched when she lied. He wondered who she liked.

He thought of Courtney. Gone was the idea of pursuing Farah himself. She only had eyes for Rockwell. He'd tested that tonight. And she'd rebuffed his obvious flirtation.

However, he'd made Farah a promise. That if society ever learned she'd been in Ireland with Rockwell, alone and unchaperoned, and if she really didn't want to marry Rockwell, he would marry her to save her from scandal.

This was the reason he didn't openly set his cap at Courtney—yet. He couldn't. He was obligated to Farah and yet, he couldn't tell anyone for fear of exposing Rockwell and Farah's scandalous journey to find him.

The sooner bloody Rockwell realized he was about to lose the best thing that ever happened to him, the better. Now there was an idea. Perhaps he could push the point at the ball Farah and her brother were hosting to welcome Lucien back to the world of the living.

He settled into bed and his thoughts drifted to Courtney. In the back of his wardrobe, hidden behind a loose board, he'd found a pencil drawing of himself lying naked on a bed with a blanket over his lower half but his chest bare. It had been drawn by Courtney, as she'd signed it. Just what had his relationship been with the woman he thought was so straitlaced she wouldn't do anything to upset society?

They must have been alone—doing what? He would have to find out as it had implications. But the drawing was definitely intimate. To say he was surprised was an understatement... That was one of the reasons he'd hesitated in pursuing Courtney. Everyone spoke of the virtuous Lady Courtney, and he didn't know how to live up to that sort of ideal. At some point, he'd put a foot wrong and then what would she feel or do? Would she end up despising him? Would she look down on him?

He unrolled the etching and stared at his image. This painting was full of passion, sex, and heat. He closed his eyes and remembered her touch, her scent and her laugh from the opera tonight. How surprising that underneath all that respectability lay a woman dying to break free. Was that why she'd loved him? Because he'd freed her inhibitions? Her desires?

He would set his plan in motion tomorrow night at the ball. He would push Rockwell into recognizing his feelings for Farah. As soon as he was free of his promise to Farah, as soon as Rockwell proposed, he would pursue Courtney. Not because he had to, but because he wanted to. He wanted to get to know her. Not the society stuffy Courtney but the woman she'd obviously been with him.

Having found this drawing, he now realized what his old self saw in her. He was so overwhelmed by his situation, he'd not really looked at the woman he'd once loved.

He fell asleep with visions of Courtney in his bed, her long auburn hair sliding over his chest, her creamy breasts bouncing and her hardened nipples in his mouth, as she rode him into oblivion.

CHAPTER SIX

THE NEXT NIGHT, as Courtney descended the stairs of her home, her gown and hair perfect, it was a different Lucien who greeted her. The way he looked at her, the way he kissed the knuckles of her gloved hand, the way he handed her into the carriage for their ride to the ball, all screamed flirtation.

The carriage swayed gently as it made its way through London's darkened streets. Courtney's heart fluttered at Lucien's proximity; his thigh pressed warmly against hers. Something had changed in him since last night at the opera. The way he looked at her now held an intensity she remembered from before—before Ireland, before his memory loss, before everything changed.

"You look very beautiful tonight."

She could feel her face blush. "Thank you. You look very handsome too."

His hand moved to his jacket pocket, and she saw him withdraw a familiar parchment. Her breath caught in her throat as she recognized it in the passing glow of the streetlamps. The drawing. *Her* drawing. Heat flooded her face as she remembered that intimate morning, the way the early sunlight had played across his bare chest as she'd sketched him, both of them still warm and languid from their lovemaking.

"I found this," he said softly, "hidden in my wardrobe behind a loose board." His voice held a note of curiosity rather than accusation. "You signed it."

"I—yes." Her voice trembled slightly. "It was the morning before you left for Ireland. We had…" She broke off, unable to continue.

"Were we lovers?" The direct question, spoken in that slight Irish lilt he'd acquired, made her shiver.

"Once," she whispered. "Just once. That night. We were to be married anyway, and you were leaving, and I—" She stopped, gathering her courage. "I didn't want to risk you dying without having known me completely. And afterwards, I never regretted that choice."

His thumb traced the edge of the paper, and she could see him studying the drawing in the intermittent light. "It's quite…intimate."

"I drew you without your permission," she said softly, lost in the memory. "But you loved it. You said it was proof of how I saw you and of our love for each other." A tear slipped down her cheek. "When you didn't return… I have worried that someone might have found it. But Lauren never mentioned it. I didn't know if you'd kept it at all."

"I did keep it." He turned to look at her then, and she saw something flare in his eyes—not memory but understanding. "That's why you never married. Not just because you mourned me, but because we had…" He trailed off, clearly trying to find the right words.

"Because I had given myself to you," she finished quietly. "Yes. How could I marry another when my heart—and my body—belonged to you?" More tears fell, but she didn't try to hide them. "But I don't want you to feel obligated. I want to marry for love. And after watching Tiffany and Wolf, I suddenly realized that if a man loved me, he wouldn't care. I had started to allow men to court me. I'm getting to an age where I can't wait much longer if I don't wish to be alone for the rest of my life. And I don't."

His hand found hers in the darkness, his callused fingers threading through hers. "The woman who drew this," he said slowly, "who gave herself to me that night…she wasn't the proper society lady everyone describes. She was passionate. Brave. Willing to risk everything for love."

"I was different with you," she admitted. "You made me feel safe enough to be myself. To want things. To take them. To share my dreams and longings with you. I want that again."

The carriage hit a rough patch of road, pressing them closer together. Courtney felt the familiar heat of his body, so achingly similar to that last morning together. But this wasn't her Lucien, not really. This was a new man, one who looked at her drawing with fresh eyes, seeing not the memory of their passion but the promise of what might still be possible.

"I've been a fool," he said finally. "Looking at you and seeing only what society sees—the perfect, proper lady. But this…" He held up the drawing. "This shows me who you really are. Who we were together."

"Perhaps we could find that again," she whispered before she could stop herself. "If you wanted."

His fingers tightened on hers. "I was scared of you. I'm so far from the perfect gentleman. And you, you seemed such a perfect lady."

"Nobody is perfect, Lucien. But people can be perfect together. Or perfect for each other."

The carriage was slowing as they approached their destination. She held her breath waiting to see what he said.

"Will you save me both waltzes tonight?" he asked, tucking the drawing carefully away.

"Always," she replied, and for the first time since his return, her smile held no sadness, only hope.

Then his smile died. "I have something else to confess. It involves Farah and Rockwell."

"I already know she was in Ireland with him and helped find you. Ashley, Rockwell's sister, let it slip."

He looked out the window, seeming lost in thought. "I can't remember ever being Viscount Furoe, but I remember what it means to be a man. To be a good man. Farah risked her reputation coming to rescue me. I don't know if I'd have made the transition home without her. She was less threatening than Rockwell somehow and she was kind to Ava-Marie and Caitria."

She held her breath, her heart getting ready to shatter. He was in love with Farah.

He turned to face her. "She's in love with Rockwell but the stupid man is running scared. She doesn't want to marry him, believing he will leave her behind as he sails the world. So, I made her a promise. If it becomes common knowledge that she was in Ireland with Rockwell, and she does not wish to marry him, I will marry her to protect her reputation."

He didn't love her. It was merely a promise. Thank the lord.

"So, you see, I can't openly court you until I know I will never have to make good on that promise. Since my return, I'm constantly reminded about what honor means to a gentleman."

Her heart gave a kick. Farah would never take Lucien up on that offer, but she would not say that. He was trying to show her he could be a gentleman, even though he'd forgotten he ever was one.

"When will that be, do you think?" His smile was so sensual she wanted to grab him and kiss him.

"I have a plan to make Rockwell face his real feelings. But it might mean I have to look as though I'm interested in Farah. Jealousy is a powerful emotion. And it may hurt you."

I'd be okay with anything if it meant you could focus on me, she wanted to scream. "Perhaps I can help too. If I make Rockwell believe your intentions are real."

"We could do this together. The pair of them won't realize what's going on, but we will." He pressed a kiss to her knuckles. "I shall pay Farah special attention tonight and you will warn Rockwell about the fact he has a rival for her affections."

Courtney's resolve wavered slightly as she prayed this plan didn't backfire on them both.

Backfire? It bloody well more than backfired… Courtney had never experienced a more mortifying moment in all her life.

One moment, she had been sharing secret smiles with Lucien across the ballroom, both reveling in their clever scheme to push Rockwell and Farah together. The next, her world had crumbled as Lucien announced his engagement to Farah before the entire *ton*.

A lady friend of Rockwell's, who had seen him and Farah in Ireland, realized the lie Rockwell had told her. In Ireland, he'd tried to pass Farah off as his sister Ashley. The lie was exposed when the lady turned up at the ball…and met the real Ashley! Now everyone knew Farah had been in Ireland with Rockwell and Lucien.

The whispers had started immediately, rustling through the crowd like wind through autumn leaves. And while Courtney understood Lucian had no choice and was protecting her friend, her insides clenched as she analyzed how this could turn out.

"Wasn't he engaged to Lady Courtney before his disappearance?"

"Poor dear, jilted by the same man."

"How utterly humiliating."

She maintained her composure with remarkable fortitude, smiling placidly as if the announcement was of no consequence whatsoever. Even as her pride splintered in her chest, she had nodded graciously, accepting condolences with a practiced laugh and dismissive wave of her fan. *Please, please Rockwell, do the right thing…*

"How extraordinary," she'd murmured to Lady Worthington, who had practically sprinted across the ballroom to offer her sympathies. "I wish them every happiness."

Courtney could stand it no longer and followed Lucien as he strode from the ballroom, her heart still reeling from the public humiliation of his engagement announcement. She found him on the moonlit terrace, his hands braced against the stone balustrade, his shoulders rigid with tension.

"Lucien," she began softly, approaching him with careful steps. "We need to talk about what just happened."

He didn't turn around. "I've ruined everything. My life. My family's life and now Farah's and your life. If not for me, Rockwell would never have gone to Ireland and Farah would never have been on that damn boat."

"I'm proud of you for doing the right thing. Maybe it's for the best. You make a new life, and I can make one, too, without burdens from our past. There is someone else I was considering. I'll be all right. And you will be all right, because you don't love either me or Farah. It's Farah I'm worried about."

"Someone else?" How could he sound so hurt when they hardly knew each other and he'd just proposed to another woman?

"Mr. Axton Fancot, Valora's brother." She shrugged her shoulders. "He's nice and he has taken an interest in me."

"So, were you ever going to take my return and a relationship between us seriously? Or were you only humoring me in the carriage tonight?"

"If the love of your life returned from the dead, even with no memories of you, would you walk away?"

"Probably, if they were damaged? Broken?" His voice cracked slightly.

Tears pricked at Courtney's eyes. "Well, I'm not you—"

"But am I a man you want to try again with?" He stepped closer, his expression raw with pain and frustration. "When you look at me, you see him. When I fail to remember something that was important to us, you look disappointed. When I don't react the way you expect, you try to remind me of who I used to be. Everything will be new with Mr. Fancot. No memories of how it used to be, just new memories. It's hard to compete with that."

"You aren't competing—"

"Aren't I?" The words hung between them. "The Lucien you loved died in Ireland five years ago. I'm what's left—a farmer who doesn't know how to be a lord, a man who can't remember loving you, someone who's failing every test you never told me I was taking."

"But we spoke in the carriage on the way here and I said I wanted to try."

His shoulders slumped and he looked away. "I really want that chance, too. But now I've ruined everything with my public proposal."

He spun to face her and the pain in his eyes broke her heart. "I'd best go and sort this out. Hopefully Rockwell will come to his senses."

He left her standing in the dark, and that was how she felt about him. He was cloaked in darkness, and she had no idea if he'd ever step into the light so she could get to know the new man he was. He was here, but hiding pieces of himself.

Perhaps second chances were just a dream. She didn't even know if she liked this new Lucien. One minute he wanted to try, and the next he'd ruined everything by making a scene trying to save Farah's reputation. Perhaps Axton was a better option for her. Lucien was right. Axton was new and there was no doppelganger for her to compare him to.

NOW SAFELY ENSCONCED in a small antechamber off the main ballroom, Courtney allowed herself a moment of weakness. She pressed her forehead against the cool glass of the window, grateful for the momentary relief it provided against her flushed skin.

"At least he realizes he's created a terrible scandal," she whispered, her breath fogging the glass. "What's worse, even if Rockwell does the right thing and Lucien is free to marry, who will believe he's marrying me for love? They will think he loves Farah and marries me merely for my money."

Did she care what the *ton* thought? If Lucien had said he loved her, that would be enough. But he hadn't said any such thing.

Behind her, the door clicked open. She straightened immediately, schooling her features into a mask of indifference. When she turned, however, her composure faltered at the sight of Lucien standing in the doorway, his face ashen.

"Courtney," he said, his voice rough. "I need to apologize."

"I think what you did was wonderful. You were protecting our friend. But I hope you are right, and Rockwell comes to his senses. But was this part of your plan? If so, it's going to cause a huge scandal."

Lucien knelt at her feet and took her hand in his. "I'm sorry to make you the subject of more gossip."

"At least the focus will be on Rockwell and Farah, and it might give us a chance to learn more about us."

"Rockwell will marry her," he insisted, as if talking to himself. "Once he realizes he might lose her to me, he'll come to his senses. This is just… a temporary measure."

"Farah won't marry you, Lucien. She knows that would hurt me and Farah is too nice to do that. You seem so sure Rockwell will marry Farah, but my fear is she won't marry either of you. And if not, she's ruined. I'm not sure I can live with that on my conscience."

"What are you saying?"

"I might have to convince her to marry one of you. I won't see my friend ruined for something that is not her fault."

Lucien's jaw tightened. "Are you saying that if Farah declines Rockwell, you'll expect me to honor my word?"

"Yes." A tear slid down her face.

"Is this because of Mr. Fancot? You would prefer him?"

Before she could respond, the door opened again, and Tarquin entered, his expression thunderous.

"There you are," he said, his gaze locking on Lucien. "I've been looking everywhere for you both. We need to discuss what happened before the gossips tear my sister's reputation to shreds."

Lucien straightened, facing Tarquin with admirable composure. "I was just explaining the situation to Lady Courtney."

"Were you?" Tarquin's voice dripped with skepticism. "And what situation might that be? The one where you publicly announce your engagement to Lady Farah mere days after returning to London and reconnecting with my sister—your former fiancée?"

"It's not what it seems," Lucien began, but Tarquin cut him off with a sharp gesture.

"Save it. Wolf has informed me of the…circumstances surrounding Lady Farah's trip to Ireland. While I commend your gallantry in protecting her reputation, I can't help but wonder if there might have been a less damaging solution. Or did you have an ulterior motive?"

"Such as?" Lucien challenged, his posture stiffening.

"Such as actually marrying Farah rather than allowing Lord Ware to do the honorable thing and offer for her himself," Tarquin replied smoothly. "After all, he was the one who compromised her in the first place, however accidentally."

Courtney could see where this conversation was heading—a challenge. She wanted to defuse the tension between these men. "What's done is done," she continued. "Lord Furoe acted to protect Farah, and I can't fault him for that. Now we must decide how to proceed from here with minimal damage to all parties."

"You're being remarkably understanding," Tarquin observed, his brow furrowed.

"What am I supposed to do? Cause a scene? That would certainly give the gossips something to talk about. Besides, Lucien had already told me of a promise he'd made to protect Farah's reputation. He is a man of honor. Would you prefer I collapse into hysterics?" she countered, arching an eyebrow.

A reluctant smile tugged at the corner of Tarquin's mouth. "No, I suppose not."

"Good. Then let us be practical." She turned to Lucien. "You believe Rockwell will come to his senses and offer for Farah, thus rendering your engagement unnecessary?"

Lucien nodded, some of the tension leaving his shoulders. "He's stubborn, but he's not stupid. He loves her—he's just afraid."

"Afraid of what?" Tarquin asked.

"Of disappointing her. Of not being the husband she deserves." Lucien's expression softened. "He believes his desire to travel the world would make him a poor husband, leaving her alone for months at a time."

"Perhaps that's a decision Farah should make for herself," Courtney suggested. "Rather than having it made for her."

Something flickered in Lucien's eyes—realization, perhaps, or regret. "You're right. Just as you should have the opportunity to decide for yourself whether you want to continue our…association, rather than having it decided for you by my circumstances."

Hope flickered again in Courtney's chest, stronger this time. "What are you saying, Lucien?"

"You are a beautiful woman, and you deserve a man who loves you," he replied, his voice low and earnest. "I can't offer you much of anything."

Tarquin cleared his throat pointedly. "As touching as this is, might I remind you both that Lord Furoe is currently engaged to Lady Farah before all of society? We need a plan to extricate him from this situation without further damage to anyone's reputation."

"Which leaves us with one question," Lucien said, turning to Courtney. "Will you wait for me to resolve this situation? Or have I finally tested your patience beyond endurance? Do you want to get to know me? Not my ghost but me? The man returned from Ireland with nothing?"

The question hung between them, weighted with significance. Courtney searched Lucien's face, looking for any hint of the man she had once loved so desperately. He was different now—harder, more direct, less constrained by society's expectations. But there was still that same intensity in his gaze, that same unwavering focus that had drawn her to him from the first.

"I've waited five years," she said finally. "I suppose I can manage a few more days. But Lucien—" She met his gaze steadily. "I won't wait forever. Not again. Mr. Fancot deserves better from me, too."

Relief washed over his features. "Thank you. I promise, this will be resolved quickly."

"See that it is," Tarquin said, his tone making it clear the words were as much a threat as agreement. "Now, shall we return to the ballroom? Your absence has already been noted, and continued seclusion will only fuel the gossips further."

Courtney nodded, smoothing her skirts and checking her reflection in a small mirror on the wall. Her eyes were bright, her cheeks flushed, but she looked composed—a woman in command of herself and her situation.

"Lead on, brother," she said, taking Tarquin's offered arm.

As they moved toward the door, Lucien caught her free hand, pressing a swift kiss to her knuckles. "I will fix this," he murmured, his eyes intense. "I promise."

She nodded, unable to speak past the sudden tightness in her throat. As they reentered the ballroom, she held her head high, ignoring the curious stares and hushed whispers that followed their progress.

Let them talk, she thought defiantly. The story was far from over.

The orchestra struck up a waltz, and to her surprise, Lucien appeared at her side, hand extended in invitation.

"May I have this dance, Lady Courtney?" he asked, his voice carrying just far enough for those nearby to hear.

A hush fell over their immediate vicinity, all eyes turning to witness her response. She knew what they expected—for her to rebuff him publicly, to display her wounded pride through a cutting rejection.

"You do like causing scandal," she replied. She placed her hand in his, her smile serene. "You may, Lord Furoe."

The shocked murmurs that rippled through the crowd brought a certain satisfaction. Let them wonder. Let them speculate. The truth would reveal itself in time.

As Lucien led her onto the dance floor, his hand warm and steady at her waist, she leaned in and whispered, "You realize what you've done? By dancing with me so soon after announcing your engagement to Farah, you've set the *ton* abuzz with new speculation."

"The *ton* is talking about me no matter what I do. I intend to be myself. They will learn I'm not the same man who left to fight in the Irish rebellion. I am a man who follows my own path."

Despite everything, Courtney found herself laughing. "How very...direct of you."

"I've found directness has its advantages," he replied, his expression sobering. "If I'd been more direct with you from the beginning about my promise to Farah, perhaps we could have avoided some of this evening's drama."

"Perhaps," she agreed. "Though I'm beginning to think drama follows you wherever you go, Lord Furoe."

"An unfortunate side effect of returning from the dead, I'm afraid." His eyes glinted with humor, but it quickly faded. "In all seriousness, Courtney...thank you for understanding. And for giving me another chance to prove myself worthy of you."

The simple sincerity in his voice touched her deeply. "You don't need to prove yourself worthy, Lucien. You need to decide what you want. Who you want. The man I loved was never uncertain about that."

A shadow crossed his face. "I'm not him anymore."

"No," she agreed softly. "You're not. But perhaps the man you've become is someone I could love just as deeply, if given the chance. I need to know that as much as you. I have a choice to make as well."

The music swelled around them, and for a moment, it was as if they were alone on the dance floor, cocooned in a bubble of possibility. Lucien's hand tightened slightly at her waist, drawing her a fraction closer than propriety allowed.

"I don't know if I can ever love again," he murmured.

"I don't believe that," she replied with a hint of her old spirit and a cheeky smile. "I'm very lovable, or so I've been told."

As the waltz ended, Lucien reluctantly released her, though his eyes remained fixed on her face. "I will fix this mess," he promised again. "And then, if you'll allow it, I'd like to court you properly. No schemes, no pretenses. Just us, discovering who we are together now."

Courtney felt a curious lightness in her chest, a fragile hope taking root. "I'd like that," she said simply.

Around them, the ball continued, the musicians striking up another lively tune. Gossips huddled in corners, speculating on the evening's dramatic events, while couples whirled across the dance floor, blissfully ignorant of the drama unfolding in their midst.

"If it's any consolation," she said as they made their way off the dance floor, "I've always believed you think better in a crisis."

He laughed, the sound warm and genuine. "Let's hope that holds true. Because this, my dear Courtney, is most definitely a crisis."

Her smile in response was both challenge and promise. "Then by all means, Lord Furoe, show me how well you can think."

CHAPTER SEVEN

BARON LOCKWOOD SLUMPED in the crimson velvet chair, swirling amber liquid in a crystal tumbler that had seen better days. The Golden Pheasant was one of London's most reputable establishments, but he rarely used its services. Too vanilla for his tastes. But the proprietress was always a mine of information.

"Another, my lord?" the proprietress, Mrs. Bellamy, asked, her aging but still striking features creasing with practiced concern.

"The whole damn bottle," Lockwood growled, sliding coins across the polished mahogany table. His usual good humor had abandoned him since that disastrous night at Crockford's. The memory of Furoe's cold smile as he'd reclaimed his father's vowels still burned like acid in Lockwood's gut.

"Something troubling you?" Mrs. Bellamy settled her considerable frame into the chair opposite, signaling to a serving girl to bring the requested bottle. Despite her questionable profession, Mrs. Bellamy possessed a shrewd intelligence that had kept her establishment thriving for fifteen years.

"Furoe!" He spat the name like a curse. "The damned prodigal viscount returns from the dead."

"Ah, yes." Mrs. Bellamy's painted eyebrows rose. "Word has spread through half of London already. Lord Lucien Furoe, miraculously alive after five years. Quite the sensation. But I have to inform you he has not partaken of the services my house offers."

"Quite the inconvenience, you mean." Lockwood tossed back his drink, relishing the burn. "I had plans, Bellamy. Five long years of careful planning, down the privy in a single evening."

The serving girl, barely more than sixteen, with a face still retaining traces of innocence despite her surroundings, approached with the bottle. Mrs. Bellamy dismissed her with a flick of her bejeweled fingers.

"Plans involving the Danvers residence, I presume?" Mrs. Bellamy inquired, pouring Lockwood another generous measure. Though proprietress of a brothel, she kept abreast of society's machinations better than most peers' wives.

"The earl was nearly mine," Lockwood muttered. "Another month—two at most—and he'd have lost everything. The London house is all I want. It used to belong to my grandfather, and the Danvers virtually stole it from him." His eyes took on a feverish gleam. "I was to be the savior, you understand. The benevolent creditor, willing to forgive his debts in exchange for certain...considerations."

"Such as?"

"His eldest daughter's hand, for starters." Lockwood smiled unpleasantly. "Lady Lauren Cavanaugh—beautiful, accomplished, and with no dowry to speak of. A perfect arrangement. I'd gain entrée to the highest circles of society through marriage to an earl's daughter, and she'd gain financial security that I'd won from her father. And of course, the town home would be mine, as it always should have been."

"How very charitable of you," Mrs. Bellamy remarked dryly, likely tempted to remind him that it was his grandfather's gambling that lost it in the first place.

"The London house," Lockwood continued, ignoring her tone. "I've wanted that property since I was a boy. My grandfather used to point it out to me when we rode through Mayfair. Danvers House, used to be Lockwood House, elegant Georgian lines, prime location. 'That,' he'd say, 'was our home. One day you will get it back for us.' And now, just when it was within my grasp…"

"The son returns." Mrs. Bellamy nodded sympathetically.

"Not just returns," Lockwood snarled. "Returns and humiliates me before half the peerage at Crockford's. Called me a predator to my face! Me, who was merely pursuing legitimate business interests."

Mrs. Bellamy's expression suggested she might have her own opinion on that characterization, but she wisely kept it to herself. "Well, I'm sure a man of your…resourcefulness…will find another path to your ambitions."

Lockwood stared moodily into his glass. "The son was supposed to be dead. I made inquiries five years ago when rumors first surfaced that he might have survived the Irish Rebellion. My sources assured me he perished in the fighting."

"Evidently not."

"No." Lockwood's eyes narrowed. "Instead, he's been living in some Irish backwater all this time, playing at being a farmer while his family slowly disintegrated. And now he returns like some conquering hero, full of righteous indignation about his father's gambling debts." He drained his glass again. "It's intolerable."

A commotion near the entrance drew their attention. He heard a burst of feminine laughter, followed by the slamming of a door. A stunningly beautiful young woman with flaming red hair and a gorgeous smile, swept into the parlor.

"Kitty!" Mrs. Bellamy called. "What a lovely surprise. I didn't expect to see you so soon."

"Oh, I didn't know you were entertaining," Kitty said. "I just wanted to say goodbye."

Mrs. Bellamy's smile lacked substance. "Yes, well, I am unhappy that I've lost you, but I suspected that would eventually happen for a young woman with your looks and demeanor." She turned to the baron. "Kitty has managed to become the mistress of a man of quite significant social standing."

"Ah, the aspirations of whores."

Mrs. Bellamy frowned at his rude comment. "Pardon the baron's demeanor. Baron Lockwood could use some cheering. His lordship's had a trying week. Lord Furoe returning from Ireland has disrupted his plans."

Kitty kept her professional smile firmly in place.

Lockwood barely acknowledged her, still lost in his brooding. "The worst of it is, he's brought a child with him. Thank God it's not a son and heir to solidify his position."

Mrs. Bellamy asked, "A daughter is no threat to your plans?"

"Of course not." He shook his head. "A man wounded in the Irish Rebellion, with no memory of his past life, finds love. How ridiculous. Apparently, he married while in Ireland. The daughter is, what, four years old now? Ava-Marie, I believe they call her."

Kitty's eyebrows shot up at the name, and she exchanged a quick glance with Mrs. Bellamy.

"Do you know something, Kitty? Kitty is from Ireland," Mrs. Bellamy explained.

"Ava-Marie?" Kitty repeated, her voice suddenly devoid of its practiced seduction. "And you say he came from Ireland? Where?"

"How the devil should I know?" Lockwood snapped, irritated by her questions. "Some village or other. What does it matter?"

"Malahide, perhaps?" Kitty persisted, earning a warning look from Mrs. Bellamy.

Lockwood's attention sharpened. "Yes, I believe that was mentioned. Malahide." His eyes narrowed. "What do you know of it?"

Kitty hesitated, glancing at Mrs. Bellamy, who gave an almost imperceptible nod.

"I might know something, my lord," Kitty said carefully. "About an Ava who lived near Malahide."

Lockwood sat up straighter, suddenly alert. "Go on."

"She was a friend, you see. Worked with me before I came to London." Kitty twisted her hands in her lap. "We were close, for a time. She hated the life, always talking about finding a way out, a respectable life."

"And did she?" Lockwood asked, leaning forward.

"So, the story goes." Kitty lowered her voice, though there was no one nearby to overhear. "Word came back that she'd found herself a gentleman. Injured, he was, with no memory of who he really was. She nursed him back to health; told him he was her husband."

Lockwood's glass froze halfway to his lips. "No memory, you say?"

"None at all, according to what we heard. Head injury from the rebellion, they said. Found him half-dead in the street right outside our place of business." Kitty shrugged. "Ava always was clever. She saw her opportunity and took it. Set herself up as his wife, moved them both to a little cottage near Malahide."

"And the child? This Ava-Marie?"

"Could be hers, I suppose." Kitty frowned. "You say the girl is four? The timing works."

Lockwood's mind raced, calculating possibilities. "Perhaps she was already with child when she found him. Or shortly after." His lips curled in a predatory smile. "This is…most interesting."

"Now see here," Mrs. Bellamy cut in, her tone sharp. "Kitty's just repeating gossip. We don't know if it's the same man or the same Ava."

"But it could be," Lockwood insisted. "An amnesiac gentleman, found after the Irish Rebellion, nursed back to health by a woman named Ava, moving to Malahide with a child named Ava-Marie… The coincidence would be extraordinary."

"Even if it is the same man," Mrs. Bellamy said carefully, "what of it? He's returned to his family now."

"Ah, but under what pretenses?" Lockwood leaned back, a calculating gleam in his eye. "Society believes he married this Ava legitimately, that his daughter is his lawful issue. What if that's not the truth? What if Ava never went through with a wedding? How could she, when she'd already told him they were married?

Could it be that their precious Viscount Furoe was living in sin with a common whore, that his beloved daughter is a bastard?"

Kitty paled. "My lord, I never said—"

"You didn't have to." Lockwood waved away her protest. "The implications are clear enough. Tell me, this Ava of yours, is she still in Ireland?"

"She's dead," Kitty replied flatly. "Consumption took her about two years ago. That's the last I heard, anyway."

"Convenient," Lockwood murmured. "Very convenient indeed. No one to contradict whatever story Furoe has concocted."

"Except perhaps those who knew Ava," Mrs. Bellamy pointed out. "Those who might recall her boasts about finding a gentleman with no memory. Surely there must be church records of any marriage."

"Excellent," Lockwood said, his smile growing wider. "There should be a record of his marriage."

Kitty shrank back slightly. "I don't want trouble, my lord. Ava was my friend."

"And you can honor her memory by telling the truth," Lockwood coaxed. "For suitable compensation, of course."

"Baron," Mrs. Bellamy interjected, her tone warning, "What's in it for me? You have this information because of me and Kitty. And as you know, everything comes at a price."

"Come now, Bellamy." Lockwood fixed her with a knowing look. "I'm sure we can come to an agreement."

The proprietress's lips thinned. "Kitty, dear, fetch us some fresh glasses, would you?"

Once the younger woman had departed, Mrs. Bellamy leaned across the table, her voice dropping to a dangerous whisper. "Tread carefully, Baron. I don't take kindly to being double crossed."

"Nor do I," Lockwood growled. "You best remember to keep quiet about this until I'm ready."

"What are you going to do? Travel to Ireland and look for

evidence—or should I say, lack of evidence—of their marriage?" Mrs. Bellamy retorted. "Furoe would probably pay anything to keep the details of his bastard from going public. He's in need of a wealthy wife. No father would want a man with a bastard daughter." Her eyes hardened. "This could be most profitable for both of us. I want out of this life too. I'm getting on in years. A nice cottage in the country would suit me."

Lockwood's smile never wavered, though a muscle ticked in his jaw. "You misunderstand me, dear lady. I merely seek to restore what's mine. Lord Furoe robbed me of my rightful winnings, humiliated me before my peers and I want my family home back. If his past offers a means of redress, who am I to ignore such providence?" His lips formed a sly smile. "And if I can use this information to become wealthy, why shouldn't I? It's not my fault Furoe was a sucker."

"And the child? Would you destroy her future for your petty revenge?"

Something flickered across Lockwood's face, a momentary hesitation, quickly suppressed. "Maybe I can keep the child's secret if it's worth it to me," he said dismissively. "What have you heard about his ex-fiancée, Lady Courtney?"

Mrs. Bellamy regarded him with undisguised contempt. "She is letting him court her, I believe. Furoe needs her dowry, and she's mourned him for five years. I suspect she's still madly in love with the man."

He tapped his fingers together. "Interesting. That might be a way in."

"What are you thinking now?" Mrs. Bellamy asked.

But before he could answer, Kitty returned with fresh glasses, her expression carefully neutral, though her hands trembled slightly as she set them down.

"Thank you, my dear," Lockwood said, his voice silky. "Now, tell me more about your friend Ava. Everything you can remember. Leave nothing out."

As Kitty began her reluctant recitation, Lockwood's mind

whirred with possibilities. This could be the leverage he needed not just to recoup his losses, but to destroy Furoe entirely. The scandal would be delicious: the noble viscount, living in sin with a brothel girl, passing off his bastard as legitimate. Society would devour him alive. What would he pay to stop that secret coming out? His London house and sister's hand in marriage?

Or could he take a different tack. Lady Courtney loved Furoe. She had a very large dowry and was the daughter of a Marquess. What would she pay to keep her lover's secret? Lockwood wouldn't mind Lady Courtney as his wife. What a rise in status that would be.

And more importantly, Furoe would learn what it meant to cross Baron Lockwood. He might still be able to get Danvers House by buying it from Furoe when he didn't find a wealthy wife in time. Hell, once he married Lady Courtney and had her dowry in his hands, he could still reveal Furoe's secret and see the man ostracized and lose everything.

"One more thing," he said, interrupting Kitty's narrative. "Did this Ava ever mention a cousin? Someone who might have accompanied her and the child to London?"

Kitty's eyes widened slightly. "I believe her cousin, Caitria, arrived to care for Ava-Marie when she became ill."

"And this Caitria—would she recognize you? Would she know of Ava's…profession?"

"I don't know. She lived in Cork, a long way away from Dublin. She might not know the story." Kitty shrugged.

Lockwood's mind whirled. "I'll send someone to Ireland immediately." He raised his glass in a mocking toast. "To Lord Lucien Furoe and the house of cards he's built around himself. May it collapse spectacularly."

Mrs. Bellamy's body hummed too. She'd survived in her business by knowing when to speak and when to remain silent. And something in Lockwood's eyes tonight—a merciless gleam, cold as winter—suggested silence was the wiser course. She would bide her time and get what she wanted from Lockwood when she found out how much he received for this knowledge. Alternatively, she could do some blackmailing of her own.

Kitty, however, could not contain herself. "What are you planning, my lord? I don't want Ava's child harmed. Whatever Ava did, the girl is innocent."

"Innocent?" Lockwood repeated, the word twisting on his tongue as if it were foreign. "No one is innocent, my dear. We're all tainted by the circumstances of our birth, the choices of our parents." He leaned forward, his voice dropping to an intimate murmur. "But don't fret. I won't harm the child...physically. I'll simply ensure that society knows exactly who—and what—she is, if I have to. But I believe Furoe will pay to keep her secret."

"That's cruel," Kitty whispered.

"That's justice," Lockwood said, correcting her. "His justice, for what he's done to me." His eyes gleamed with unholy satisfaction. "And when I'm finished, when the mighty Viscount Furoe is brought low by his own deception, when his precious daughter bears the stain of illegitimacy that no amount of wealth or privilege can erase...then perhaps he'll understand the cost of humiliating Baron Lockwood."

He drained his glass in one fluid motion, setting it down with a decisive click. "Now, Kitty, I'll need you to write down everything you remember about Ava and this gentleman she claimed as her husband. Every detail, no matter how small."

Glancing briefly at Mrs. Bellamy, Kitty said, "I can't write, Baron."

Lockwood merely grunted. "Then I'll get my lawyer to draft up a note that you can leave your mark on."

Kitty looked even more uncomfortable. She jumped to her feet. "I must depart, Mrs. Bellamy. You won't see me here again—I hope. Good day, Baron Lockwood."

Once Kitty had left, Mrs. Bellamy watched Lockwood with growing unease. She'd seen many men consumed by revenge during her years in the demimonde. Noblemen, merchants, soldiers, all twisted by their thirst for retribution. Few ever found the satisfaction they sought, and many destroyed themselves in the process.

But Lockwood...there was something different about him. A cold calculation beneath the veneer of wounded pride. A patience that boded ill for young Lord Furoe and his little family. Lockwood would find a way to line his pockets with this information. Appeasing his wounded pride would always be secondary to money because the baron needed coin more than pride. And she intended to get her fair share of whatever the baron earned from this information she'd help reveal.

Or perhaps there was another way. Perhaps she should call on Lord Furoe.

CHAPTER EIGHT

LUCIEN ADJUSTED HIS cravat for the third time, studying his reflection in the glass of Lord Rockwell Ware's ballroom windows. The evening's celebrations were in full swing—a grand affair to mark Rockwell and Farah's wedding. The gentle strains of a Mozart piece floated through the air as couples swirled across the polished floor, their movements elegant and practiced. Candlelight glimmered off crystal chandeliers, casting a warm glow over the assembled cream of society.

He should have been elated. After all, his plan had worked to perfection. Rockwell had finally come to his senses when faced with the possibility of losing Farah to another man—even if that man had been Lucien himself. The scene played out in his mind like a theatrical production: Rockwell storming into Danvers House the morning after the ball, practically frothing at the mouth, demanding to know what Lucien thought he was doing by proposing to Farah.

"You don't even love her," Rockwell had snarled, pacing the library like a caged beast.

"Perhaps not," Lucien had replied coolly, leaning against the mantelpiece. "But I care for her deeply, and I'll give her the security and position she deserves. Which is more than you're offering at present."

Rockwell had looked as if Lucien had struck him. "You know why I can't—"

"Can't what? Love her? Because that's patently false. Can't

marry her? Why not? Because you're afraid she'll be lonely while you sail the world? Have you asked what she wants, or are you making that decision for her too? Or is it that you are too scared to face what it is you really want?"

It had been a calculated strike, designed to pierce Rockwell's armor of noble self-sacrifice. And it had worked spectacularly. Within days, Rockwell had proposed properly to Farah, offering her not just his heart but a partnership. Farah had accepted with tears and laughter, and Lucien had been graciously released from his "engagement" with minimal damage to anyone's reputation. After all, society always swooned over a love story.

So yes, he should have been elated. His friend was married to the woman he loved. The scandal had been contained. And most importantly, Lucien was now free to pursue Courtney without complications or divided loyalties.

Yet as he scanned the ballroom, searching for her auburn hair among the crowd, he couldn't quell the restlessness churning in his gut. Or was it fear? The fear that his motives were not honorable, driven by his need to save his family. Or the fear he wasn't good enough for her? Or the fear that she would demand more than his heart could give?

"Admiring yourself, brother?" Lauren appeared at his side, resplendent in a new gown of pale blue silk—a gift from Lucien after he'd finally gained control of the family finances and paid off the most pressing debts. "Or plotting your next social catastrophe?"

Lucien smiled despite himself. "I believe I've met my quota of scandals for the season."

"Pity. I was just getting used to them." She followed his gaze across the ballroom. "She hasn't arrived yet."

"Who?" he asked, feigning ignorance.

Lauren raised an eyebrow. "Cinderella? Who do you think? Courtney, of course."

"Ah." He tugged at his cuffs, aiming for nonchalance. "I hadn't noticed."

"Of course not. That's why you've been watching the door like a hawk for the past half-hour." She patted his arm. "She'll come. Tarquin promised he'd escort her."

His head jerked up. "Did she not want to attend?"

Lauren sighed. "Lucien, the woman has waited five years for you, endured believing you dead, watched you announce an engagement to her friend, and still showed remarkable grace through it all. I think she's entitled to a little hesitation."

He winced. When laid out so starkly, his behavior seemed abominable.

"I know," he said quietly. "I'm lucky she's still speaking to me at all."

"Yes, you are." Lauren's voice softened. "But for what it's worth, I think she loves you still, including this new version of you. Though heaven knows why."

"Your confidence is overwhelming."

"My confidence is perfectly calibrated to the situation." She nodded toward the entrance. "And now, brother dear, I suggest you put your most charming foot forward, because your lady love has just arrived."

Lucien turned, and the sight of Courtney nearly stole his breath. She stood in the doorway, a vision in deep emerald silk that complemented her auburn hair, which was arranged in an elegant knot with loose curls framing her face. Diamonds glittered at her throat and ears, and her graceful neck held her head high.

Tarquin stood beside her, tall and imposing in his formal wear, his expression making it clear he was still reserving judgment on Lucien's worthiness. But it wasn't Tarquin's disapproval that made Lucien's blood run cold.

It was the man on Courtney's other side—Mr. Axton Fancot, the notoriously charming younger brother of Viscount Vale. Even from across the room, Lucien could see Fancot's easy smile, the attentive tilt of his head as he leaned in to whisper something that made Courtney laugh.

A strange heat seared through Lucien's chest. Not quite anger, not quite fear, but something more primal. Something that made him want to stride across the room and insert himself between Courtney and the handsome rake currently monopolizing her attention.

"Careful, brother," Lauren murmured, apparently reading his thoughts. "Your farmer is showing."

The comment jerked him back to awareness of where he was and who he was supposed to be. Lord Lucien Furoe, Viscount, heir to an earldom. Not John Collins, Irish farmer, who might have simply marched over and staked his claim without ceremony.

"I see nothing wrong with directness," he muttered.

"Neither do I," Lauren agreed. "But perhaps consider a more subtle approach than glowering from across the room?"

Lucien nodded, took a steadying breath, and made his way through the crowd with measured steps. He was conscious of the eyes following him. Society still hadn't tired of observing the 'resurrected viscount'. But he focused solely on reaching Courtney before Fancot could claim her for the first dance.

"Lady Courtney," he said, executing a perfect bow as he reached her. "You look absolutely stunning this evening."

Her amber eyes met his, warm but slightly guarded. "Lord Furoe. Thank you for the compliment."

Though her tone was pleasant enough, he sensed a careful distance in her manner. Their last conversation had been thoughtful but unresolved, with Courtney making it clear that while she understood the necessity of his ruse with Farah, she needed time to determine if they still suited one another after all that had happened.

"I would have to be blind not to," he replied honestly. "The color suits you remarkably well."

"Doesn't it?" Fancot interjected smoothly. "I was just telling Lady Courtney that emerald brings out the gold in her eyes. Like sunshine through whiskey."

Lucien's jaw tightened at the familiar comparison, one he himself had made the day he'd re-met her. "How poetic."

"Mr. Fancot has a gift for observation," Courtney said, her smile giving nothing away.

"Among other gifts," Fancot added with a wink that made Lucien's fingers itch to form a fist.

"Lord Furoe," Tarquin cut in, ever the diplomat, "I trust you're enjoying the celebrations?"

"Immensely." Lucien never took his eyes off Courtney. "Though I find myself in need of a partner for the first waltz. Lady Courtney, would you do me the honor?"

He saw the hesitation flicker across her face, followed by a glance at Fancot that set Lucien's teeth on edge. But then she nodded, extending her hand. "I would be delighted."

Relief washed through him, followed by a surge of something that felt dangerously like triumph as he led her away from the disappointed Fancot. But as they took their positions for the dance, he noted the careful distance Courtney maintained between them, the guarded expression in eyes that had once looked at him with unguarded adoration.

"I wasn't certain you would come tonight," he said as the music began, and they moved into the steps of the waltz.

"And miss Lady Farah's wedding celebration? I would never." Her tone was light, but her spine remained rigid under his hand. "Besides, Tarquin insisted."

"I'm glad he did." Lucien guided her through a turn, aware of the watchful eyes around them. "You've been avoiding me."

"Have I?" She arched an eyebrow. "I've been rather busy this past week helping to organize this event."

"With Mr. Fancot, it seems."

The words escaped before he could stop them, and he immediately regretted them when he saw the spark of irritation in her eyes.

"Mr. Fancot has been kind enough to escort me to several events," she replied coolly. "In the absence of other invitations."

The pointed remark landed like a physical blow. "I've been occupied with family matters," he said, which was true enough. Between sorting out his father's debts and helping Rockwell navigate the aftermath of their faux engagement, he'd had precious little time for courtship.

"Of course. Family matters must take precedence." Her gaze drifted briefly over his shoulder toward where Axton stood. "I understand completely."

There was no accusation in her tone, but rather a gentle acknowledgment of their complicated situation. She wasn't bitter about Farah—they'd already worked through that misunderstanding—but he sensed she was keeping her guard up, protecting herself from potential disappointment.

"Axton has been a good friend to me," she added quietly. "During the years when I thought you were dead, and even now…he worries about me."

"Worries?" Lucien asked, carefully guiding her through a turn.

"He's concerned that…" She met his gaze directly. "Well, to be frank, he's not certain if you're good for me, Lucien. Given how much has changed and how easily I could be hurt."

The music swelled around them, and he drew her a fraction closer, lowering his voice. "And what do you think? Am I good for you?"

She considered this thoughtfully as they moved through the steps of the waltz. "I don't know yet. That's the truth of it. The man I knew and loved is gone in many ways. You're someone new. Someone I might come to care for deeply, but I can't be certain."

"Farah is my friend," he said, understanding her caution. "She helped me when I was lost and confused, returning to a life I couldn't remember. But what I feel for you is different."

"And what exactly do you feel?" Courtney asked, not challenging but genuinely curious. "Because from where I stand, Lord Furoe, we're both still discovering who we are to each other. Mr.

Fancot, however, has been quite clear about his regard."

"And what exactly are Mr. Fancot's intentions?" Lucien asked, unable to keep a slight edge from his voice.

A small, thoughtful smile touched her lips. "Yesterday, Axton paid me a call and he's asked permission to court me formally. He's been a steadfast friend these past years and believes we might suit."

Suit? If she merely wanted a marriage based on friendship, he could do that. But her words landed with unexpected weight, and Lucien nearly missed a step in the dance. "And have you granted it?"

"I told him I would consider it." Her eyes met his directly, honest rather than challenging. "I'm not closing doors, Lucien. I spent five years believing you dead, and now everything has changed. I'd just started to move on with my life and suddenly here you are. You, but not you. I would be foolish not to keep my options open while we determine if there's still something between us worth pursuing."

"I understand that," he said, though the admission cost him. "But I hope you know you're not merely a convenient solution to me. I'm not sure I can do convenient solutions when thinking of marriage."

"I know your intentions aren't mercenary. Many families would be more than happy to align with your family through a marriage even though your family's financial situation is dire," she replied gently. "But the truth remains that you don't remember loving me. You may have once, but that man is gone. And we both need to be certain of what we want out of a union before making any decisions about our future."

The last accusation stung worst of all, perhaps because it was the truth. His family did need the security her fortune would provide. But that wasn't why he wanted her.

"You're right," he said finally. "I don't love you. I can't. That love was built on shared experiences I no longer remember." He took a breath, guiding her through another turn. "But I'm not that man anymore. And you're not the same woman. We've both changed. Yet I find myself drawn to you still. Drawn to who you are now, not who you were in my forgotten past."

Her steps faltered slightly, but she recovered quickly, her expression guarded. "Pretty words, Lucien. But I need more than words."

"Then let me show you," he said simply. "Give me the chance to court you properly. To discover who we might be together now."

"While Mr. Fancot does the same?"

A flash of possessiveness surged through him, but he forced it down. "If that's what you require."

The music was drawing to a close, and Courtney stepped back as the final notes faded. "Life has taken some unexpected turns for us both," she said thoughtfully. "The gossips have had their fill discussing our situation, of course. Though I understand why things happened as they did with Farah, it's been…complicated to navigate socially."

Lucien felt a pang of remorse.

"I'm sorry for that additional burden," he said sincerely.

Her expression softened. "You did what was necessary for Farah's reputation. I don't fault you for that. But now, I need to proceed carefully, for my own sake."

"I understand completely," he assured her. "You're protecting your heart, as you should."

"And reputation." She stared at him, her amber eyes studying his face. "Axton has been patient and kind through all of this. He deserves consideration."

"And what do you deserve, Courtney?" he asked gently.

A small, genuine smile touched her lips. "A chance at happiness, whether that's with you, with him, or perhaps with neither. I am resolute on that."

Something flickered in her eyes, a softening, perhaps, or at least a willingness to listen.

"I'm leaving for Dorset in two days' time," he said, seizing the moment. "To inspect the estate and introduce Ava-Marie to her ancestral home. Would you consider accompanying us? Perhaps your brother Julian and his wife Serena could join as chaperones."

Surprise registered on her face. "You want me to travel to the country with you?"

"I want the chance to know you away from London's prying eyes. Away from the gossip and expectations. Just us, discovering who we are together now." He took her hand, his thumb brushing over her knuckles. "Lauren says we were happy at my estate. You used to visit to see Lauren and then to see me."

"That's true." He watched her as memories he could not share with her rolled across the expressions on her face.

He coaxed. "I won't press you for more than friendship at first. But I want the opportunity to show you that my interest is genuine and not born of convenience or necessity, but of genuine admiration and affection."

She studied him for a long moment, her amber eyes searching his face. "And Ava-Marie? How does she feel about this?"

"She asked specifically if you might come. She quite adores you." He smiled, remembering his daughter's excitement when he'd mentioned the possibility. "She said you promised to tell her more stories about the stars."

A genuine smile softened Courtney's features. "I did, didn't I?" She hesitated, then nodded slowly. "Very well. I'll speak with Julian about it. If he and Serena are willing, I...I would like to come."

Relief washed through him. "Thank you."

"Don't thank me yet, Lord Furoe," she warned, though the ice in her tone had thawed somewhat. "I haven't decided anything beyond a country visit."

"I understand," he assured her. "One step at a time."

As he led her off the dance floor, he spotted Fancot watching them from across the room, his expression a mixture of concern and calculation. Lucien met his gaze steadily, an unspoken message passing between them. He might not remember loving

Courtney, might not recall their shared past, but he knew with bone-deep certainty that he was unwilling to lose her before they'd had a proper chance.

"Axton seems to be waiting for the supper dance," Courtney observed, following his gaze.

"He's protective of you," Lucien acknowledged, managing a more measured tone than his instincts wanted.

A small smile played at the corners of her mouth. "As are you, it seems."

"I am." He turned to face her fully. "I may not remember our past, Courtney, but I know I want the chance to discover what we might be to each other now. If Mr. Fancot is also part of that journey while you decide, I understand. But I hope you'll give me a fair opportunity to show you who I am today. He's had five years."

"I want that too," she admitted, a spark of something— interest, warmth, perhaps even hope—kindling in her eyes. "But you do hold an advantage. My heart still loves you. That's why I haven't simply walked away."

"Despite having plenty of reasons you could have," he added with a rueful smile.

She laughed then, a genuine sound that lightened his heart. "Perhaps I'm simply curious to see what else you might say to redeem yourself."

"I can be very persuasive when motivated," he promised.

"We'll see." She glanced across the room. "I should go speak with the bride. I haven't had a chance to offer my congratulations."

"Of course." He bowed, brushing his lips against her knuckles in a gesture that lingered just a moment longer than propriety dictated. "But save me another dance before the evening ends?"

She hesitated, then nodded. "The last waltz."

As he watched her walk away, moving gracefully through the crowd toward where Farah stood radiant beside her new husband, Lucien felt a curious lightness in his chest. Not the passion he'd once felt for Ava, nor the desperate need of safety he'd briefly harbored from Farah, but something steadier. Something that felt, despite the complications and his lost memories, remarkably like coming home.

"You look pleased with yourself," Lauren commented, appearing at his side with uncanny timing. "I take it the conversation went well?"

"She's considering accompanying me to Dorset," he replied, still watching Courtney's progress through the ballroom.

"Ah. And what of her handsome admirer?"

"Mr. Fancot is welcome to try his luck," Lucien said, surprised by his own confidence. "But I don't intend to make it easy for him."

Lauren studied him thoughtfully. "You know, brother, I believe Ireland has made you more direct and less patient with society's games than you were before. The old Lucien would have maneuvered and plotted. This new version simply stakes his claim."

"Is that bad?"

She smiled, linking her arm with his. "No. In fact, I think it might be exactly what Courtney needs. She doesn't have time to play games. She's reaching a certain age... Perhaps she needs to experience the attentions of one who doesn't play by society's rules."

Across the room, Courtney turned, her eyes finding his through the crowd. Even at a distance, he could see the question in them, the careful consideration. She wasn't won yet and might never be, if he couldn't prove his feelings were genuine. But for the first time since returning to London, Lucien felt he had a clear path forward.

A small niggle of doubt hit him squarely in his chest as he made his way to talk to Rockwell. He wondered what Courtney wanted from a match with him. While he found her physically appealing, and intelligent, and he really liked her, and he hated the idea of another man wooing her, Lucien was very aware that his battered heart may refuse to open and let any woman in. What if she wanted words of love he could never say to her, or to any woman? Ava's lies had destroyed his heart and he didn't know how to recover.

❧ ❧ ❧

CHAPTER NINE

THE NOISE OF the ballroom had grown overwhelming. Courtney slipped through the French doors onto the west terrace, breathing deeply of the cool night air, grateful for the momentary respite. Rockwell's wedding ball was a splendid affair, but after her dance with Lucien, she needed a moment to collect her thoughts. Her heartbeat had only just begun to steady when Lauren appeared at her side.

"Seeking sanctuary?" Lauren asked, her blue eyes knowing.

"Just a breath of fresh air," Courtney replied, smiling at Lucien's sister. In the soft glow of the terrace lanterns, Lauren's resemblance to her brother was striking—the same dark hair, the same direct gaze, though Lauren's held the sparkle that Lucien's had lost during his years in Ireland.

"I saw you dancing with my brother." Lauren's tone was casual, but Courtney detected the undercurrent of curiosity. "He looked…intense."

"That would be one word for it," Courtney agreed, smoothing an invisible wrinkle from her emerald silk skirts. The memory of Lucien's hand at her waist, the earnestness in his gaze as he asked her to accompany them to Dorset lingered like the warmth of a hearth fire against winter's chill.

"Well, if you're hiding from him, you've chosen the wrong spot," Lauren teased. "He's been watching the doors since you left the ballroom."

"I'm not hiding," Courtney protested, though perhaps she

was, a little. Not from Lucien, but from the intensity of her own feelings. "I just needed a moment to clear my head."

"You and half the ladies of the *ton*, it seems," Lauren observed as their friend Valora appeared at the terrace doors, followed by Ivy and Ashley. Claire emerged a moment later, looking flushed from dancing. Ivy and Ashley, Rockwell's sisters, always tried to keep Valora's behavior in check. Valora was Axton's sister, and he had a hard time keeping infatuated men away from the great beauty and ton diamond. Claire was the most sensible of them all. Her brother was the Earl of Marlowe, the biggest rake in all England and the main reason Claire always declared she never wanted to marry. Her brother's heartbreaking ways made her believe love was for fools. All the ladies were part of the sisterhood investment club and the best of friends.

"There you both are," Valora said, her dark eyes bright with mischief. "Discussing Lord Furoe's sudden interest in courtship, I presume?"

Heat rose in Courtney's cheeks. "We were discussing the loveliness of the evening, actually."

"Mmm, very lovely indeed," Valora agreed, her smile teasing. "Especially the part where the recently returned viscount couldn't take his eyes off you during the waltz."

"Oh, leave Court alone," Ivy chided, though her own eyes sparkled with interest. "After everything she's endured, she deserves some peace."

"Thank you, Ivy," Courtney said, grateful for the intervention.

"Though," Ivy added thoughtfully, "I must say, the man does cut a fine figure in evening wear. Those shoulders have certainly broadened since his gentleman days."

"Farm work," Lauren explained, a touch of pride in her voice. "He's grown quite strong. Papa says he can outride any of the grooms now."

Courtney tried to reconcile this image, Lucien with rolled-up shirtsleeves, hair tousled, muscles straining as he hauled timber, with the polished viscount she'd fallen in love with five years ago. Both versions made her heart race, but in decidedly different ways.

"It is rather remarkable, isn't it?" Claire mused, leaning against the stone balustrade. "How this season has unfolded. First Serena and Julian, then Tiffany and Wolf, and now Farah and Rockwell—all married to men they've known their entire lives."

"It's as if Cupid suddenly remembered a stack of unfinished business," Ashley agreed with a laugh.

"Speaking of unfinished business," Valora said, turning to Claire, "where is that disreputable brother of yours tonight? I haven't seen Fane anywhere."

Claire rolled her eyes. "Probably somewhere he shouldn't be, with someone he shouldn't be with. I wouldn't wait on my rakish, man-whore brother if I were you, Val. He's not looking at settling down anytime soon."

"As if I'd wait on him," Valora scoffed, though Courtney noticed the slight flush that crept up her neck. "I was merely curious."

"Curiosity is a dangerous thing where Fane is concerned," Claire warned. "Just ask any debutante from the last three Seasons. He broke many a heart."

"Well, I'm certainly not in danger of becoming the next bride this season," Ashley said, a hint of resignation in her voice. "Not with the 'scandal' still hanging over me."

"Don't be so certain," Ivy countered, nudging her friend gently. "Society's memory is shorter than we give it credit for. I've noticed the Duke of Blackstone speaking with you twice this evening." Her eyes widened meaningfully. "Farah's brother, no less!"

Ashley waved dismissively, though her eyes brightened. "He was merely being polite. His Grace would never consider a match with someone like me."

"Someone intelligent, beautiful, and accomplished?" Lauren asked innocently. "How dreadful for him."

They all laughed, and Courtney felt a rush of affection for these women. Even with everything that had happened, her supposedly deceased fiancé returning from the grave with a child and no memory of their love, they had rallied around her, offering support without judgment.

"What about you, Court?" Ivy asked. "Will you give Lucien another chance? Or is Mr. Fancot the frontrunner for your affections now?"

All eyes turned to her, curious but not unkind. Courtney hesitated, uncertain how to articulate her conflicted feelings. "I honestly don't know," she admitted. "Lucien is…different now. Not the man I remember, but perhaps someone I could come to care for just as deeply."

"And Axton?" Valora prompted.

"He's been a steadfast friend," Courtney said carefully. "He helped me through some of my darkest days after Lucien was presumed dead. He's kind, thoughtful, and straightforward about his intentions."

"Unlike some men we could mention," Claire muttered.

Lauren bristled slightly. "My brother's circumstances are hardly typical. He lost his memory, Claire. It's not as if he intentionally abandoned Courtney."

"No, just unintentionally fell in love with someone else, fathered a child, and then announced an engagement to Farah the moment he returned to London," Claire countered, then immediately looked chagrined. "I'm sorry, Courtney. That was unkind."

"But not entirely inaccurate," Courtney acknowledged with a wry smile. "Though to be fair, the engagement to Farah was merely to protect her reputation after it came to light that she'd accompanied Rockwell to Ireland unchaperoned."

"How scandalously convenient," Valora remarked, arching an elegant eyebrow.

"Valora," Ivy admonished.

"What? I'm only saying what everyone's thinking. The whole

situation is extraordinary. Like something from a Jane Austen novel."

"Life rarely follows the neat patterns of fiction," Ashley observed quietly. "People make mistakes, hearts change, circumstances intervene. What matters is how we face what comes next."

The wisdom in her words settled over the group. Courtney found herself nodding. "That's precisely it. I can't change what's happened, but I can decide how to proceed. And right now, that means taking time to know who Lucien is now, while also keeping my heart...cautious."

"Very sensible," Lauren approved. "Though I hope you don't mind my saying that I'd be delighted to call you sister one day. I always thought you and Lucien perfectly suited, even before...everything."

Courtney squeezed her hand gratefully. "You're very kind. And I've always adored you, Lauren. Whatever happens with your brother, that won't change."

"So, you're truly considering traveling to Dorset with them?" Ivy asked, eyes wide. "That seems rather significant."

"Only if Julian and Serena will be with us as chaperones," Courtney clarified quickly. "And it will be good for me to spend time with Ava-Marie and Lucien away from London's prying eyes."

"Ah yes, the child," Claire said, her tone softening. "What is she like?"

"Wonderful," Courtney replied without hesitation. "Spirited, curious, unaffected by society's rules. She has Lucien's eyes and his directness. She's quite enchanting, actually."

"And you don't find it difficult?" Ashley asked gently. "Caring for the child he had with another woman?"

The question gave Courtney pause. In truth, she'd struggled with that initially. She had to face the stark evidence that Lucien had loved someone else, built a life without her. But from the moment Ava-Marie had thrust those cherry blossoms into her hands, eyes bright with innocent generosity, she'd been unable to hold the child or Lucien responsible for circumstances beyond her control.

"I love her for herself," she said finally. "She's not responsible for the past. And she's suffered losses too—her mother, her home in Ireland."

"You have a generous heart, Court," Valora said, her usual teasing manner subdued. "Not many women would be so understanding."

"Understanding, yes. But foolish? I hope not." Courtney sighed. "That's why I'm proceeding cautiously. I need to be certain of what I want before making any decisions. And perhaps Tiffany's investments can earn enough money for Lauren that Lucien could take his time and find a woman he really wants rather than one he just needs."

"I don't believe he's paying you attention just because he needs you," Ashley said. "There are plenty of rich mothers looking for a man of his social standing to marry their daughters to. He could take an easier path." Ashley shook her head. "No. He is drawn to you, Court."

The conversation might have continued, but a shadow fell across the terrace as the door opened once more. Baron Lockwood stepped into the lantern light, his attire impeccable but his eyes moved over the ladies with calculated interest. Courtney felt an instinctive chill when his gaze found her and lingered.

"What a delightful gathering," he remarked, strolling toward them with a confidence that bordered on arrogance. "The loveliest flowers of the *ton*, all conveniently assembled. I must be in fortune's favor tonight."

While undeniably handsome, with his golden hair and aristocratic features, there was something in Lockwood's smile that put Courtney on edge—a coldness that never quite left his ice-blue colored eyes.

"Baron," Lauren acknowledged coolly. "What brings you to the terrace? Surely the card rooms would hold more appeal for a gentleman of your…interests."

If he registered the slight, Lockwood gave no indication. "The pleasure of ladies' company far exceeds that of cards, Lady Lauren. Though I hear your father may disagree."

Courtney saw Lauren stiffen and moved closer to her friend, distaste rising. Lucien had mentioned his confrontation with Lockwood at Crockford's; the baron's reference to the earl's gambling problem was a deliberate barb.

"How fortunate we are to be graced with your preference," Courtney interjected, her tone deliberately light but her eyes frosty. "Though I'm afraid we were just discussing matters unlikely to interest you."

"On the contrary, Lady Courtney," Lockwood replied, stepping closer to her, "I find everything about you fascinating."

The directness of his gaze made her skin crawl. There was nothing of genuine admiration in it; rather, it held the calculating assessment of a predator.

"How flattering," she replied, not bothering to hide her disinterest. "Though I imagine your fascination is rather newly acquired."

His smile thinned. "Not so newly as you might think. I've long admired your…resilience."

"My resilience?" she echoed, baffled by his choice of words.

"Indeed. To endure the loss of a fiancé, to stay true to him, then witness his miraculous return with a new child and no memory of your engagement, then observe his immediate proposal to your friend… Most women would crumble under such circumstances." His voice dripped with false sympathy.

The other ladies moved subtly closer around Courtney, a protective wall of silk skirts and steely glares.

"Lady Courtney's strength is well known," Ivy said firmly. "As is her good judgment."

"Of course," Lockwood agreed smoothly. "I merely offer my admiration. And perhaps…a sympathetic ear, should you ever tire of Lord Furoe's inconstancy."

Claire scoffed audibly. "I believe Lady Courtney has no shortage of confidants, Baron."

"No doubt. Though perhaps fewer who understand the true character of the returned viscount." Something glinted in Lockwood's eyes—knowledge, or the pretense of it. "I've been making some inquiries about his time in Ireland, you see. Most enlightening."

Despite herself, Courtney felt a flicker of curiosity. "Inquiries?"

"Court," Lauren murmured in warning, but Lockwood had already seized upon her interest.

"I find it curious," he continued, lowering his voice theatrically, "that a man of Lord Furoe's background would adapt so seamlessly to life as a simple farmer. One might almost think he'd had…assistance."

"Lucien suffered a traumatic head injury," Lauren said sharply. "He had no memory of his former life."

"So, we've been told," Lockwood replied, his tone suggesting skepticism. "And yet, he managed to find a wife almost immediately. Most convenient."

Courtney's dislike deepened into outright aversion. "I fail to see what you're implying, Baron, but I find your interest in my former fiancé rather excessive."

"Not in him, my lady," Lockwood corrected, his gaze still fixed on her face. "In you. I merely thought you deserved to know the truth about the man who abandoned you."

"Abandoned?" Valora repeated incredulously. "He nearly died in the Irish Rebellion."

"Is that the story?" Lockwood's smile was chilling in its insincerity. "How very dramatic. Almost as dramatic as returning with a child in tow." He turned back to Courtney. "Tell me, Lady Courtney, have you met the little girl? Ava-Marie, isn't it? Such an unusual name. I understand she looks just like her father."

"She does," Courtney replied stiffly, increasingly uncomfortable with his line of questioning.

"And the mother? What was she like, this Irish farmer's daughter who captured the heart of a viscount?"

"She was his wife," Courtney said, wondering why he would ask such a question. "And she is deceased. It's hardly appropriate to discuss her."

"His wife," Lockwood repeated, as if testing the word. "Yes, of course. How unfortunate that she passed before she could join London society."

"I believe we've entertained your conversation long enough, Baron," Ashley said firmly. "If you'll excuse us."

Lockwood bowed, but his eyes never left Courtney's face. "Of course. I wouldn't dream of imposing further. But Lady Courtney, should you ever wish to learn more about your returned fiancé's…adventures in Ireland, I would be most happy to share what I've discovered."

There was something disturbing in his tone, a hint of malice thinly veiled as concern. Courtney felt the hairs on the back of her neck rise.

"I doubt you could tell me anything of value that Lucien could not tell me himself," she replied icily.

"Perhaps not," he conceded, though his smile suggested otherwise. "But it's always wise to know the truth about those closest to us, wouldn't you agree? Especially when children are involved."

Before she could respond, Ivy stepped forward, deliberately placing herself between Courtney and the baron. "I believe Lord Blackstone was looking for you in the card room, Baron. Something about a wager from last week's races."

It was a blatant fabrication, but an effective one. Lockwood hesitated, clearly weighing the potential advantage of continuing his conversation against the risk of offending a duke.

"I should hate to keep His Grace waiting," he said finally. "Ladies, it has been a pleasure. Lady Courtney—" he bowed over her hand, his grip lingering uncomfortably "—until our next meeting."

As he disappeared back through the terrace doors, the tension among the women eased tangibly.

"What an odious man," Claire declared, shuddering slightly.

"He's dangerous," Lauren added, her expression troubled. "Lucien said as much after their confrontation at Crockford's. My father, who was well in his cups, lost a significant sum to the baron and he was deliberately attempting to win more when Lucien intervened."

"And now it seems he's seeking some form of revenge," Ivy observed. "Though what he hopes to accomplish by making vague insinuations about Lucien's time in Ireland, I can't imagine."

More concerning was his evident interest in Ava-Marie. What possible reason could he have for asking about the child's mother?

"Are you all right, Court?" Ashley asked gently. "You've gone quite pale."

"I'm fine," she replied automatically, though her mind was racing. "Just tired. Perhaps I should return to the ballroom."

"We'll all go," Valora declared, linking her arm through Courtney's. "Safety in numbers. That man is vile."

As they made their way back inside, Courtney scanned the crowd for Lucien. She spotted him across the room, deep in conversation with Rockwell. His expression was serious, intent, so different from the carefree viscount she'd known before. Yet there was something compelling in that seriousness, a depth that drew her, even as it reminded her how much he had changed.

Whether Lockwood was merely being malicious or truly knew something about Lucien's time in Ireland, one thing was clear: she needed to proceed with care. Not just to protect her own heart, but perhaps Lucien's as well. Whatever Lockwood was planning, he clearly meant harm to the Furoe family.

And despite everything that had happened, despite her lingering uncertainties, she found herself unwilling to allow that. If Lockwood thought he could use her as a pawn in whatever game he was playing, he would soon discover his mistake. She might be cautious with her heart these days, but her loyalty—once given—was not easily shaken.

As if sensing her gaze, Lucien looked up, his eyes finding hers across the crowded ballroom. Something passed between them, a silent recognition, a connection that transcended memory. He excused himself from Rockwell and began making his way toward her, his expression warming as he drew near.

"You look troubled," he said without preamble when he reached her side. "Has something happened?"

The concern in his voice was genuine, and Courtney found herself momentarily at a loss for words.

"It's nothing," she said finally, deciding that Lockwood's insinuations could wait for a more private moment. "Just a tiresome conversation on the terrace."

Lucien studied her face, clearly unconvinced. "I see." His gaze moved to where Lockwood had entered the ballroom behind them, and his expression hardened. "Did the baron have something to say that upset you?"

His perception surprised her. "How did you know it was Lockwood?"

"The way you're looking at him," Lucien replied simply. "Like he's a particularly unpleasant insect you found in your tea."

Despite herself, Courtney laughed. "What a charming analogy."

His smile in response was warm, genuine, and wholly his own—not an echo of the man she'd lost, but something new and equally compelling. "I may have lost my aristocratic polish in Ireland, but I gained a certain clarity about people's characters."

"So, it seems," she agreed, finding herself relaxing in his presence despite the lingering unease from her encounter with Lockwood. "It's not an entirely unwelcome change."

"No?" His eyes held a tentative hope that tugged at her heart.

"No," she confirmed softly. "It isn't."

The orchestra struck up the opening notes of the final waltz, and Lucien offered his hand. "I believe you promised me this dance, Lady Courtney."

As she placed her hand in his, Courtney was acutely aware of Lockwood watching them from across the room, his cold gaze assessing. Whatever game the baron was playing, whatever he thought he knew about Lucien's past in Ireland, she would not allow him to use it to hurt Lucien or his daughter.

Some things were worth protecting, even when one's own heart remained uncertain.

"So, I did, Lord Furoe," she replied, allowing him to lead her onto the dance floor. "So, I did."

CHAPTER TEN

THE CARRIAGE ROCKED gently as it wound along the coastal road, and Courtney leaned forward to catch her first glimpse of Danvers Hall through the window. The Dorset countryside unfurled around them in a tapestry of emerald fields and wild hedgerows, the late summer light bathing everything in golden warmth. Beside her, Ava-Marie bounced in her seat, her small face alight with excitement.

"Are we nearly there, Lady Courtney? Will we see the sea?" The little girl had been asking variations of this question since they'd left London two days prior.

"Almost there, darling," Courtney replied, smoothing a wayward curl from the child's forehead. "If I remember correctly, yes, you can see the sea from the house. It sits on a cliff overlooking the water."

As they crested the final hill, the hall and grounds came into view, and Courtney's breath caught in her throat. Five years had done little to change its weathered stone facade, the ivy climbing its walls perhaps a bit more abundant, the gardens somewhat less tended. But it was still the place where she and Lucien had spent countless summer days, where she had first realized she was in love with him.

"Goodness, it's bigger than our London house. It looks like a castle," Ava-Marie said in awe, pressing her small nose against the glass.

"It's so big you can get lost in it," Courtney said. "There are meadows where you can run, and a path down to a small cove where we can swim when the weather is warm enough."

"I love swimming," Caitria said. "I shall swim everyday while we are here. I'll teach Ava-Marie."

Courtney wondered if that was Caitria's way of saying Ava-Marie was hers to look after? Was she going to have a problem with the young woman where Ava-Marie was concerned? She couldn't blame her. Caitria had been a mother to Ava-Marie.

"I'd forgotten how big their estate is," Julian said. "I'm looking forward to riding and swimming with you, my love," he said, picking up his wife's hand and pressing a kiss to her knuckles.

"Thank you both for coming with me."

"What are big brothers for but to ensure my sister is chaperoned properly?"

Serena laughed at Courtney's stricken look. "Not too properly, I suspect Courtney is hoping."

Her brother didn't reply as Courtney's face heated. She turned to look out the window.

A memory washed over her unbidden. Lucien pulling her by the hand down that same path, both of them laughing as they raced toward the water. She had been wearing her oldest dress, one she didn't mind ruining with salt water, and he had rolled up his trousers to wade into the surf beside her. They'd been so carefree and innocent then, before his departure for Ireland, before the years of believing him dead.

"Papa says there are ponies," Ava-Marie said, her green eyes, so like Lucien's, wide with anticipation. "He promised I could learn to ride."

"Your father loves horses," Courtney replied, grateful for the distraction from her memories. "He taught me to ride properly, you know. When I was younger, I was terribly afraid of falling."

"Were you?" Ava-Marie looked skeptical, as though she couldn't imagine the composed Lady Courtney being afraid of anything.

"I was," Courtney admitted with a smile. "But your father

was very patient. He chose the gentlest mare in the stables and walked beside me for hours until I felt confident enough to ride alone."

What she didn't share was how those lessons had led to long rides across the estate, galloping side by side over open fields, stopping to picnic by the stream that marked the estate's eastern boundary. How Lucien had taught her to jump fences, his pride in her accomplishments warming her from within. How he had stolen kisses from her for the first time after one such ride, both of them windswept and exhilarated.

The carriage began its descent toward the hall, and Courtney caught sight of two figures waiting at the entrance. Her heart sped up at the sight of Lucien and she also spied Mr. Roberts, the new estate manager whom Lord Wolfarth had recommended after Lucien's father had been forced to dismiss the previous one. Her heart quickened at the sight of Lucien, still unaccustomed to the miracle of his return despite the weeks that had passed since the scandal at Farah's ball had been resolved.

"Look! There's Papa!" Ava-Marie cried, waving enthusiastically though the men couldn't possibly see her through the carriage windows.

"Yes, dear, we're nearly there," Caitria said, adjusting the child's bonnet which had gone askew during her excited bouncing.

Julian, seated across from Courtney, glanced out the window with interest. "The place has good bones, though it's clear it's been neglected. I'm curious to hear what Mr. Roberts has already assessed."

"I'm just looking forward to a proper walk after being cooped up in this carriage," Serena remarked, smoothing her skirts. As Courtney's companion and chaperone for the visit, she had borne the journey with remarkable patience.

As they pulled to a stop before the house, Lucien stepped forward to open the carriage door himself, his smile warm as he greeted them. "Welcome to Dorset," he said, his voice carrying that slight Irish lilt that still startled her occasionally. "I hope the journey wasn't too taxing?"

"It was worth every bump in the road," Courtney replied, allowing her hand to linger in his as he helped her descend. "The estate looks almost the same."

It was a slight exaggeration. Up close, she could see how the years of neglect had taken their toll. The gravel drive was overgrown with weeds, the fountain in the center courtyard was dry, and several shutters hung askew. But the bones of the place remained sound, and she could see the potential for restoration.

Julian followed, then helped Caitria down with Ava-Marie practically leaping out after her, while Serena descended last with the dignified air of someone determined to maintain decorum, despite the journey's difficulties.

Mr. Roberts stepped forward, a stocky man with the weathered complexion of someone who spent much of his life outdoors. "Welcome to Danvers Hall, my lady, Lord and Lady Montague," he said with a slight bow to Courtney, Serena and Julian. "I've been familiarizing myself with the property these past few days."

"Mr. Roberts has been invaluable," Lucien added. "His knowledge of estate management is impressive. We've already identified several areas for immediate improvement."

Julian nodded appreciatively. "I'd be very interested to hear your assessment, Mr. Roberts. Perhaps I can provide advice to Lucien if he requires it."

"Of course, my lord," Mr. Roberts replied. "I've prepared some notes on the tenant farms and the southern fields that I believe will interest Lord Furoe. A second opinion never hurts."

Ava-Marie tugged at Lucien's coat. "Papa, you promised to show me the sea! Can we go now, please?"

Lucien bent to kiss the top of her head. "Soon, darling. First, we must let everyone settle in. The journey has been long."

"I'll take her to wash up and change," Caitria offered. "Perhaps Lady Serena and Lady Courtney would like to rest as well?"

"An excellent suggestion," Lucien agreed. "The housekeeper has prepared rooms for everyone. Meanwhile, Lord Milburn, if you'd care to join Mr. Roberts and me for a brief tour of the immediate grounds?"

"I would indeed," Julian replied with enthusiasm. "I'm particularly interested in seeing what stock you have on the property."

As the men prepared to depart on their inspection, Courtney exchanged a warm glance with Lucien. "Don't keep my brother too long," she said lightly. "We've been promised a view of the sea, after all."

"I wouldn't dream of disappointing you," Lucien replied, his eyes lingering on hers for a moment longer than was strictly proper. "We'll return shortly."

The small party separated, with the ladies and Ava-Marie being led inside by the housekeeper while the men strode off toward the fields, already deep in conversation about crop rotation and soil quality.

Inside, the huge hall was cool and dim after the bright sunshine, the familiar scent of beeswax and lavender bringing a rush of memories. Courtney paused in the entrance hall, overwhelmed for a moment by the sense of the past pressing in around her. This was where she and Lucien had danced during the midsummer party, where he had first told her he loved her, where they had planned their future together.

"Lady Courtney?" Serena's voice gently pulled her back to the present. "I hope it's not too overwhelming for you?"

"It's only happy memories," Courtney assured her, gathering herself. "Just taking in the familiar surroundings. It's been some time since I visited."

Ava-Marie looked around with undisguised curiosity, her bright eyes taking in the portrait gallery that lined the staircase. "Who are all these people, Lady Courtney? Are they Papa's family?"

"Yes, they are," Courtney replied, leading the child toward the stairs. "That's your grandfather when he was young, and next to him is your grandmother. And there—" she pointed to a portrait of a young, dark-haired woman, "is your aunt Lauren when she was just sixteen."

"She's pretty," Ava-Marie observed, then wrinkled her nose. "The house smells funny. Like old books."

Courtney laughed softly. "That's because there are a great many old books here. Perhaps Caitria can show you the library after you've rested." She didn't want to have to tell Ava-Marie that the house had all but virtually been shut up and servants released due to finances.

"Oh yes, please!" Ava-Marie's enthusiasm was immediate. "Papa says I can learn to read properly now that we're settled. Can you help teach me, Lady Courtney?"

The simple question touched Courtney deeply. "I would be honored to help you learn to read, Ava-Marie. The library here has some wonderful books for children that I think you'll enjoy." She wondered if Caitria could read. Perhaps she could teach them both.

The housekeeper led them to their rooms, which had been prepared with evident care despite the manor's general state of disrepair. Lucien had obviously hired more staff with some of the money Rockwell had loaned him. Courtney's chamber was exactly as she remembered it from her last visit. The same blue and cream wallpaper, the same view of the gardens and, beyond them, the glittering expanse of the sea. And, as usual, she was placed just down the hall from Lucien's rooms. How convenient.

Once alone, she moved to the window, drinking in the familiar vista. How many times had she stood at this very window, watching for Lucien to return from one of his rides? How many dreams had she woven here, imagining their future together in this house?

Those dreams had been shattered by his disappearance, then reshaped by his return. The pressure to see what their relationship could be now made her shoulders sag under the weight of hope and expectations. The one question she had yet to find the courage to ask was, was Lucien still in love with his wife?

A soft knock at the door interrupted her reverie.

"Come in," she called, turning from the window.

Caitria entered, her expression apologetic. "Forgive the intrusion, my lady, but Ava-Marie is desperate to see the sea. She's been cooped up for a few days so a walk should tire her out for the afternoon. She's washed and changed already, and I wondered if perhaps you might accompany us to the cliff path? She's quite insistent that we wait for you."

Courtney smiled. "Of course. I'd be delighted to show you both the view. It truly is spectacular."

As they walked together down the hall to collect Ava-Marie, Courtney felt a sense of rightness, of pieces falling into place. This grand old house, weathered but enduring, seemed to welcome her back like an old friend. And if the memories it held were bittersweet, they were also precious. They contained the foundations on which to build new remembrances with this changed Lucien and his delightful daughter.

Standing at the cliff's edge a short while later, with Ava-Marie's small hand clasped trustingly in hers as they gazed out at the endless blue of sea meeting sky, Courtney allowed herself to hope.

She showed them the narrow path to the shore below, warning them both to be careful of the drop and that Ava-Marie was never to go down to the beach or go in the water alone. The rip tides were dangerous.

Caitria took Ava-Marie to paddle in the water while Courtney sat on the sand, remembering spying on Lucien swimming naked when she was a young girl and visiting with Lauren. On her first visit here, she'd decided to marry Lauren's handsome older brother, and a few years later when he proposed, she knew her dreams had come true.

Just then, a body plonked down in the sand next to her. She knew who it was before she turned to look at him. "My daughter's going to love it here."

She turned to smile at him. "It's a beautiful place."

His smile died. "It will be when I set it to rights. What were you thinking about before I sat?"

She laughed and felt her cheeks heat. "I was remembering spying on you swimming in this cove when I was fifteen. That's the day I knew I wanted to marry you."

"I was a good swimmer then?" he laughed.

"More like the fact you were nude, and as you were the first naked man I'd ever seen, my head was turned."

This time, Lucien's cheeks flushed with color.

She carried on. "We often swam here after we were engaged. And swimming clothes were often absent."

Before he could reply, Ava-Marie spotted her father. "Papa!" She raced across the sand and threw herself into her father's open arms. "I love it here. I want to swim every day."

Lucien hugged her tight and kissed the top of her head. "As long as a grown up is with you, then you may come here as often as you like. And of course, if you are a good girl."

Courtney loved how he didn't care that Ava-Marie's dress was wet and covered in sand. He still hugged her tight.

"Now, I think it's time Caitria took you home. I want to have a talk with Lady Courtney, if that's all right?"

The little girl must have been tired as she didn't put up a fight. Soon, only the sound of the gulls and waves filled the silence.

"Lord Danvers accompanied you here," she asked. "How has your father settled in? Lauren was worried about him." It was lame conversation, and she wondered if they would ever get to that place where they could talk about anything and know what the other would say before they spoke.

Lucien lay back on the sand with his hands behind his head. "He seems to be better away from town. He's still drinking too much, but I don't think he's gambling. I've let it be known around the area that no one is to let him gamble. He's even seeing a widow in the village."

"That must be a weight off your shoulders. I know you've only been here for ten days, but what else have you uncovered since you've been here alone?"

He closed his eyes against the glare of the sun. "That I understand estate management but I'd still welcome Julian's input to a few ideas I have. Rockwell also mentioned that I should follow him in developing a Merino herd, but I'm not sure I can afford to take a risk."

Courtney bit her lip and wondered if she could tell him about the mills the ladies were investing in. The sisterhood followed Tiffany's advice. She'd done her research regarding the demand for the fine wool. Their share price was racing up on the idea of a more consistent supply of Merino wool. "I believe Rockwell is right and the risk is worth taking."

His eyes flew open. "And how would you know that? Have you been studying the share market?" He laughed…but his laughter died as he looked at her face.

She swallowed hard. "If we are to have any chance at seeing if this relationship can evolve into something both of us want, we must trust each other. Don't you agree?" She looked into his eyes.

He rose up on one elbow but took his time in answering. "I think trust would be an advantage, certainly."

"So, we shouldn't keep secrets between us."

He shrugged his shoulders. "Depends on whose secrets they are. Sometimes a person can't share, even if they want to, because it's not their secret."

She nodded. "That makes sense. Then maybe I can't share this secret, as it's not just mine. But you'll just have to trust me when I say follow Rockwell's advice. You won't regret it."

He reached up and brushed an escaped curl from her cheek. "I'm glad you're here."

Lucien watched the waves lap against the shore, their rhythmic motion almost hypnotic. The afternoon sun had begun its slow descent toward the horizon, painting the sky in strokes of gold and amber that reminded him of Courtney's eyes. Beside him, she sat with her knees drawn up, arms wrapped around them, her skirts spread around her on the sand like the petals of a flower. The breeze lifted tendrils of her auburn hair, and he resisted the urge to reach out and tuck them back into place.

"It's beautiful here," she said, breaking the comfortable silence that had settled between them after Caitria had taken Ava-Marie back to the house. "I'd forgotten how the light changes everything at this time of day."

"It reminds me a bit of the Irish coast," he found himself saying. "Though the cliffs there were rougher, wilder somehow."

She turned to look at him, curiosity in her amber eyes. "Do you miss it? Ireland?"

He considered the question, surprised to find the answer wasn't simple. "Parts of it," he admitted. "The simplicity, perhaps. Knowing exactly who I was and what was expected of me each day. No complicated social obligations, no family fortune to restore."

"No memories to recover," she added softly.

He nodded, feeling a familiar twist of guilt in his chest. "No ghosts of a man I can't remember being."

Courtney drew idle patterns in the sand with her fingertips, her expression thoughtful. "Tell me about her," she said after a moment. "About Ava."

The request caught him off guard, and he tensed slightly, unsure how to respond. So far, he'd managed to avoid this conversation, but here, with the sun setting and the sea whispering secrets to the shore, it seemed impossible to deflect.

"Why would you want to know about her?" he asked, watching Courtney's face carefully.

"Because she was important to you," Courtney said simply. "Because she gave you Ava-Marie. And because I think understanding your life in Ireland might help me understand who you are now."

Lucien sighed, picking up a smooth pebble and turning it over in his hands. "She was…vibrant," he said finally. "Full of life, always laughing or singing, with this wild copper hair that seemed to catch fire in the sunlight. She found me after I was injured—nursed me back to health."

He paused, choosing his words carefully. The truth about how Ava had deceived him, pretending they were married when they weren't, creating an entire fictional past for them, was something he couldn't tell her. Only Rockwell and Farah knew the truth, and he intended to keep it that way. The shame of it, the implications for Ava-Marie's legitimacy—the consequences for his family, for Lauren and Madeline finding good matches… Hell, even he needed a good match. It would be devastating if society ever learned the truth. He didn't really know this woman.

"Did you love her?" Courtney asked, and though her voice was steady, he caught the slight tremor in her hand as she brushed sand from her skirt.

CHAPTER ELEVEN

"I DID," HE answered honestly, staring out at the horizon. "She was my anchor when I had nothing else. And when she died..." His throat tightened. "When she died, I grieved for her. For the mother of my child, for the woman who'd made me feel alive."

He glanced at Courtney, saw the gentle sympathy in her eyes, and continued, "But looking back now, knowing what I know about who I was before..." He shook his head. "It was a different kind of love than what we apparently had. Simpler in some ways but also built on a foundation of emptiness where my memories should have been. She didn't care who I was but only what I could do for her. She just wanted out of her horrible life of destitution, and I can't blame her for that."

"I can't imagine how disorienting this situation is for you," Courtney said, her voice soft with genuine compassion.

"The hardest part was learning she kept things from me," he admitted carefully. "Not just about who I might have been, but about our life together. Small things at first, that grew larger over time."

Lucien let out a bitter laugh. "The irony is, I still don't know all of it. There are still pieces of the puzzle that don't quite fit." He thought of the truth he could never share. That he'd never actually married Ava, that Ava-Marie was illegitimate and he felt the familiar twist of shame and fear in his gut.

Courtney seemed to sense there was more he wasn't saying.

"Is that why it's hard for you to trust now? Because she wasn't completely honest with you?"

Her perception startled him. "Perhaps," he admitted. "How can you trust your own judgment when it's been proven fallible? How can you trust others, when the one person you relied on completely wasn't entirely forthcoming?"

"People have different reasons for keeping things to themselves," Courtney said gently. "Not all of them malicious."

"No," he agreed, meeting her gaze. "They're not."

The unspoken question hung between them: *But how do I know I can trust you?* It wasn't fair to her, he knew. She'd given him no reason to doubt her sincerity. But the wounds Ava had left were still raw, still bleeding whenever he prodded them.

"What are you looking for now, Lucien?" Courtney asked, drawing her shawl more tightly around her shoulders as the evening breeze picked up. "In a wife, I mean. I know you have no choice but to marry, due to your family's finances, but surely you want to be happy?"

The directness of her question caught him by surprise, but then, this new Courtney seemed more forthright than the society lady he'd been told about. He found he rather liked it.

"Honesty," he said immediately. "Above all, honesty." The irony of this response, given his own carefully guarded secret about Ava-Marie, wasn't lost on him. Shame burned in his chest, but he pushed it aside. It wasn't truly dishonesty, he told himself. And it wasn't just his secret—it was Ava-Marie's too. It was protection for his daughter, for his family name. "Someone who sees me as I am now, not as the man I was before. Someone who understands that I may never remember my past, and who doesn't expect me to become someone I'm not. Someone who would be content to live a simple life on the estate and share the burden of my title and place in this world."

"That seems reasonable," she said, a small smile playing at the corners of her mouth.

"And kindness," he continued, warming to the subject.

"Someone who could love Ava-Marie as her own. Someone intelligent, who can challenge me, make me think."

"And passion?" Courtney asked, a hint of mischief in her eyes. "Surely that matters too?"

Heat crept up his neck. "Yes," he admitted. "That too." Ava had been as wild in bed as she had been outside of it.

She laughed, the sound carried away by the wind. "At least you're honest about that."

Not as honest as you deserve, he thought bitterly.

"What about you?" he asked instead. "What are you looking for in a husband? Mr. Axton Fancot seems quite attentive."

Something flickered in her eyes—amusement, perhaps, or exasperation. "Axton is charming and kind, and yes, attentive. But…" She trailed off, looking out at the sea.

"But?" he prompted, surprised by the flicker of jealousy he felt at the mention of Fancot's name.

"But I'm not looking for charm or attention," she said slowly. "I want someone who sees beyond the proper Lady Courtney that society expects. Someone who understands that I have thoughts and desires of my own, that I'm more than just a suitable match or a convenient solution to a problem. And I want a husband who captures my heart."

His heart was broken, and he doubted any woman could mend it.

"And passion, of course," she added with a small smile, echoing his earlier admission.

"Of course," he agreed, returning her smile despite the turmoil in his chest.

She turned to face him fully, her expression suddenly serious. "How do we know, Lucien? How do we know if we could build something real together, when we're both so different from who we were before?"

It was the question that had been haunting him since his return to London. Since the moment he'd realized that the elegant, reserved Lady Courtney might still hold feelings for him, despite everything that had happened.

"I don't think we can know," he said honestly. "Not with certainty. But perhaps we can discover it together."

"How?" she asked, her voice barely audible above the sound of the waves.

Lucien shifted closer, drawn by the vulnerability in her eyes. "We have two weeks here, away from London's prying eyes, away from society's expectations. Let's use that time to truly get to know each other as we are now. To talk, to laugh, to see if there's still something between us worth building upon."

"A trial period?" she asked, a hint of amusement in her voice. "How pragmatic, Lord Furoe."

"I prefer to think of it as thorough," he countered, matching her tone. "No one builds a house without first examining the foundation."

She laughed again, and the sound warmed him more effectively than the setting sun. "Very well. Two weeks to discover if we suit. But I have conditions."

"Of course you do," he said dryly, though his lips twitched with suppressed amusement. "Let me hear them."

"Complete honesty," she said, holding up one finger. "We must promise to speak our minds, even when it's difficult. No hiding behind politeness or social niceties."

He nodded, ignoring the guilty twist in his gut. He couldn't promise complete honesty, not yet. Not about Ava-Marie. But he could be honest about everything else. "Agreed. What else?"

"No pressure," she continued, raising a second finger. "If, at the end of these two weeks, either of us feels this isn't right, we part as friends. No recriminations, no wounded pride."

"That seems fair," he agreed. "Anything else?"

A mischievous glint appeared in her eyes as she raised a third finger. "Passion. Desire. I can't live without knowing you want me in your bed."

Lucien's breath caught in his throat. "I beg your pardon?"

"You heard me," she said, a becoming blush spreading across

her cheeks despite her bold words. "How can we possibly determine if we suit without testing passion? It's a matter of scientific inquiry."

He laughed, surprised and delighted by this unexpected side of her. "Scientific inquiry, is it? Well, far be it from me to stand in the way of science." He leaned closer, his voice dropping to a murmur. "How would you propose we conduct this experiment?"

Her blush deepened, but she met his gaze steadily. "When it feels right. Not forced, not planned. Just…right. We indulge. It's not as if you can ruin me twice."

Something shifted between them, a tension that hadn't been there before, or perhaps it had always been there but hadn't been acknowledged. Lucien suddenly found himself acutely aware of the fading light, the isolation of the beach, the way her lips parted slightly as she waited for his response.

"Agreed," he said softly. "All three conditions."

He could have kissed her then. Part of him wanted to, wanted to bridge the small distance between them and discover if her lips were as soft as they looked, if she would respond with the same surprising boldness she'd shown in making her request.

But it wouldn't be right. Not yet. Not with the weight of his secret about Ava and Ava-Marie still haunting him.

Instead, he rose to his feet, offering her his hand. "We should head back. The tide will be coming in soon, and dinner will be waiting."

She took his hand, allowing him to help her up, but didn't immediately release him. "Lucien," she said quietly, "I meant what I said about honesty. Whatever happened in Ireland, whatever secrets you're still keeping, I won't judge you for them. When you're ready to share, I'll listen."

The simple offer, made with such genuine compassion, nearly undid him. For a moment, he was tempted to confess everything about Ava's greater deceptions that he'd discovered after her death, about his fear that he might never be capable of the kind of love Courtney deserved. But the truth about Ava-Marie's birth remained locked away, a secret he'd never reveal.

Instead, he squeezed her hand gently. "Thank you," he said, the words inadequate for the emotions churning inside him. And to take her mind off of secrets, he pulled her into his arms and kissed her.

He ran the tip of his tongue over her bottom lip. Courtney drew in a deep breath, surprised at her body's sudden, feminine reaction to his attentions. Her stomach clenched into a tight, silken fist and desire bloomed. His lips worked tenderly over hers. It was as if a strong ocean tide was pulling at her—she knew she wanted to swim, but she was scared she'd drown in the undertow. And she still didn't know if this man was her savior or a man who could break her heart.

Her mistake was to look into his clear green eyes, for they trapped her with pure heat. Unable to resist, she leaned in, and her tongue slipped out to touch his. At the small sigh that unintentionally escaped from her, the normally cool and contained Lucien disappeared, and with a groan filled with longing, he pulled her deep into an embrace and his lips firmly but gently took hers in a kiss that was—oh, goodness—familiar and different at the same time. It thrilled and frightened her. Frightened her because she was consumed with want and need and hunger . . . and this was a man who didn't remember her.

His hands were wrapped tightly in her hair, holding her head exactly right for his invasion. His body pressed into hers, and she welcomed the heat he generated. She felt something hard and long pressing against her stomach; she knew they were going too fast, but his mouth was creating such amazing sensations that she simply pressed closer, wrapping her arms around his neck and whimpering for more.

He gave her more. His tongue thrust deep into her mouth in a dance that demanded she follow. She dueled for dominance, her tongue entering his mouth like a queen at the head of her army. He welcomed the invasion, and another groan echoed deep in his throat as he ground his hardness against her.

This was heaven. She never wanted the kiss to end, but when his clever fingers found her hardened nipple, her knees gave out and she sagged in his arms.

Only then did he break the kiss. He took a deep breath and with his forehead touching hers, he murmured in a voice like smooth brandy, "I'm sorry. I got a bit carried away."

She thought that a good thing. He desired her. "I guess we can cross off passion and desire as something to test."

"Or maybe it needs a thorough evaluation while you are visiting." He set her on her feet and took her hand. "Come. We need to get home before it gets too dark."

As they made their way back up the cliff path, the setting sun casting long shadows before them, Courtney found herself wondering what the next two weeks might bring. Could he learn to trust again, to open his heart? Because unless he could, Courtney saw no possibility of a future together. Could they build something true and lasting, or would he forever hide himself behind this fortress of fear?

She didn't know. But for the first time since his arrival back to England, she found herself hoping—truly hoping—that he could find a way forward. But would two weeks be enough time?

CHAPTER TWELVE

T HE MORNING SUN filtered through the lace curtains of Courtney's bedchamber at Danvers Hall, casting delicate patterns across the polished wooden floor. She had woken early, her mind still full of the previous day's kiss. The memory of Lucien's hand in hers as they'd walked back to the hall made her pulse quicken even now.

After dressing in a simple morning gown of soft green muslin, she made her way downstairs, hoping to find Serena for a quiet breakfast before the household fully stirred. The corridors were still hushed with early morning tranquility, and she moved quietly, not wanting to disturb the peaceful atmosphere.

As she passed the library, she noticed the French doors leading to the terrace stood ajar, letting in the warm summer air. Voices drifted through the opening—masculine voices engaged in what sounded like serious conversation. She paused, recognizing Julian's measured tones and Lucien's deeper voice with its slight Irish inflection.

They must be taking an early morning walk in the gardens, she thought, moving toward the doors to greet them. But something in their tone made her hesitate just inside the library, hidden from view by the heavy velvet curtains.

"The figures are sobering, I'll grant you," Julian was saying, his voice carrying the careful neutrality he used when discussing particularly delicate matters. "But not insurmountable, given proper investment and time."

"Time is something I have precious little of," came Lucien's reply, tinged with frustration. "The creditors grow more insistent by the week. Some have already threatened legal action."

Courtney's hand flew to her throat. Legal action? She had thought Rockwell's loan had kept them at bay.

"How much would you estimate is needed?" Julian asked. "To restore the estate to full productivity and satisfy the immediate debts?"

There was a long pause, during which Courtney could hear the soft crunch of gravel beneath their feet as they walked. When Lucien spoke again, his voice was heavy with the weight of responsibility.

"Three thousand pounds, at minimum. Perhaps more, depending on how extensive the repairs to the tenant cottages prove to be. The roof of the main barn needs complete replacement, and the drainage system in the south fields has failed entirely."

Courtney's breath caught. Three thousand pounds was an enormous sum—more than many families saw in a lifetime. But her investment fund run by Tiffany was higher than that. Her own dowry was substantial, at fifteen thousand pounds. Her money would be enough.

"And without that investment?" Julian prompted gently.

"The estate will continue to decline," Lucien said flatly. "The tenant farmers will be unable to pay their rents, more will abandon their holdings, and within a few years, there will be nothing left but empty fields and crumbling buildings. My sisters will have no prospects, and Ava-Marie…" His voice trailed off, the implication clear.

"I see." Julian's tone held the careful consideration Courtney knew well. "And you believe marriage would provide the necessary capital?"

The directness of the question made Courtney's heart hammer against her ribs. She pressed herself deeper into the shadows, knowing she should retreat but unable to tear herself away from a conversation that so directly concerned her future.

"A marriage to a woman of substantial means would certainly help," Lucien replied carefully. "The question is whether I can find someone willing to take on such a burden."

"Someone like my sister?"

The words hung in the air between them, and Courtney felt the world tilt beneath her feet. Julian's question was asked without accusation, but with the protective concern of a brother who needed to understand the motives of any man courting his sister.

Lucien's response was so long in coming that Courtney began to wonder if he would answer at all. When he finally spoke, his voice was barely audible.

"Your sister deserves better than a man who needs her fortune to save his family from ruin."

"That's not what I asked," Julian pressed, his tone sharpening slightly. "I asked if that's why you brought her here. If her dowry is the primary attraction."

Another long pause, during which Courtney could hear her own heartbeat thundering in her ears. She gripped the curtain so tightly, her knuckles turned white.

"I won't lie to you, Julian," Lucien said finally, his voice rough with emotion. "When I first considered pursuing Courtney, her dowry was…a significant factor. My family's situation is desperate, and I have responsibilities I cannot ignore. Ava-Marie's future, my sisters' prospects—they all depend on my ability to restore our fortunes."

The admission hit Courtney like a physical blow. She had known, intellectually, that financial considerations played a role in most marriages of their class. But to hear it stated so baldly, to know that her worth had been calculated in pounds and shillings…

"But," Lucien continued, his voice growing stronger, "if money were my only concern, there are other heiresses who would be far more practical choices. Lady Pemberton's daughter has ten thousand pounds, and she's made it clear she'd welcome my attentions. Miss Hartwell has twenty-five thousand and fewer family complications. And neither woman looks at me as if I'm a ghost."

"Then why Courtney?" Julian asked quietly.

"Because she's the only woman I've met since returning from Ireland who makes me feel like I might be capable of love again," Lucien said, the words seeming to be torn from him. "Because when I'm with her, I want something more than mere survival. Because while she can look at me as if I'm someone she knows, she also looks at me and sees my flaws and still wants me."

Tears sprang to Courtney's eyes, her anger at his mercenary considerations warring with joy at his confession of deeper feelings.

Lucien's voice cracked slightly. "Society keeps reminding me I'm a gentleman, not a common farmer. Yet it doesn't feel honorable to court a lady for her dowry when I don't know if I can offer her the one thing she wants—my heart."

"But you're not preying on her," Julian said gently. "You're being honest about your circumstances. There's a difference."

"Is there?" Lucien's laugh was bitter. "When I'm courting a woman whose dowry could solve all my problems? When I'm inviting her to my estate, showing her what could be hers, knowing that her attachment to me might cloud her judgment about the financial realities?"

Courtney pressed her hand to her mouth, stifling a sob. She could hear the genuine anguish in his voice, the conflict between his feelings for her and his family's needs.

"You're assuming she's naive about money," Julian pointed out. "Courtney has always been practical about financial matters. She understands the reality of your situation."

"I hope so." Then Lucien asked, "Or is she wondering if my feelings are genuine, or merely the result of desperation? Would she question every word of affection, every gesture of tenderness, wondering if it's motivated by love or by my need for her inheritance?"

The question struck at the heart of Courtney's own fears. Even now, listening to his conflicted confession, she wondered how much of his growing warmth toward her was genuine and how much was influenced by his financial desperation.

"Just be honest with her," Julian said with understanding. "Love takes time. Look at Serena and I. It took Serena an age to realize she loved me. Be patient with yourself. Relax and see if you can develop feelings for my sister. She deserves a chance at winning your heart again."

"I'm afraid my heart is irrevocably broken," Lucien admitted. "I care for her, Julian. More than I thought possible, after everything I've been through. But I can't separate my feelings from my family's needs. They're tangled together in ways I don't fully understand myself."

"Courtney is strong. Stronger than you or I."

"Marrying me means taking on burdens that aren't hers to bear," Lucien said quietly. "That her dowry would go not to providing comfort for our future children, but to paying for my father's gambling debts and my estate's neglect. What woman would choose that willingly?"

"A woman who loves you," Julian said simply.

"Love shouldn't require such sacrifice," Lucien replied. "She deserves better than a husband who needs her fortune to survive."

Courtney's heart clenched at the self-loathing in his voice. Here was a man torn between his growing feelings for her and his sense of honor, between his family's needs and his desire not to burden her with problems that weren't of her making.

"Perhaps," Julian said carefully, "you're underestimating my sister. Perhaps you're so focused on protecting her from yourself that you're denying her the choice to make her own decision."

"Or perhaps I'm protecting her from making a decision she'll regret," Lucien countered. "When the romantic glow fades and she realizes what she's taken on, what then? When she sees how much of her inheritance has gone to patching up crumbling walls and paying old debts, will she still look at me with the same warmth?"

The pain in his voice was unmistakable, and Courtney felt her anger at his mercenary considerations begin to soften. This wasn't a calculating fortune hunter coldly pursuing her dowry. This was a man tormented by circumstances beyond his control, struggling to balance his feelings with his responsibilities.

"You're borrowing trouble," Julian observed. "Assuming the worst before giving her a chance to prove you wrong."

"Am I?" Lucien asked. "Or am I being realistic about what marriage to me would mean? She could have any man in London. Why should she settle for one who brings nothing but problems and debts?"

"Because," Julian said with quiet conviction, "she sees something in you that you don't see in yourself. Because she's already chosen you, financial complications and all. The question is whether you're brave enough to trust her judgement."

Silence fell between them, and Courtney could hear the distant sound of morning birds and the rustle of leaves in the garden. Her mind raced with everything she'd heard, trying to sort through the tangle of emotions Lucien's words had stirred.

"I don't know if I can," Lucien said finally, his voice barely audible. "I don't know if I can bear to see the disappointment in her eyes when she realizes what she'd be taking on."

"Then you don't know her as well as you think you do," Julian replied. "My sister has faced disappointment before. You died and I watched her rebuild herself after utter desolation. She's stronger than you give her credit for."

"Perhaps," Lucien conceded. "Sometimes I think it would be easier to marry a woman I didn't care about and who didn't care about me."

Their voices began to fade as they moved further into the garden, and Courtney realized she'd been holding her breath. She released it slowly, her mind reeling from everything she'd overheard.

She gripped the curtain, her knuckles white. Part of her was hurt by his frank admission that her fortune had been a consideration in his courtship. But the anguish in his voice, his fear that he wasn't good enough for her—that spoke to something deeper than mere calculation.

The sound of footsteps on gravel grew closer. They were returning.

Courtney quickly moved away from the windows, her heart hammering. She needed time to think, but not here where she might be discovered eavesdropping. She slipped from the library and hurried toward the breakfast room, her mind churning with everything she'd learned.

Lucien wasn't a fortune hunter—he was a man struggling with impossible choices. The question was: what was she going to do about it?

She paused in the doorway of the breakfast room, hearing voices approach the library behind her. Whatever her decision, it would define not just her future but the kind of woman she chose to be.

"Courtney?" Serena appeared at the other end of the corridor, already dressed for the day. "You're up early. Shall we break our fast together?"

"Yes," Courtney said, forcing a smile. "I think I could use some company this morning."

But even as she followed Serena into the breakfast room, her thoughts remained fixed on the conversation she'd overheard. Lucien had called his heart "irrevocably broken"—but what if he was wrong? What if hearts could heal, given the right circumstances?

What if she was willing to take that risk?

CHAPTER THIRTEEN

PUTTING HER EAVESDROPPING behind her, shortly after breaking fast, Courtney descended the wide staircase to find Lucien waiting in the entrance hall, dressed in riding clothes. Lucien looked so like his old self in his clothes that her heart couldn't help but beat a little faster.

"You're up early," she said, feeling guilty. "Where is everyone else?"

"Lord Julian and Mr. Roberts left at dawn to inspect the northern boundaries," Lucien explained, his eyes seemingly appreciating the simple blue walking dress she'd chosen. "Serena is helping Ava-Marie with a drawing project, and Caitria is organizing the girl's wardrobe. She's growing so fast, and needs new clothes."

"So, we're alone," Courtney observed, a slight flush rising to her cheeks as she recalled their intimacy on the beach yesterday. She couldn't get their kiss out of her head and had tossed and turned all night.

Lucien's smile held a hint of mischief. "Not entirely. There are servants about. But I was hoping you might join me for a ride. There's something I'd like to show you. A cottage I found the other day. You might know who resides within, as it's not listed as one of the tenant properties, but I think it's on my land."

Curiosity piqued, Courtney readily agreed. "I'll need to change."

"No need," he said. "I thought you could ride with me on my

horse. Like we used to when you were learning. Thank you for telling me that, by the way."

The suggestion sent a flutter of anticipation through her. "Double? That's hardly proper, Lord Furoe."

"As I recall, you hinted that propriety never concerned us when we were here?" he challenged, his green eyes dancing with amusement. "Besides, the place I want to show you is difficult to find if you don't know the way."

Half an hour later, they were mounted on Lucien's sturdy bay gelding, Courtney seated sideways before him, her back supported by his strong arm. The intimacy of the position was not lost on either of them. She arranged her skirts as modestly as possible over her legs, his arm encircling her waist to balance her, their bodies pressed close from necessity.

They rode away from the house, taking a path through the home woods that opened into rolling meadows. The day was gloriously warm, the countryside alive with summer abundance. Birds darted through the hedgerows, rabbits scattered at their approach, and wildflowers nodded in the gentle breeze.

"I've been exploring the estate since I arrived," Lucien explained as they climbed a gentle hill. "Trying to reconnect with the land, to understand what it might have meant to me before."

"And has it helped?" Courtney asked, enjoying the solid warmth of him behind her. "Do you feel connected to it now?"

He considered this for a moment. "Not in the way my father does—not with the weight of generations of memories. But I feel...responsible for it. Protective." He guided the horse around a fallen log. "It's strange. I have no memory of growing up here, yet I feel at peace."

"You did always say it was the one place you could be yourself," Courtney observed.

"Exactly." The appreciation in his voice warmed her.

As they crested the hill, Courtney knew where they were heading, and her pulse raced. Soon Lucien drew the horse to a halt. Before them, nestled in a small, sheltered valley, stood a picturesque stone cottage. A stream gurgled past it, and a small garden, overgrown but still showing signs of careful planting, surrounded the dwelling. Smoke rose from the chimney, suggesting someone was in residence.

"It's exactly as I remember it," Courtney said.

"You've been here before?" he asked. "Who lives here?"

"Your old gamekeeper and his wife. Your father gifted them the cottage for his years of service. They own it," Courtney replied. "They…" She couldn't tell him. Not yet.

He dismounted and lifted her down, his hands lingering at her waist longer than necessary before releasing her. Taking her hand, he led her down the gentle slope toward the cottage, the horse following behind them.

"Three days ago, I was riding alone, letting my mind wander," he explained as they walked. "I wasn't following any particular path, just allowing the horse to choose his own way. And somehow, we ended up here."

As they approached the cottage, the door opened, and an elderly woman emerged, wiping her hands on her apron. Her weathered face broke into a wide smile at the sight of them.

"Lord Lucien! You've returned!" she exclaimed. "And you've brought Lady Courtney, just like old times!"

"Mrs. Baxter," she said warmly, "good morning. It's been so long since I was last here. It's good to see you looking so well."

The woman bustled forward; her blue eyes bright with emotion. "It does my heart good to see you both together again. When we heard you'd returned from the dead, I told George straight away, 'Now he'll bring his lady back to see us, mark my words.' And here you are!"

Lucien cast Courtney a questioning glance, and she stepped forward. "Mrs. Baxter used to make your favorite game pie, and we used to visit with the Baxters just so you could have a slice. And how is Mr. Baxter?" she asked while taking the woman's work-roughened hands in her own.

"Kind as ever, my lady. George is fighting fit if not a bit stiff when it's cold." Mrs. Baxter beamed. "Come in, come in! I've just taken a rabbit pie from the oven, and I'll put the kettle on."

Inside, the cottage was neat and cozy, with a small sitting room dominated by a sturdy oak table and comfortable, if worn, furniture. Dried herbs hung from the ceiling beams, and a collection of carved wooden animals lined the mantelpiece. A large ginger cat dozed by the hearth, opening one eye lazily to assess the visitors before returning to its nap.

Mrs. Baxter busied herself preparing tea while Lucien and Courtney took seats at the table. "George is out checking the rabbit snares," she explained. "He'll be sorry to have missed you. He always said you were the best shot among the young gentlemen, my lord."

Lucien accepted this information with a nod, though Courtney could see the questions in his eyes. She leaned closer, keeping her voice low.

"George taught you to shoot. You loved him and missed him when he retired, so you would visit a lot," she explained. "You would bring game from your hunts, and I would bring yarn for Mrs. Baxter to spin and knit. You taught their grandson, Tommy, to fish."

Understanding dawned in his eyes. "Thank you," he murmured.

Mrs. Baxter returned with a tray laden with tea, fresh bread, and a golden crust pie cut into slices. "Now then," she said, settling across from them and offering a plate to Lucien, "tell me everything. We've heard such strange tales that you were in Ireland all this time, with no memory of who you were! Poor Lady Courtney has been so steadfast, waiting for you."

Courtney felt heat rise to her cheeks, but Lucien answered smoothly.

"It's true, I'm afraid," he said. "I was injured during the rebellion and lost all memory of my previous life. I've only recently found my way home. And I'm sorry to say I don't remember you or George."

Mrs. Baxter clicked her tongue sympathetically. "How dreadful for you both. But you've found each other again, and that's what matters." She beamed at them as if they were reconciled lovers. "This cottage has seen its share of your happy times, hasn't it?"

Courtney's blush deepened, and she took a hasty sip of tea to hide her embarrassment. Lucien seemed equally disconcerted. "Has it?" he asked carefully.

Mrs. Baxter chuckled. "Oh, don't worry, my lord. George and I have always been discreet. Young love needs its private moments, after all." She winked at Courtney, who nearly choked on her tea. "We'd often leave for the village on market days and return to find the cottage had been…visited. But everything was always left neat, and there'd be a brace of pheasant, or a fine fish gifted as thanks."

Courtney avoided Lucien's gaze, mortified and fascinated in equal measure. She could see the questions in his eyes. Had they used this cottage for trysts? The drawing she'd done of him, their one night together before he left for Ireland, had it occurred here?

"How kind of us," Lucien managed, a hint of amusement in his voice.

"Kind indeed," Mrs. Baxter agreed. "And we've kept your secret all these years, even after you were believed dead, my lord. Not a word to anyone."

"And we're grateful for your discretion," Courtney said, regaining her composure. She shot Lucien a look that clearly said, *don't you dare ask what secret.*

They spent another half-hour with Mrs. Baxter, listening to her village gossip and tales of local happenings during Lucien's absence. By the time they took their leave, promising to return with yarn and some chewing tobacco for Mr. Baxter, Courtney could see that Lucien was both charmed by the woman's obvious affection for them and increasingly curious about what exactly had transpired in that cottage during their courting days.

As they remounted the horse and began the return journey,

Lucien's arm seemed to hold her more securely against him, his hand curving possessively around her waist.

"So," he said, his voice low near her ear, "it appears we have a history of impropriety, Lady Courtney."

She could hear the smile in his voice and couldn't help but respond to it. "It appears so, Lord Furoe."

"Care to enlighten me on exactly what secret Mrs. Baxter has been keeping all these years?"

Courtney turned her head to look up at him, their faces now inches apart. "I have no idea," she said, though her pink cheeks suggested otherwise. "I don't recall anything...untoward."

"Liar," he said softly, his eyes dropping to her lips. For a moment, she thought he might kiss her again, but instead, he urged the horse forward, his arm tightening around her. "No matter. I suppose we'll have to create new memories to replace the ones I've lost."

The suggestion hung between them, tantalizing and full of promise. Courtney turned forward again, leaning back slightly into his embrace, enjoying the solid strength of him behind her.

"Perhaps we will," she agreed, her voice carrying on the summer breeze. "After all, we did agree to a thorough evaluation."

His chuckle rumbled against her back, and for the rest of the ride home, they traveled in companionable silence, each lost in their own thoughts about what secrets the cottage might have witnessed and what new ones it might yet keep.

Reality broke the daydreaming as soon as they reached the stables. The head groom said there was a problem with one of the mares, so Courtney made her way back inside the house alone. Soon Caitria had roped her into playing a game of hide and seek in the garden with Ava-Marie.

As the day drew to an end and she dressed for dinner, Courtney realized she loved it here. She could see herself building a wonderful life with Lucien, Ava-Marie and any children they might have in the future.

She hoped Lucien was thinking the same thing. As she descended the stairs to dinner, she admitted that she was falling in love with Lucien again. She was fooling herself. She'd never fallen out of love with him, even when he couldn't remember her. She had enough memories for both of them. She prayed he had room in his damaged heart to love her back.

THE FOLLOWING DAY brought steady rain, confining the house party indoors. After breakfast, Julian and Serena announced their intention to write letters in the morning room, while Caitria took Ava-Marie to the nursery to measure up for new clothes. Left to their own devices, Lucien suggested a tour of the house with Courtney.

"But I know the house already," she pointed out, amused.

"Yes, but I don't," he countered. "Not really. It would be nice to hear stories."

The request touched her deeply. "I'd like that, although I'm not party to all your family secrets," she said softly.

They began in the portrait gallery, where Courtney pointed out ancestors whose stories she remembered Lucien telling her. Next came the music room, where she recalled evenings spent with Lauren at the pianoforte while Lucien and his father played chess by the fire.

"You were terrible at chess," she told him, smiling at the memory. "Your father would beat you in ten moves, and you'd declare it was because you were distracted by Lauren's playing."

"Was I truly that bad?" he asked, looking skeptical.

"Dreadful," she confirmed with a laugh. "You much preferred cards—you had an excellent memory for which cards had been played."

"That's still true," he admitted. "I discovered it in Ireland during games at the local pub. It's one of the few skills that seems to have survived my memory loss."

They moved to the library next, a grand room with floor-to-ceiling shelves and comfortable seating arranged near the large windows. Despite years of neglect, it remained impressive, though dust covers shrouded most of the furniture and the air held the musty scent of closed rooms and old books.

"This was always my favorite room," Courtney said, running her fingers along the spines of leather-bound volumes. "We spent hours here, discussing books, arguing about philosophy." She paused at a shelf of poetry. "You used to read Keats to me on rainy days like this."

Lucien approached, standing close enough that she could feel the warmth radiating from him. "Did I?" he asked, his voice low. "Which poems did I favor?"

She pulled a volume from the shelf, the binding familiar beneath her fingers. Opening it, she found a pressed flower—a forget-me-not—marking a page. A wave of emotions engulfed her. She remembered putting the flower in the book to mark their favorite poem. 'Bright Star,' she said, a tremor in her voice as she handed him the book. "This one was your favorite."

Lucien took the book, his fingers brushing hers in the exchange. He looked down at the marked page, his expression thoughtful as he began to read.

"Bright star, would I were steadfast as thou art—Not in lone splendor hung aloft the night..." His voice, deeper now with its slight Irish lilt, gave the familiar words new resonance. Courtney closed her eyes, letting the poem wash over her.

When he finished, the silence in the library seemed charged with emotion. She opened her eyes to find him watching her, something indefinable in his gaze.

"You used to say it reminded you of how you felt about me," she said quietly. "Steadfast, unwavering."

"It's a beautiful poem," he acknowledged. "Though I find it rather melancholy now. The desire to remain forever in one perfect moment, knowing that time must eventually sweep it away."

She stepped closer, drawn by the honesty in his voice. "Perhaps that's why it resonated with you then. You were thinking of going to Ireland, and we were trying to hold onto our last moments together before returning to the glare of London society."

He set the book aside, his eyes never leaving hers. "And now? What resonates with you now, Courtney?"

The directness of his question caught her off guard. "Hope. Hope for a new future," she said after a moment. "The hope that we might create new moments worth preserving, even if they're different from what came before."

Something shifted in his expression—a softening, a vulnerability she hadn't seen before. He reached out, his calloused fingers gently brushing a strand of hair from her face. "I think I would have liked the man I was with you," he said quietly. "He sounds more thoughtful than the reckless young lord everyone else describes."

"He was both," she answered honestly. "Thoughtful in private, charming and sometimes reckless in public. But always sincere in his affections."

His hand lingered at her cheek. "And what of the man I am now? How does he compare?"

"He's more direct, with a hint of mystery," she said, leaning slightly into his touch. "More grounded. Less concerned with society's expectations but more burdened by responsibility. And…" she hesitated, then continued, "he carries wounds that make him cautious, especially with his heart."

He didn't deny it. "Those wounds may never fully heal," he warned, his palm now cupping her cheek. "I can't promise to be the man you remember."

"I'm not asking you to be," Courtney replied, her heart quickening at his proximity. "All I want is to know the real man who is contained within the old Lucien. Just be you."

For a moment, she thought he might kiss her again, but instead, he dropped his hand and took a step back. "Show me more of the house," he said, his voice slightly rougher than before. "I want to understand all the places we made memories together."

She led him through the main floor, sharing anecdotes and recollections, watching his face for any flicker of recognition. There was none, but his interest was genuine, his questions thoughtful. He seemed determined to understand the shared past he couldn't remember.

Their tour eventually led them back to the portrait room, where generations of Danvers gazed down from gilt frames. Lucien paused before an image of himself at twenty, dressed formally in his viscount's finery, his expression serious, save for a hint of mischief in his green eyes.

"I look like a pampered lordling," he observed with a touch of irony. "Not a callus to be found, I'd wager."

Courtney studied the portrait, seeing it through his eyes. "You were raised to be a viscount," she said gently. "Not a farmer. But you always had more substance than most young lords of the *ton*."

He moved to a portrait of a beautiful dark-haired woman— his mother, the countess, painted in the prime of her life. "Lauren says I have her eyes," he remarked.

"You do," Courtney confirmed. "And her stubbornness, according to your father."

A ghost of a smile touched his lips. "That I can believe."

They had nearly completed their circuit of the room when they came upon a portrait Courtney had forgotten—herself at eighteen, painted shortly after her debut. She wore a gown of pale gold silk, her auburn hair styled in fashionable ringlets, her amber eyes bright with youth and promise.

"You were—are—lovely," Lucien said, studying the portrait with evident appreciation.

"Lord Danvers commissioned it after our engagement was announced," she explained, feeling oddly self-conscious. "He wanted a portrait of his future daughter-in-law to hang alongside the family."

Lucien glanced at her. "And now? Will you sit for another?"

CHAPTER FOURTEEN

T HE QUESTION CARRIED implications that made her pulse quicken. This was the time to talk about his feelings. "That would depend on whether there's a reason for me to be included in the family gallery again," she replied carefully.

His gaze was steady, searching. "I think there might be," he said, his voice low. "Like you, suddenly I'm hopeful."

"I know money is a necessity in your marriage, but I'm not the only woman with a decent sized dowry."

"That is very true. If I simply wanted money from a marriage, I would not be courting you. There are less complicated options. I want more from a marriage that will span the rest of my life and involve Ava-Marie."

Joy blossomed in her chest, tempered with caution. "We still have much to learn about each other," she reminded him. Mostly she wanted to learn what was in his heart, but she was too scared to push. Besides, they had promised each other two weeks.

"Yes," he agreed, "we do."

A comfortable silence fell between them, broken only by the patter of rain against the windows. Courtney was acutely aware of him beside her—his height, his presence, the subtle scent of sandalwood and leather that seemed to cling to him.

"I should check on Ava-Marie," he said finally. "Thank you for the tour. It's given me much to think about."

"You're welcome," she replied, watching as he moved toward the door. He paused on the threshold, turning back to her.

"Courtney," he said, his voice serious. "I know I can't give you certainty yet—about us, about what I feel. But I want you to know that I'm trying to open my heart again, to trust. It's not easy for me."

The simple honesty of his statement moved her deeply. "I know," she said softly. "Most things worth having rarely come easily."

He nodded, his expression thoughtful, then left her alone with the portraits of his ancestors—and her younger self, whose painted eyes seemed to hold secrets and hopes that her present self was only beginning to rediscover.

The rain continued into the evening, drumming steadily against the windows as they gathered in the small family dining room for dinner. The space was intimate compared to the grand formal dining room, with a table that seated just ten comfortably. Candles flickered in silver holders, casting a warm glow over the assembled party.

Conversation flowed easily through the meal. Julian spoke enthusiastically about the condition of the estate's northern fields, while Serena described the book she was currently reading to Ava-Marie—a tale of knights and dragons that had captivated the child's imagination. Caitria, usually reserved, shared amusing anecdotes about Ava-Marie's attempts at hiding from her in the big house.

Courtney found herself watching Lucien throughout the meal. He seemed more relaxed than she'd seen him since his return to England, laughing at Julian's hunting stories and asking thoughtful questions about the estate's potential. The role of country lord suited him, she realized—perhaps better than that of London gentleman had ever done. He fitted here but he seemed to find fitting into London life much harder. She realized if they married, he'd want to spend most of his time here. Would she be happy with that kind of life?

As the final course was cleared away, Ava-Marie tugged at her father's sleeve. "Papa, may I play the pianoforte for everyone?

Aunt Lauren has been teaching me, and I hope to practice while I am here so I can show her how much I have improved when we go home."

Silence greeted Ava-Marie's mention of home being in London. Courtney knew Lucien thought of this country estate as home. He smiled down at his daughter. "If you think you're ready." Ava-Marie clapped her hands in glee.

They adjourned to the music room, where Ava-Marie, with Serena's assistance, played a simple tune with remarkable concentration. Her small fingers were still clumsy on the keys, but her determination was evident in her furrowed brow and the tip of her tongue caught between her teeth in concentration.

When she finished, they all applauded enthusiastically, making the child beam with pride.

"My sister plays beautifully too," Julian said, giving Courtney a warm glance. "Perhaps she might favor us with a piece?"

"Oh yes, please!" Ava-Marie exclaimed, sliding from the bench to make room. "Papa says all young ladies need to learn how to play so I know you must be able to because you are a proper lady."

Proper lady? She'd have to talk with Ava-Marie about her comment. Had someone made her feel inadequate? Courtney took her place at the instrument, her fingers finding the keys with practiced ease. "Any requests?" she asked, looking up at Lucien.

"Whatever moves you," he replied, his eyes holding hers for a moment longer than necessary.

She began with a Mozart sonata, one she knew well enough to play without complete concentration, allowing her to observe the room as she performed. Julian and Serena sat close together on a small settee; their hands entwined. Caitria had taken Ava-Marie onto her lap in a comfortable armchair near the fire. And Lucien—Lucien stood by the pianoforte, watching her with an intensity that made her fingers nearly falter on the keys.

As she played, she recalled evenings just like this on her first and last trip to his home as his fiancée before he'd left for Ireland.

How he would stand in that exact spot, turning the pages of her music, occasionally reaching out to brush his fingers against hers when the others weren't watching. Those stolen touches had been thrilling then—the promise of more intimate caresses to come when they were finally wed.

When she finished the piece, Lucien was the first to applaud, his expression appreciative. "Beautiful," he said simply. "Would you play something else?"

She nodded, transitioning into a church song by Bach, the melancholy notes filling the room with sweet sorrow. This had been their piece—the one she'd played on the night before he left for Ireland, the night they had finally given in to the passion that had been building between them for months. The semi-innocent foreplay and kissing at the cottage was no longer enough. Not if he was leaving.

Glancing up, she saw he was moved by her playing. He moved closer, his hand coming to rest on the pianoforte, inches from her shoulder.

"This was important to us," he said quietly, his voice pitched for her ears alone.

"Yes," she confirmed, not breaking the flow of the music. "I played it the night before you left. Our last night together."

Understanding dawned in his eyes. "The night we—"

"Yes," she interrupted, a flush rising to her cheeks. "That night."

His gaze darkened, dropping briefly to her lips before returning to her eyes. "I wish I could remember it," he murmured.

"So do I," she replied softly. "It was a very special moment for me—for us." It was the first time she'd shared a regret, but she didn't care. He needed to understand how she felt.

The nocturne built toward its climax, her fingers drawing emotion from the keys that reflected the tumult in her heart. When the final notes faded away, the room remained silent for several heartbeats, as if everyone present had been transported by the music.

"I think it's past someone's bedtime," Caitria observed eventually, noting how Ava-Marie's head had drooped against her shoulder.

"But I'm not tired," the child protested, her words immediately contradicted by a wide yawn.

Lucien crossed to his daughter, lifting her into his arms with practiced ease. "Say goodnight to everyone, little one."

Ava-Marie dutifully bid them all goodnight, her small arms wrapped around her father's neck as he carried her from the room. Courtney's heart squeezed at the sight—the tenderness with which he held his child, the gentle way he pressed a kiss to her forehead. The way he still took his daughter to bed as he would have done in Ireland, regardless of the fact that he had staff to do that.

"Well," Julian said, rising from his seat, "I believe I'll retire as well. It's been a long day."

"I'll be up in a little while," Serena replied. "I haven't had a chance to catch up properly with Courtney."

Courtney smiled at her sister-in-law for her kindness. It would be good to talk to Serena about the emotions swirling within her.

Once the ladies were alone, Serena asked, "Shall I call for tea or would something a bit stronger do, like a sherry?"

"Sherry, I feel."

"Like that, is it?"

She shrugged her shoulders and sighed. "Sometimes I look at him and see my old Lucien and then other times, I see the haunted look in his eyes and see his pain. I don't know how to help him or what he wants from me."

Serena handed her a sherry. "I think he's still the honorable man he was all those years ago and he feels trapped. He needs money and he knows a marriage to you brings him that, but he likes you and doesn't want to trap you in a marriage you may grow to regret."

"That's not it. He could marry for money tomorrow. I know several wealthy families with marriageable daughters who would jump at the chance for a title—and he's handsome enough to turn any woman's head. No. There is something else worrying him. If I didn't know better, I'd say it is something about me that troubles him." Courtney couldn't help but feel he was keeping something from her. "Have you heard anything that I'm unaware of?"

Serena shook her head. "Nothing."

She sighed. "Maybe it's nothing to do with me, but that he is still so in love with his wife that the idea of remarrying is repugnant to him."

"You might be right. But his wife has been dead for two years." Serena slapped her hand to her forehead. "Sorry, that's me speaking without thinking. You have mourned him for five years." They sat in silence before her sister-in-law added, "Maybe you're right. Maybe he thinks it would be easier to marry someone who doesn't love him because he may not be able to love them back."

She knew Serena was right. She had to be. "Do you think if he loved me before, he could love me again? Do people get second chances?"

"I have no idea. He's not the same man, but you have to ask yourself if he's worth the risk of trying?"

The answer flew into her head before Serena had even finished the sentence. "Yes. He is. I lost him once before and I'm not going to lose him again." She'd never voiced that thought before. But it was how she felt. They had friendship. They had desire and passion. Surely, in time, love would come. Or maybe she'd love him enough for both of them.

Serena stood and placed a kiss on her cheek. "I believe deep down you know what you want to do." As she walked to the door, she added, "He's a good man. He has a lovely daughter. And with your dowry, you could turn his family's fortune around. You could have the life you always dreamed of. I'd say that's worth fighting for."

And that was the truth.

After Serena had departed, Courtney remained at the pianoforte, idly playing snippets of various pieces as she contemplated the day's events. Lucien's willingness to explore their shared past, his openness about his struggle to trust again—these were promising signs. Yet she sensed he was still holding something back. His love for his wife was the fortress between them.

"That was lovely," Lucien's voice startled her from her reverie. He had returned to the music room and now stood in the doorway, watching her.

"Thank you," she said, her fingers stilling on the keys. "Is Ava-Marie settled?"

"Almost instantly asleep," he confirmed, moving into the room.

He came to stand beside the pianoforte, his tall figure outlined by the firelight. In his riding clothes earlier, he had looked like the farmer he'd been in Ireland—capable, practical, strong. Now, dressed for dinner in evening attire, he seemed more the aristocrat again, though the two identities no longer seemed at odds within him.

"Julian seems impressed with the estate's potential," Courtney observed, filling the silence that had settled between them.

"He's been incredibly helpful," Lucien agreed. "He has a head for agricultural improvements that I admire. We're discussing the possibility of introducing new breeding stock for the sheep, though the investment required is significant."

"The Merino crosses Rockwell mentioned?" she asked, recalling their earlier conversation on the beach.

He nodded, his expression curious. "I listened to your advice and discussed it with Julian."

She smiled, offering no explanation for her knowledge. "One picks things up in ballrooms. Plus, Julian is always discussing his latest farming venture at family gatherings."

Lucien studied her for a moment, as if trying to reconcile this practical knowledge with the accomplished lady who played Bach so expressively. "You continue to surprise me, Lady Courtney."

"I hope that's not unwelcome," she replied, her fingers idly playing a soft chord.

"On the contrary." He took a seat beside her on the bench, the proximity sending a shiver of awareness through her. "I find I enjoy being surprised by you."

They were close enough that their shoulders brushed, her silk sleeve against the fine wool of his evening coat. Courtney was acutely conscious of his thigh pressed against hers through the layers of her gown, of his clean masculine scent mingled with the faint aroma of brandy from after dinner.

"Play something else," he requested softly. "Something you enjoy."

She began a gentle Mozart impromptu, the notes rippling like water under her fingers. Lucien watched her hands, his expression thoughtful.

"You mentioned we spent time in Mrs. Baxter's cottage," he said suddenly. "What were we doing there, exactly?"

Courtney nearly missed a note at his direct question. "We…spent time together," she said evasively, concentrating on the music.

"Alone?" he pressed, his voice holding a hint of amusement.

"Yes," she admitted, her cheeks warming.

"Unchaperoned?"

She sighed, giving up any pretense of propriety. "Yes, Lucien. Unchaperoned. We would ride out, ostensibly to hunt or sketch or collect botanical specimens, and sometimes we would stop at the cottage."

"To do what, exactly?" His tone was teasing now, his eyes alight with mischief.

Courtney stopped playing, turning to face him fully. "If you must know, we would talk, read, sometimes just sit together by the fire. And yes, occasionally we would…kiss."

"Just kiss?" he asked, his voice dropping lower.

"Mainly," she replied, maintaining eye contact despite her blush. "Though there may have been some…exploration.

Nothing that would compromise my virtue," she added hastily. "Not until that last night before we left to go back to London and you to Ireland."

Lucien's expression softened; the teasing replaced by something more profound. "I wish I could remember it," he said again, his voice tinged with regret. "Not just the physical aspect, but the intimacy of it—knowing you so well, being so comfortable together that we could share those private moments."

His honesty touched her deeply. "We can build that again," she said softly. "It doesn't have to be the same, but it can be equally meaningful."

He reached out, his fingers gently tracing the curve of her cheek. "You're extraordinarily patient with me," he observed. "Most women would have given up by now."

"Perhaps I'm not most women," she replied, leaning slightly into his touch.

"No," he agreed, his thumb brushing her lower lip. "You're certainly not."

The tension between them was palpable, a living thing that seemed to pulse with each beat of her heart. His eyes dropped to her mouth, and she knew he was thinking of kissing her again.

Instead, he pulled back slightly, though his hand remained at her cheek. "We should retire," he said, his voice rougher than before. "It's getting late."

Disappointment flickered through her, but she nodded. "Of course."

He stood, offering her his hand to help her rise from the bench. When she placed her fingers in his, he didn't immediately release her, instead bringing her hand to his lips for a kiss that was both gentlemanly and somehow deeply intimate.

"Goodnight, Courtney," he said, his eyes holding promises his words didn't express. "Sleep well."

"Goodnight, Lucien," she replied, reluctantly withdrawing her hand from his. As she made her way upstairs to her bedchamber, she could still feel the imprint of his lips on her skin, a phantom sensation that followed her into her dreams. Was she ready to push for more? Not when his heart was still full of his love for Ava. How did she compete for his affections with a ghost? She hoped she wouldn't have to. Could a man love twice in his lifetime or in Lucien's case, three times? He had loved Courtney once; of that she was certain.

They said time heals and she had to admit that after five years, she had finally begun to look at the idea of marrying again, but she hadn't expected to love again. Lucien's ghost still filled her heart, so she could understand his situation. Could Lucien love again? Or would he only offer affection? She rolled over in her cold bed and knew it would not be enough. Not when he once again was beginning to fill her heart.

LUCIEN WATCHED COURTNEY walk up the stairs, her cute bottom swaying provocatively, and the desire to follow and pull her into his room, into his bed almost overwhelmed him. But how could he, when he was still too scared to tell her the truth? What would she think of him? Of Ava-Marie?

After this time with Courtney, he knew in his heart she would never use the knowledge of Ava-Marie's birth to hurt him or his daughter. But now he didn't know how to tell her without revealing his initial distrust.

Or was it simply that he feared what she would think of him? A man duped by a woman. A man who fell in love with that woman and still loved her after all she'd done. Was there ever a bigger fool?

He'd tell her when they got back to London. He didn't want to ruin the memory of their time here.

As he lay in bed—alone—thoughts of kissing every inch of Courtney's delectable creamy skin filled his mind. It wasn't lost on him that, for once, it wasn't thoughts of Ava who kept him awake to near dawn.

CHAPTER FIFTEEN

T HE DAYS THAT followed fell into a pleasant rhythm. Mornings were often spent exploring the estate, with Lucien proudly showing Courtney the improvements he'd begun implementing, based on Julian's suggestions. Afternoons might bring a visit to the village, where Lucien was gradually reacquainting himself with the local inhabitants, or quiet hours spent with Ava-Marie, who delighted in Courtney's stories and patient instruction at the pianoforte.

Each day, Courtney observed subtle changes in Lucien. His smiles came more readily, his laughter more frequent. He spoke more openly about his time in Ireland, sharing amusing anecdotes about village life and his struggles to master farming techniques. When he talked about Ava, it was with a wistful honesty that acknowledged both the love they had shared and the agony of her death.

A break in the persistent Dorset rain prompted Julian to suggest a fishing expedition. The men departed with tackle and high spirits, leaving the ladies to their own devices.

Serena, pleading a headache, retired to her room, while Caitria took Ava-Marie to the kitchen gardens to harvest vegetables for dinner. Finding herself unexpectedly alone, Courtney decided to explore the estate further, drawn to the bluebell woods that lay beyond the formal gardens.

The woods were peaceful, with dappled sunlight filtering through the canopy to create patterns on the forest floor. Though the bluebells had long since faded, the undergrowth was lush with ferns and late summer wildflowers. Courtney followed a narrow path, enjoying the solitude and the opportunity to gather her thoughts.

Her mind kept returning to Lucien—to the growing ease between them, the moments of connection that suggested they might indeed forge something meaningful from the ruins of their past. Yet she sensed he was still holding back, still guarding some part of himself. Guarding his battered heart. She understood loss better than anyone—she'd lost Lucien five years ago. Hearts were delicate organs. It took a lot for them to recover.

So deep was she in contemplation that she nearly missed the small clearing ahead. It was only when she emerged from the trees that she realized where her feet had carried her—to a secluded glade with a stone bench overlooking a small, natural pond. The spot was achingly familiar, a private retreat where she and Lucien had often escaped during her visits to Danvers Hall.

Taking a seat on the bench, Courtney closed her eyes, memories washing over her. Here, away from the house and its ever-watchful servants, they had shared confidences, dreams, and increasingly passionate embraces. It was in this very spot that Lucien had first told her he loved her, nervous despite his usual confidence, his green eyes earnest as he confessed feelings that had been growing for months.

"I thought I might find you here."

Lucien's voice made her start. Opening her eyes, she found him standing at the edge of the clearing, fishing rod in hand, his expression unreadable.

"Julian and I finished early," he explained, approaching the bench. "He's headed back to the house, but I saw you walking into the woods and followed."

"How did you know about this place?" she asked, making room for him beside her.

He sat, setting his fishing rod aside. "I discovered it a few days after arriving here," he said. "It felt…peaceful. I've come here several times to think."

"We used to come here together," Courtney told him. "It was our special place, away from everyone else."

He nodded, unsurprised. "I suspected as much. There's a carving on the back of this bench—our initials within a heart. Very romantic."

She smiled, remembering. "You did that after I accepted your proposal. I scolded you for damaging your family's property."

"Did I apologize?" he asked, a hint of mischief in his eyes.

"Eventually," she replied, her smile widening. "After you'd finished kissing me senseless."

He laughed, the sound echoing in the clearing. "I'm beginning to think I was quite the rogue before my memory loss."

"Only with me," she corrected, enjoying the ease between them. "In public, you were the model of propriety. That was why no one suspected how passionately we felt about each other."

A comfortable silence fell between them as they gazed out at the still waters of the pond. Birds called from the trees, and the occasional splash marked a fish rising to the surface.

"I caught nothing," Lucien admitted, nodding toward his empty fishing basket. "Apparently my skills have not survived my memory loss."

"You were never particularly patient with fishing," Courtney told him. "You preferred hunting—something more active."

He nodded, considering this. "That makes sense. I've found I prefer being in motion to sitting still. In Ireland, I could never stay indoors for long, even in poor weather. I needed to be working the land, feeling like I was accomplishing something tangible."

"Is that what you want now?" she asked. "A life of activity and purpose?"

He turned to look at her, his expression thoughtful. "Yes, but not just physical labor. I want to restore this estate, to make it productive again. I want to provide security for my daughter, for my sisters—for any other children I might have, if God is kind, hopefully sons." He hesitated, then added quietly, "For whoever shares my future."

The implication hung between them, delicate as spun glass. Courtney's heart quickened, but she maintained her composure.

"Do you have any feelings for me?" she pressed, needing to hear him articulate what seemed to be growing between them.

He reached for her hand, his fingers warm against hers. "I didn't like Fancot paying you attention," he said simply. "That must mean something. I am possessive about you, and I like you."

"And is that enough?" she asked softly.

His eyes darkened. "There's also desire," he said, his voice dropping to a low timbre that sent shivers through her. "When I'm with you, I feel things I haven't felt since…since before. Different than with Ava, but no less powerful."

Courtney's breath caught at his admission. "I feel it too," she confessed.

His grip on her hand tightened slightly. "But is it enough for you? I can't promise you the same love we apparently shared before. I don't know if I'm capable of that kind of love again."

The question was earnest, his vulnerability evident in the tension of his jaw, the searching look in his eyes. Courtney considered her answer carefully, aware that her response could shape whatever future they might have together.

"I don't need the same love," she said finally. "I'm not the same woman, and you're not the same man. What we build now will be different—but that doesn't mean it can't be equally meaningful, equally profound in its own way."

"I want to be happy. I have to marry again, and I want that marriage to be happy. I think I'd be happy with you. So, you have to really think if this is a risk you're willing to take. Will our marriage be happy if I can't give you my heart and you come to resent me? That would be the worst outcome I could imagine."

She took a step back. What an impossible position to be in. To marry him now without his heart or to walk away and give up on the possibility he could love her again. "The one thing we have always shared, and one of the reasons I fell in love with you and trusted you, was your honesty. That hasn't changed." She looked up to the sky and closed her eyes. "If I agree to marry you, I would never come to resent you because I chose this. I would live with the consequences of my choice. That is only fair."

Relief flickered across his features. "You're quite remarkable," he said, pulling her back towards him, his free hand coming up to tuck a loose strand of hair behind her ear.

"It's funny, if you think about it. You're still in love with Ava, and I'm still in love with a Lucien who doesn't exist. We're both in love with ghosts."

He did a double take at her words but didn't deny he was still in love with his dead wife. "Would you have remarried if I'd not returned?" he asked, squeezing her hand.

"I think I would have. I've had five lonely years to consider what my future could be. What I want out of a marriage."

"And what does that look like?" he asked, genuinely curious.

"Respect," she said immediately. "Trust. Companionship. Shared purpose." She paused, a blush rising to her cheeks. "And yes, physical attraction. But love is still important. Perhaps love can grow from these foundations. It doesn't need to exist fully formed from the beginning. I saw it in my parents' arranged marriage."

Lucien studied her face, as if memorizing each feature. "I do desire you," he said, his voice husky. "From the moment I saw you at the opera, there's been something…undeniable between us."

Impulsively, she leaned forward and pressed her lips to his. He responded immediately, one hand cupping the back of her neck as he deepened the kiss. Unlike their exchange on the beach, this was unhurried, exploratory—a rediscovery rather than a claiming.

When they finally drew apart, both slightly breathless, the air between them felt charged with possibility.

"We should return to the house," Lucien said reluctantly. "They'll wonder where we've gone."

"Let them wonder," Courtney replied, feeling uncharacteristically bold. "They know why I'm here and will give us our privacy."

He laughed softly. "Even so, Julian is still your brother and I don't want to upset him. I've also promised to take Ava-Marie riding this afternoon. Her first proper lesson."

The mention of his daughter brought reality back into focus. Whatever grew between them would need to include Ava-Marie—a fact Courtney was increasingly comfortable with. The child had wormed her way into Courtney's heart with her enthusiastic questions and unguarded affection. But would the child be a constant reminder of the woman he still loved?

"Then we should go," she agreed, rising from the bench. "I wouldn't want to deprive her of her lesson."

Lucien stood as well, gathering his fishing equipment. As they made their way back through the woods, he reached for her hand, entwining his fingers with hers in a gesture that felt both protective and possessive.

"Will you join us?" he asked. "For the riding lesson? Ava-Marie would be delighted."

The invitation, seemingly simple, felt significant—an inclusion in this most precious part of his life.

"I'd love to," she replied, squeezing his hand gently.

As they emerged from the woods into the afternoon sunlight, Courtney felt a lightness in her heart that had been absent for years. No, this wasn't the same love they'd shared before. But perhaps, just perhaps, it could be something even better.

"That was a big sigh," he said as he squeezed her hand.

"We leave for London tomorrow. The two weeks have gone by so quickly."

"I know we are all busy packing but tonight, after dinner, can we talk privately about our situation? In the library perhaps?"

Her heart gave a lurch. This was it. She had to make her

decision—tonight! She smiled bravely to show she wasn't afraid, but her legs were already beginning to shake. "That would be lovely."

CHAPTER SIXTEEN

L UCIEN PACED THE length of the library, the dying embers in the fireplace casting long shadows across the weathered carpet. He paused before the window, gazing out at the moonlit grounds of Danvers Hall. The estate looked peaceful, timeless—so different from his humble cottage in Ireland. Yet somehow, over these past two weeks, this place had begun to feel like home, or a place he could make a home. Probably because it was away from the eyes and vicious tongues of the *ton*.

His fingers toyed with the small velvet box in his pocket. It contained his mother's ring—a sapphire surrounded by diamonds that the earl had pressed into his hand this morning, urging him to do what was expected of him. That was just it. He wanted more from a marriage than money. He could be happy with Courtney, couldn't he? His stomach churned once more.

The irony wasn't lost on him. Here he stood, about to propose to a woman he couldn't remember loving, while still carrying the weight of Ava's deception. His heart felt like a battlefield where past and present waged an endless war.

The soft click of the door opening made him turn. Courtney stood in the doorway, a vision in a simple evening dress of deep blue that made her auburn hair glow like burnished copper in the firelight. She looked beautiful. And some of his tension left his shoulders. Her amber eyes held a question as she hesitated on the threshold.

"You came," he said, the words coming out more breathless

than he'd intended.

"You asked me to." Her simple reply held no coyness, no games—just honesty. That was what drew him to her most, he realized. In a world where he'd been deceived so thoroughly, her straightforward nature was like a beacon. He wanted to trust her.

She crossed to join him by the window, close enough that he could catch the subtle scent of roses that seemed to cling to her. "It's a beautiful night," she observed.

"It is," he agreed, though his eyes remained on her face rather than the view. "Courtney, these past two weeks—"

"Have been lovely," she finished for him, a small smile playing at her lips. "I've enjoyed getting to know you again. And I hate to say it, but you're not so different from the man you don't remember."

His throat tightened with unexpected emotion. "Really?"

She turned to face him fully. "Well, maybe somewhat the same. I suspect five years changes people, Lucien. Whether spent in Ireland living a different life, or in London grieving what I thought was lost."

He took her hands in his, marveling at how perfectly they fit within his own. "What I feel for you is…complicated," he admitted. "I admire you—your intelligence, your openness, your kindness toward Ava-Marie."

"I adore her. She's a part of you," she said simply. "She makes it easy."

"I like you," he continued, choosing each word carefully. "I more than like you. I find myself thinking of you when we're apart, watching for you when you enter a room. I respect your opinions, value your insights."

"But you're not in love with me," she said, her voice gentle rather than accusatory.

The truth of it hung between them, painful but necessary. "I don't know if I'm capable of that kind of love again," he confessed, the admission costing him dearly. "After losing Ava, after everything that happened in Ireland…"

He couldn't tell her the whole truth. Not yet. Ava-Marie's future hung in the balance. Society would destroy her if they knew the truth. He had to protect her, the innocent party in Ava's deception. He had to be absolutely certain before he shared this secret with anyone. That Ava had never been his wife. That his beloved daughter was illegitimate. That he'd been thoroughly deceived by the woman he thought he'd married. A woman who kept him from his real family—hell, Ava had kept him from Courtney. The shame of it all burned in his chest. He wouldn't tarnish this moment with those truths. London. He'd tell her in London. *Because you know that once the engagement is announced in London, she would find it difficult to cry off?* He hated that thought.

Courtney waited patiently, her thumb brushing reassuringly across his knuckles.

"My heart is…damaged," he finally said, settling for a truth that wasn't the whole truth. "Not just because of Ava's death, but because of things I'm not ready to speak of yet. Things I promise to tell you when I'm ready."

To his surprise, there was no hurt in her eyes at his secrecy, only understanding. "We all have wounds that take time to reveal," she said. "I don't need all your secrets tonight."

Where was her judgment? Her disappointment? Instead, she offered understanding he wasn't sure he deserved.

"Courtney," he said, releasing one of her hands to retrieve the box from his pocket, "I can offer you respect, admiration, trust, and companionship. I can promise to be faithful, to cherish you, to build a life together that has meaning and purpose." He swallowed hard, confronting his deepest fear. "But will that be enough for you? Can you accept a man who may never give you the kind of all-consuming love we once shared?"

Her eyes widened as he opened the box, revealing the ring nestled within. "Lucien…"

"I know it's not the romantic proposal you might have imagined," he said, his voice rough with emotion. "But it's honest. You deserve nothing less."

To his surprise, tears filled her eyes, though she was smiling. "When I thought you were dead, I believed I would never marry," she said softly. "The idea of giving myself to someone else felt impossible. But eventually, I came to understand that there are many kinds of love—each valuable in its own way."

She touched his face, her fingers warm against his cheek. "I don't need all-consuming love, Lucien. I need a partner who respects me, who sees me for who I truly am, who walks beside me rather than ahead or behind. Someone who will be kind to me, and whom I can be kind to in return."

Hope flickered in his chest, fragile but persistent. "And you believe that could be me? Even with my…limitations?"

"I believe," she said with quiet certainty, "that we can build something beautiful together, if we choose to. Love isn't just a feeling that strikes like lightning. It can grow slowly and deepen over time. It's also a choice—one we make every day."

She trusted him. The knowledge was both a balm and a burden. Would she still look at him with such acceptance when she knew the full truth? He had to believe she would.

"Lady Courtney Montague," he said formally, taking the ring from its velvet nest, "would you do me the great honor of becoming my wife? Not because of what we once were to each other, but because of what we might become together?"

Her smile was radiant through her tears. "Yes, Lord Furoe. I would be honored to be your wife."

His hands trembled slightly as he slid the ring onto her finger. It fit perfectly.

He raised her hand to his lips, pressing a kiss to her knuckles just above where the sapphire now rested. "Thank you," he whispered, the words inadequate for the gratitude flooding through him.

She stepped closer, eliminating the distance between them. "Kiss me," she requested softly, "I won't break."

He didn't hesitate, drawing her into his arms and claiming her lips with a gentleness that quickly gave way to something deeper, more primal. Her body molded against his perfectly, her hands sliding up to tangle in his hair as she responded with equal fervor.

When they finally broke apart, both breathless and flushed, he rested his forehead against hers. "I may not remember loving you before," he said roughly, "but we will be happy together. I promise you that."

"We have all the time in the world to build a life," she assured him, then bit her lip, a becoming blush spreading across her cheeks. "Though perhaps…we needn't wait for everything."

He drew back slightly, searching her face. "What do you mean?"

Her blush deepened, but her gaze remained steady. "Come to my bedchamber tonight," she whispered. "After the household is asleep."

The invitation sent heat coursing through him, desire pooling low in his abdomen. "Courtney, are you certain? We don't have to—"

"I want to," she interrupted, her voice holding no hesitation despite her blush. "I want you, Lucien. I feel like I've been waiting forever."

The thought that she had wanted him, waited for him all these years while he had been oblivious to her existence, humbled him profoundly. He cupped her face in his hands, overwhelmed by the trust she placed in him.

"Then I will come to you tonight," he promised, sealing the vow with another kiss.

As he pulled her into his arms, Courtney felt tears welling. Did he know this was her ring? The same ring he'd given her when he'd last proposed. She'd given it back to Lord Danvers after the news that Lucien had been killed had arrived. It was his family's ring. Besides, she couldn't bear to look at it every day and know what might have been and now, here it was, back on her finger. She had never been so happy.

She'd also given herself to Lucien here—in this house. She wanted her second first time with Lucien to be here too. She tried to tell herself it wasn't because she wanted to see if lying in his arms would feel the same, but it was. If it was the same, she knew things would work out. She shuddered and he held her tighter. If it was different…she didn't know what that might mean.

"Are you all right?" he whispered in her ear.

"I'm fine." She wasn't fine. This all seemed so easy. So familiar and yet Lucien was a virtual stranger. She hoped her memories, or dreams of what their life could have been, weren't clouding her view of reality. Should it be this easy?

He picked her up in his arms and whispered, "Let's go to bed."

She buried her face into his jacket and merely nodded, too overcome with emotions to even speak. After tonight there would be no going back, and they both knew it.

She barely noted when Lucien laid her gently on her bed. Her heart pounded in her chest.

She wanted her body to remember. But she also wanted new memories.

She was beginning to despair that this would not be the same when Lucien followed her down, the weight of his body pressing her into the mattress. He made a sound low in his throat and began kissing down her neck.

And that was when her body remembered. She felt it begin in her toes, a tingling sensation, a warmth that traveled up her legs, pooled in the most sensitive areas between her legs, making her hot and aching, then moving on to her breasts and her neck and her face. It was as if she were awakening from a long winter nap. Perhaps here, in bed, would be the one place he was the Lucien she had known.

Her body was awake and aware. Oh, how aware. How gloriously, wonderfully, exquisitely aware.

She realized now that for the past five years, she'd not been living. She'd been merely existing. How had she ever thought she could remain a spinster? Or was it only in Lucien's arms she could feel this heat, this desire—feel so alive?

She lay beneath him as he slowly undressed her, barely noting the cold air as each layer was removed. Every nerve ending was on fire, desperate for his touch. His lips trailed over her bare skin as if in worship. When she finally lay naked under his gaze, she watched with heat building as he lifted a shaky hand and ran it down her side.

"So soft…" He bent and pressed his lips to one bared breast.

The tenderness was what got her. This was the Lucien she'd known before. His touch wasn't that of a stranger. It was the touch of her Lucien. His hand traveled down her body, stopping at her womanhood. He lay his hand there and drew in a deep breath.

She rose up onto her elbows. "Are you having second thoughts?"

He looked at her with heat and desire flaring in his eyes. "I was just thinking how lucky I am to have you. How you make my return bearable. And how I want this night to be special."

He was beautiful and she'd not yet seen him completely naked. Her heart beat frantically, her attraction to him overwhelming her. The thought of one day lying with this man every night, was intoxicating. A small thought entered her head, especially if he gave her his heart…

Tonight, she would freely give herself to the man she loved, and she would then savor the memory for eternity. She'd enjoy Lucien's touch, and she'd give everything of herself to ensure he was satisfied. To wipe away the memory of any other.

"You're beautiful, Lucien. I've always remembered you as beautiful," she added wistfully. "It's your turn to undress."

"I've wanted you since we arrived here." The deliberate plea in his voice saw her reach for the placket of his trousers. Her fingers fumbled and she heard him issue a curse before he swept her hands aside and freed his rigid erection into her waiting hands.

Her hand firmed around the thick length, and at her first stroke, he sighed and tilted his head back. She explored him and realized her touch pleased him.

Finally, he let out a groan and he pushed her down on the bed. "You have far too many clothes on," she huskily murmured. "Remove them and let me watch."

When he complied, she drank her fill. There were a few more scars on his body that hadn't been there before, and he'd filled out. All muscle. No longer the softness of youth.

"You're even more beautiful than I had ever imagined." She brushed a hand over his chest. "You're worth waiting for, but I've waited far too long. And I'm hungry for you."

He took her hand and dragged it down over every ridge and muscle of his torso to his groin. She was startled by the warmth pooling in her stomach at the feel of him, hard and hot beneath her palm.

"See what you do to me. My body wants you. I want you."

The earthy rawness of his words sent a shudder down her spine. She loved how he encouraged her hand to explore more of him.

He cupped her chin and the suddenness of his kiss started a fire raging in her belly. She gave herself up to pleasure as his hands explored her naked flesh.

He kissed her. It was a demanding kiss, possessive and con-trolling. Hot and needy, his tongue swept into her mouth. The taste of maleness on it tantalized her taste buds as it swirled around hers until she lay weak and needy on the pillow. A strong hand ran over every inch of her goose-bumped skin, igniting the heat of passion within her. He deepened the kiss. It tugged at her, demanding a response and she gave it willingly.

The feel of his soft chest hair upon her sensitive nipples shot tiny frissons of sensation across her skin. He felt so large, so big and so overwhelming as she lay in the protective shadow of his massive frame.

The skillful touch had her melting. His dark, spicy scent was like an aphrodisiac, urging her on. She pushed even closer, exploring further.

Cool air brushed her mouth as his lips danced across her cheek in search of first her ear lobe, and then her neck.

"You have the graceful neck of a swan."

An instant later, a large hand intimately cupped her, while his thumb brushed across her nipple. She shuddered in his embrace and with a low moan of pleasure, her head fell backward, allowing and encouraging his lips to glide down her throat. His teeth gently nipped her as he moved his mouth ever closer to where his thumb continued to circle around the stiff peak of her breast. She was soon craving his mouth upon her nipple.

It was heaven, it was hell, it was everything she'd fantasized about and then more... Heaven to allow herself to succumb to his tantalizing touch; hell, to have so much hunger.

The second his mouth gave her relief, and he captured and sucked firmly on her sensitive nipple, another moan poured out of her. The wet heat of his mouth reignited another wild need and she demanded satisfaction. Her fingers sought the hard length of him and circled around his thickness.

Her touch drew a moan of delight from him, and he moved his body so that his member thrust in and out of her grasp. The thought of him, the size of him, sliding deep within her, made her shiver with a mixture of trepidation and excitement.

This was not as she remembered but then it had been her first time, and he had been a gentleman. This Lucien was as rough and raw in bed as he was out of it. And she loved it.

A sigh of bliss slid past her lips as he massaged her other breast and his mouth continued to devour her engorged nipple. Never in her wildest imaginings had she experienced such deliciously sinful sensations. He aroused her completely. Fire flooded wildly through her veins, and the moment his teeth bit down, her insides grew slick with her desire.

The palm of his hand caressed her throat before moving down to her belly. A tremor rocked her to her core.

"Are you hot and wet for me? You're my beautifully responsive girl, my dream come true."

His lungs burned as if on fire as he sent his fingers seeking the warmth and heat between her legs. She did not disappoint. As she released a soft sound of excitement, possessiveness surged through him and he kissed her again and again, lusting after the fresh sugary taste of her tongue against his.

With an eagerness that pleased him, Courtney pressed herself upon his hand, her damp curls enticing his throbbing cock. Christ, her abandoned passion made his gut lurch with desire yet again. He wanted her like nothing he'd ever experienced before. No woman had affected him like Courtney did. The memory of Ava fled before the sensual innocence of the lady lying beneath him.

Her fingernails lightly scored the skin on his back as she murmured his name in an aching plea. He'd never heard anything so sweet in all his life.

"God, the sight of you almost unmans me," he whispered as he struggled for control. It had been a long time since he'd lain with a woman.

She smiled seductively and let her legs drop open. The strong scent of her arousal assailed him and coupled with the image of her womanhood glistening in the firelight, it saw his control flee completely.

Surprise swept over her face as he grabbed a pillow and situated it beneath her bottom.

He couldn't wait any longer, so he used his thighs to part hers wider and pressed his aching cock into her, savoring her tightness as inch by inch, he slowly entered her, filling her to the hilt.

Her eyes rolled back, and she let out a deeply satisfied sigh. "This feels so right."

Gratified by her response, his body rejoiced at the hotly aroused sight of her beneath him. He held himself still above her, his arms shaking. He wanted to pound into her but knew if he did so, he would not last. Plus, it was most likely ungentlemanly. Hell, making love to her before marriage was ungentlemanly, but as she'd told him, he couldn't ruin her twice.

When he refused to move, she opened her eyes, "Are you all right?"

"I've never felt better."

She was a prize all right. God almighty, she was tight and fiery around his cock. She punctuated her words by arching her body, forcing him to withdraw and then sink back into her, penetrating her deeper. At this rate, she would make him come faster than an inexperienced youth.

He used his hands to steady her hips so he could thrust in more deeply. He pushed her legs up higher, opening her fully and at last his control evaporated. As if on the edge of insanity, he pounded into her hot depths. She tilted her hips, matching him thrust for thrust, her bountiful breasts jiggling enticingly as he slammed into her. He could feel his sacs become tight and full as they brushed against her. He could not last....

A sharp cry broke from her lips, as her fingernails dug deep into his buttocks, and her tight sheath contracted around him with spasms of pleasure, her breath coming in loud gasps.

As she continued to contract around him, the tightness drew out his own release. With a roar, he thrust one final time and spilled his seed deep inside her. He collapsed on top of her, completely spent, unable to hold himself up any longer. His body throbbed with a pleasure. It was as if every woman that had come before her had been a mere scrap, while she was the feast. She had just succeeded in wiping the memory of all others from his mind.

He drank in big gulps of air, enjoying the feel of the slowly ebbing waves of their climax. If it was always like this, he would be a happy man indeed and they would have a successful marriage.

CHAPTER SEVENTEEN

COURTNEY HAD ONLY been back in London two days and already she missed being in Lucien's company. He'd been busy with his lawyers and debtors and talking with her father about the marriage contract.

Today the sisterhood were meeting at Farah's house to discuss their investments and how the wager against the men was doing. The men were still oblivious to the fact that the ladies were behind the anonymous investment challenge placed in the betting book at White's against their brothers. Whoever earned the most profit in twelve months won it all. The sisterhood would show the men they were not helpless and could be independent.

Claire had apparently spied on her brother Fane and learned about where the men were investing their money. When Tiffany, their investment guru, heard, she'd laughed and laughed. The ladies were feeling very positive about coming out victorious.

She decided to ask Tiffany if she could tell Lucien their secret and if she could help him manage his finances. She'd thought to tell him about Tiffany's skills once they were married...if he promised not to reveal the ladies were the entity who'd challenged the men.

She was finishing a note in the drawing room and had just asked Graves, their butler, to fetch her cape when he announced she had a gentleman caller. A smile broke on her lips thinking it was Lucien before Graves added, "Baron Lockwood, my lady."

A flicker of annoyance danced along her skin. "Surely, he's here to see my father."

"No. He asked for you specifically and asked me to give you this." He held out a slip of paper.

Taking the note, she quickly began to read, and as she did, her anger built. "Show the baron up."

"Shall I organize refreshments?"

"No. He won't be here long enough. I have an appointment I must get to."

She rose from her chair and began pacing the room. The baron's note was impertinent. What information did he have that she **had** to know about Lord Furoe?. Her brother, Julian, ever the politician, had taught her to hide her emotions whenever in a conversation where you don't know what the other party is trying to gain. So, she would be pleasant until she ascertained Baron Lockwood's information.

She retook her seat by the fire and maintained her cordial smile, though it felt brittle on her face as Baron Lockwood settled himself uninvited into the chair opposite hers. His golden hair gleamed in the firelight, carefully styled to suggest casual elegance, but there was nothing casual about the calculating look in his pale blue eyes.

"How can I help you, Baron? I have an appointment with Lady Farah that I must get to."

"I'll come straight to the point, Lady Courtney," Lockwood said, leaning forward slightly. "I find myself in possession of certain information about your…fiancé. Information that would be most distressing to society should it become known."

A cold finger of dread traced its way down Courtney's spine, but she kept her expression placid. "How fascinating. And what information might that be?"

Lockwood's smile widened, like a predator sensing weakness. "It concerns his time in Ireland. Specifically, his relationship with the woman he claims was his wife."

The emphasis he placed on "claims" made Courtney's heart

stutter. Was this what Lucien had been hiding? The secret that made his eyes darken with shame whenever their conversation veered too close to his time in Ireland.

"I'm afraid I don't understand your meaning, Baron," she said, proud of how steady her voice remained. "Lord Furoe's wife died some time ago. It's hardly a secret."

"Ah, but that's just it." Lockwood settled back, clearly enjoying himself. "She wasn't his wife at all. There was never any marriage, Lady Courtney. I've had my people searching parish records throughout Ireland—particularly in Malahide and the surrounding areas. No record of any marriage between a John Collins, as he was known in Ireland, or Lucien Furoe, or any other name, to a woman named Ava."

Courtney's fingers tightened imperceptibly on her fan. "Records can be lost, Baron. Especially in a country that experienced rebellion."

"Indeed, they can," he agreed smoothly. "Which is why I also made inquiries about this Ava. It seems she was known in certain circles in Dublin before relocating to Malahide. Circles of a decidedly…improper nature. She was a lady of the night."

Understanding dawned, sharp and painful. Ava had been a courtesan, or worse.

"How opportune for your inquiries," Courtney remarked, keeping her tone light despite the thundering of her heart. "Though I fail to see why you would concern yourself with Lord Furoe's private affairs."

Lockwood's eyes glittered. "Oh, but it's not just his private affairs, is it? It affects his family, especially his sisters, and of course, you directly. After all, you're planning to marry a man who lived in sin with a common whore. A man who is presenting his bastard daughter to society as legitimate."

The crude words struck like physical blows, but Courtney refused to flinch. This was what had been weighing on Lucien. Not just the deception practiced upon him by Ava, but the implications for his sisters and Ava-Marie. The innocent child who would bear the stain of illegitimacy if the truth were known.

"If you've come merely to spread malicious gossip, Baron, I'm afraid I must ask you to leave," she said, rising from her chair. "I have an appointment I cannot miss."

Lockwood remained seated, his smile turning cold. "Not gossip, Lady Courtney. Facts. Facts that would ruin Lord Furoe if they became widely known. Facts that would taint his sisters' prospects for suitable marriages. Facts that would see his bastard daughter shunned by society." He affected a sympathetic expression. "Facts that would make you the laughingstock of society."

She gritted her teeth and refused to rise to his bait.

He continued, "Think of the poor child. Born to a common trollop, raised to believe herself legitimate, only to have that security ripped away when the truth emerges."

Bile rose in Courtney's throat. "You disgust me."

"Perhaps. But disgust doesn't change reality." He examined his fingernails with feigned nonchalance. "Society has certain expectations, especially regarding bloodlines and legitimacy. The scandal would be…devastating."

Courtney's mind raced. If what Lockwood claimed was true—and deep down, she suspected it was—then it explained so much. Lucien's reluctance to discuss his time in Ireland, his protective fierceness toward Ava-Marie… But what hurt her more than the baron's words was that Lucien hadn't confided in her. She understood his fear. But she wanted a relationship where they could tell each other everything. The old Lucien would have…no. No more old Lucien. She couldn't keep doing that. To him or to herself.

But they would need to learn how to trust before she would contemplate marriage to him. Not being in love with her was bad enough, but how could they build anything without trust? Would he have told her before they married?

"What do you want, Baron?" she asked directly, no longer bothering with pretense. "You didn't come here merely to inform me of these facts."

"Perceptive as ever," he acknowledged, finally rising. He walked to the door and closed it. Returning to stand in front of her, he said, "What I want is simple. You."

A chill swept through her. "Excuse me?"

"Marry me instead of Furoe," he said, his voice dropping lower. "Your considerable dowry would solve my financial…inconveniences. Your family connections would open doors previously closed to me. And in return, I would ensure this sordid business remains buried."

Revulsion crawled across her skin. "You cannot be serious."

"I assure you; I am entirely serious." His eyes traveled over her in a way that made her feel soiled. "You're still young, still beautiful. Lord Furoe could continue his charade, raising his little bastard without fear of exposure."

She didn't trust this man as far as she could throw him.

Courtney fought to control her breathing, to think clearly despite the shock and horror flooding through her. If she refused him outright, Lockwood would waste no time spreading his poison throughout London society. Lucien would be disgraced. His family name tarnished. And Ava-Marie—sweet, innocent Ava-Marie, who threw her arms around Courtney's neck and begged for stories about stars—would bear the cruel stigma of illegitimacy her entire life.

"You're asking me to betray the man I love," she said quietly. "My father would never allow me to marry you."

"I'm sure you'll find a way to persuade him."

"Father will know, Lucien will know, everyone will know, something is wrong."

"Why should that matter to you? I'm offering you an opportunity to save him," Lockwood countered. "To spare his family public humiliation. To protect his daughter from the harsh judgment of society. All it would cost is your hand in marriage to me."

"And if I refuse?"

His smile vanished. "Then by this time tomorrow, every drawing room in Mayfair will be buzzing with the scandalous tale of Lord Furoe's Irish deception. His sisters will find their marital prospects vanishing overnight. The child will be marked as a bastard. And you, Lady Courtney—will be an object of pity and ridicule."

The threat hung in the air between them, ugly but undeniably potent. Courtney's mind whirled with desperate calculations. She needed time—time to think, to plan, and find out if this man spoke the truth.

"This is…overwhelming," she said, allowing a tremor to enter her voice. "You're asking me to make an impossible choice with no time for consideration."

Lockwood's expression softened fractionally, though the calculation never left his eyes. "I understand your dilemma. I am not unreasonable. You may have until tomorrow evening at Lady Fenchurch's ball to make your decision. You can give me your answer at midnight on the terrace."

Relief mingled with dread in Courtney's chest. One day. Not much time, but perhaps enough to formulate a response.

"Very well," she agreed reluctantly. "Tomorrow evening."

Lockwood bowed, his manner suddenly courtly. "Until then, Lady Courtney. I trust you'll make the wise choice." He straightened, his eyes hardening. "And I needn't remind you that any attempt to flee London or warn Furoe would force my hand immediately."

She regarded him coldly. "I understand perfectly."

As Graves showed the baron out, Courtney sank back into her chair, her limbs suddenly weak. The sapphire ring on her finger—Lucien's mother's ring—caught the firelight, sending blue sparks dancing across the wall. Tears pricked at her eyes, but she blinked them back fiercely. She'd already given it back once. Would she have to give it back a second time?

Lucien *had* been keeping something from her. She'd felt it. Deep inside, she knew Lockwood's words would be true. She thought his heart was torn up by Ava's loss because he loved her. But it was more likely because she'd lied to him.

She would not believe it of Lucien—even the Lucien she didn't know that well—that he'd allow a child to be born out of wedlock. Therefore, it was a natural assumption that Ava must have lied and told him they were husband and wife. Lucien would not remember. Now she understood his trust issues.

He had never truly been married to her. That Ava-Marie, the child Courtney had grown to love during their weeks in Dorset, was born outside the sanctity of marriage and could be forever tarnished almost made her weep. That Ava had deceived him thoroughly, taking advantage of his amnesia to create a fictional life where she was his respectable wife rather than… How could Ava have been so cruel? But Courtney could hardly judge. She led a life of luxury. How desperate must Ava have been?

Whatever Ava's past, she had clearly loved Lucien and their daughter. Had clearly provided him with companionship and care when he was at his most vulnerable. Perhaps her deception had begun as opportunism, but surely it had evolved into something more genuine? But why had she never told him the truth? No wonder he struggled with trust. The woman he thought loved him had deceived him in the worst possible way.

She'd always envied Ava her time with Lucien and the child, but now she disliked her immensely. She'd stolen five years of Lucien's life. He could have come home to her sooner. Stopped his father's fall into gambling and vice and seen the family coffers remain full.

Courtney could have helped him with his memory loss… Tears welled. But then he'd not have Ava-Marie. *But they might have had their own child….*

Rising on unsteady legs, Courtney moved to the window, staring unseeingly at the street below. What was she to do? If she acquiesced to Lockwood's demand, she would save Lucien's family and Ava-Marie from scandal, but at the cost of her own happiness. If she refused, the consequences would be devastating—not just for Lucien, but for Lauren and Madeline, whose marriage prospects would be irreparably damaged by association.

And Lucien's little girl…

What if she tried to somehow warn Lucien? Lockwood would ensure the scandal broke immediately. Besides, what could Lucien do? The lack of a marriage record couldn't be remedied after the fact. Ava was dead; she couldn't suddenly produce proof of a marriage that had never occurred.

Pressing her fingers to her temples, Courtney tried to think rationally. There had to be a way out of this trap, some solution that didn't involve sacrificing either Lucien's reputation, Ava-Marie's birth, or her own future happiness.

A flash of inspiration made her straighten. Perhaps there was a third option—one that required cunning rather than surrender. Lockwood couldn't be the only one capable of gathering damaging information. Every man had secrets, vulnerabilities that could be exploited. If she could discover Lockwood's before tomorrow evening…

With renewed purpose, Courtney hastily adjusted her shawl and rang for Graves. When the butler appeared, she instructed him to summon her carriage immediately.

"I have an urgent appointment with Lord Ware," she explained, her mind already racing ahead. Perhaps Rockwell and Farah would know if this information was true because they had found Lucien in Ireland. Rockwell also had contacts throughout London society, connections that extended into spheres Courtney had never navigated. If anyone could help her uncover Lockwood's vulnerabilities quickly, it would be him.

As she waited for the carriage to be brought around, Courtney's fingers found the sapphire ring once more. She twisted it thoughtfully, her resolve hardening. She would not surrender Lucien to Lockwood's machinations. Nor would she allow Ava-Marie to suffer for circumstances beyond her control.

Learning of Ava-Marie's birth didn't change her decision to marry Lucien. If anything, it strengthened her determination to stand by him, to prove that her love wasn't contingent on the approval of society or the circumstances of his past. How could he be held responsible for Ava's deception? A man injured in battle and with no memory?

But she couldn't ignore the stabbing doubt deep in her chest.

He hadn't trusted her…

Could love blossom without trust?

In all fairness, they were not married yet. Perhaps he would tell her soon. She could give him time. But if he didn't tell her before their wedding day, could she marry him?

The carriage arrived, and Courtney descended the steps with renewed purpose. She had twenty-four hours to disarm Lockwood's threat. Twenty-four hours to ensure that the life she and Lucien were building wasn't destroyed before it truly began.

And Baron Lockwood would soon discover that Lady Courtney Montague was not a woman to be trifled with—especially when it came to protecting those she loved.

CHAPTER EIGHTEEN

"WHAT'S HAPPENED?" FARAH asked as soon as Courtney entered their beautiful drawing room.

Courtney stood frozen in the doorway, the composure she'd maintained throughout her carriage ride suddenly threatening to crumble. Farah's concerned face blurred slightly as tears filled Courtney's eyes.

"Oh, my dear," Farah said, immediately crossing the room and taking Courtney's hands. "Come, sit. You're trembling."

Courtney allowed herself to be led to a settee, sinking into its cushioned embrace as if her legs could no longer support her. Around the room, she vaguely registered the presence of their other friends—Claire and Ivy exchanging worried glances, Valora setting aside a ledger of figures, and Ashley reaching for the bell to call for tea.

"I need to speak with you privately," Courtney managed, her voice barely above a whisper. "It's…about Lucien."

Understanding instantly dawned in Farah's eyes. With a subtle nod to the others, she helped Courtney to her feet once more. "We'll be in the morning room," she informed them. "Please continue without us."

As Farah led her from the drawing room, Courtney caught a glimpse of the investor's ledger Valora had been examining. Under any other circumstances, she would have been eager to discuss their latest ventures, to celebrate the success of their bold financial strategies. How trivial those concerns seemed now, with

Lucien's future—with Ava-Marie's future—hanging in the balance.

The morning room was awash in sunlight, its cheerful yellow walls and fresh flowers a stark contrast to the darkness spreading through Courtney's heart. As soon as the door closed behind them, Farah turned to her.

"What has happened?" she asked again, her voice gentle but direct.

Courtney took a steadying breath. "Baron Lockwood came to call on me this morning."

Farah's expression immediately hardened. "What did that vile man want?"

"He…" Courtney faltered, then forced herself to meet Farah's eyes. "He claims to have information about Lucien's time in Ireland. About Ava. About Ava-Marie."

A flicker of something—alarm, recognition, guilt?—crossed Farah's face so quickly Courtney might have imagined it, but her racing heart told her otherwise.

"Is it true?" Courtney whispered. "Was Ava never truly his wife? Is Ava-Marie…" She couldn't bring herself to say the word 'illegitimate.'

Farah closed her eyes briefly, her shoulders sagging under an invisible weight. When she opened them again, they held a mixture of resignation and sorrow.

"How much did Lockwood tell you?" she asked carefully.

"Enough," Courtney replied, her worst fears confirmed by Farah's non-denial. "He said there's no record of a marriage between Lucien—or John Collins—and Ava in any parish near Malahide or Dublin. He said…" Her voice caught. "He said Ava was known in certain circles in Dublin before relocating to Malahide."

"And you believed him?" Farah asked, though her tone suggested she already knew the answer.

"I didn't want to," Courtney admitted. "But your face just now confirms it. You knew, didn't you? When you found Lucien in Ireland, you discovered the truth."

Farah moved to the window, her slender fingers fidgeting with the curtain. "Yes," she said finally. "Rockwell and I learned the truth while in Ireland. Rockwell spoke with the local vicar in Malahide. He'd never performed a wedding for them. But the vicar assumed they'd married in Dublin. Rockwell searched the local churches in Dublin but couldn't find any entries and Lucien admitted that he'd not married her after his injury. She had led him to believe they were already husband and wife, taking advantage of his memory loss."

The confirmation hit Courtney like a physical blow. She sank into a nearby chair. "And Ava-Marie?"

"Is Lucien's daughter," Farah said firmly. "Of that, there is no doubt. Just look at her. He loves her desperately. She is innocent in all of this."

"Of course she is," Courtney agreed immediately. "None of this is her fault." She twisted the sapphire ring on her finger, emotions churning inside her. "Why didn't he tell me? We're to be married, and he kept this from me. Perhaps he didn't want this information to hinder the two of us getting to know each other again."

"That's probably true." Farah returned to her side, kneeling to take Courtney's hands. "But it also could be because he was afraid," she said softly. "Terrified that this knowledge would change how you felt about him, about Ava-Marie. The shame of having been deceived so thoroughly, of having a child born outside of marriage—it weighs on him constantly."

"Then he doesn't really know me. Did he plan to tell me at all?" Courtney asked, unable to keep the hurt from her voice.

"Only he can tell you that," Farah whispered.

Courtney's mind raced, piecing together fragments of conversations, the shadows that had occasionally darkened Lucien's expression when discussing his time in Ireland, his reluctance to speak of Ava.

"I thought he couldn't bear to talk about Ava because he was so in love with her and her loss destroyed him. But I understand his fear," she said slowly. "I just wish he could have trusted me. Then Lockwood's threat wouldn't have been such a surprise. I hated that he knew more about Lucien than I did."

"Threat?" Farah's head snapped up. "What threat?"

Courtney pressed her fingers to her temples. "That's why I came. Lockwood isn't merely spreading gossip. He's attempting to blackmail me."

"Blackmail? How?"

"He demands that I marry him instead of Lucien," Courtney explained, disgust evident in her voice. "He wants my dowry and my family connections. In exchange, he claims he'll keep Lucien's secret and spare Ava-Marie and the family any scandal."

Farah's eyes widened in outrage. "That contemptible, loathsome—" She cut herself off, visibly gathering her composure. "When does he expect your answer?"

"Tomorrow night, at Lady Fenchurch's ball. He's giving me until midnight." Courtney's hand trembled as she brushed a tear from her cheek. "Farah, I have to protect them. They have suffered enough already. But I'd prefer to stop Lockwood without exposing them to the very scandal I'm trying to prevent."

Farah rose to her feet, determination replacing shock. "We need Rockwell. He has resources we can use." She strode to the bell pull and gave it a sharp tug. When a footman appeared moments later, she instructed him to send an urgent message to Lord Ware requesting his immediate presence.

"We have less than thirty-six hours," Courtney said, anxiety tightening her chest. "Even Rockwell's influence may not be enough to uncover something we can use against Lockwood in such a short time."

"It won't be easy," Farah acknowledged, beginning to pace the room. "But we must try. Lockwood has clearly been planning this for some time. He must have vulnerabilities of his own we can exploit."

"But what if we can't find anything in time?" Courtney asked, voicing her deepest fear. "I'll have to break my engagement and pretend I'm agreeing to Lockwood's plan. That would give us more time. But Lucien must remain in the dark or Lockwood will spread the news."

Farah hesitated. "Lucien will demand to know why you have called the engagement off."

"Then what do you suggest?" Courtney asked, desperation edging her voice. "Even if I pretend to accept Lockwood's proposal, my father will never consent to a match with a man of Lockwood's reputation. What do I tell my father?"

Before Farah could respond, a commotion in the hallway announced Rockwell's arrival. He entered without ceremony, his usual languid demeanor replaced by alert concern.

"Your message sounded urgent," he said to Farah, then noticed Courtney's pale face. "What's happened?"

Farah quickly explained the situation while Rockwell's expression darkened progressively. By the time she finished, he was pacing alongside her, his movements sharp with barely contained anger.

"Lockwood has overplayed his hand," he said finally. "He's made two critical errors: targeting you, Courtney, when half the ton would rise to defend you; and assuming that Lucien's secret is the only weapon in this battle."

"What do you mean?" Courtney asked, a flicker of hope igniting in her chest.

Rockwell smiled grimly. "Lockwood believes he has until tomorrow night to spring his trap. This gives us time to prepare a counter-offensive."

"But what could we possibly find to use against him in just one day?" Courtney pressed.

"Perhaps nothing," Rockwell admitted. "But we don't need evidence yet—we only need to make Lockwood believe we're pursuing his preferred course of action while we buy ourselves more time. Meanwhile, I'll put my most discreet contacts to work investigating Lockwood's affairs. The man is desperate for funds—he wouldn't resort to blackmail otherwise. There must be debts, improprieties, perhaps even crimes that could counter his hold over you."

"And what of Lucien? I'll have to break the engagement or Lockwood will become suspicious." Courtney asked, her heart aching at the thought of deceiving him, even temporarily. "What will Lucien think of me? I'm fickle and mean…"

A silence fell over the room as Rockwell and Farah exchanged glances.

"Once we tell him the truth, he will be ever so grateful," Farah said gently. "He should thank you for protecting his family."

"Agreed," Rockwell said. "He's already had a run in with Lockwood. I don't want him doing something stupid like challenging him to a duel."

Courtney twisted her engagement ring, conflicted emotions warring within her. "It feels wrong to keep him in the dark," she murmured. "Who knows what Lucien may do if he learns what Lockwood is up to? If Lucien reacts badly, it will reveal all."

"It is a difficult choice," Farah acknowledged, sitting beside her and taking her hand. "But consider this—by giving us a few days to prepare, you're protecting not just Lucien but Ava-Marie, Lauren, and Madeline. The damage Lockwood threatens would affect them all."

"Actually," Rockwell interjected, his expression thoughtful, "we may have more time than I initially thought. The Spring Assizes begin next week. I happen to know that Sir Wilfred Chambers—Lockwood's primary creditor—returns from the North specifically to attend court proceedings. If my suspicions about Lockwood's finances are correct, he'll be particularly vulnerable once Sir Wilfred is back in town."

"That gives us nearly a week," Farah said, hope brightening her face.

"But still requires Courtney to maintain the pretense with Lockwood," Rockwell reminded them soberly. "It won't be easy."

Courtney straightened her shoulders, resolve replacing uncertainty. "I can manage it. For Lucien, for Ava-Marie—I would do far more difficult things than tolerate Lockwood's company for a few days."

"You shouldn't have to face him alone," Farah insisted. "I'll ensure that either myself, Tiffany, or one of the sisterhood is always nearby at any social event. We'll create a signal. If Lockwood becomes too persistent or threatening, you can alert us."

"What am I going to tell the ladies? They will be suspicious of my being in Lockwood's company."

"Nothing. You can't tell them anything. That will just make it more believable for Lockwood. Besides, it's not our secret to share," Rockwell said firmly.

Rockwell moved to the writing desk, pulling paper and ink toward him. "I'll contact my man of business, Mr. Harrington. He's discreet, highly effective, with connections throughout London's financial and legal circles. I'll also reach out to your brother Tarquin—he has acquaintances in less savory establishments who might know of Lockwood's vices."

"I need one more assurance," Courtney said, her voice steadier now that a plan was forming. "Once we have stopped Lockwood, we do so in a way that ensures he has to leave England. If he stays here, I fear he could still ruin Lucien."

"You have my word," Rockwell said solemnly. "Once we've gathered sufficient leverage against Lockwood, we will put him on a ship going far away. Isn't it lucky that I have such a fleet of vessels?"

"And in the meantime," Farah added, "we'll have to maintain appearances."

"The prospect of deceiving Lucien, even briefly..." Courtney shook her head, her heart heavy. "It feels like a betrayal."

"It's protection, not betrayal," Rockwell corrected gently. "Sometimes the most loving action isn't the most direct one."

The door opened then, and a maid entered with a tea tray. The conversation paused as she arranged the service and departed, but the brief interruption gave Courtney a moment to collect her thoughts.

As she accepted a cup from Farah, she contemplated the sapphire ring still adorning her finger. Despite her hurt at Lucien's lack of trust, despite the shocking revelations about Ava and Ava-Marie, her love for him remained unshaken. If anything, understanding the burden he'd been carrying—the fear for his daughter's future, the shame of having been so thoroughly deceived—only deepened her compassion for him.

"There's something else," she said suddenly, looking up at Rockwell. "Something that might help us understand Lockwood's timing. He seemed particularly interested in whether I knew about Ava's background—that she had worked in 'certain circles' in Dublin before meeting Lucien. Could he have evidence beyond simply the absence of marriage records?"

Rockwell frowned. "It's possible. Lockwood has connections in London's less reputable establishments. If Ava worked in similar places in Dublin, he might have learned about Ava from a woman working at such places."

"Which means there might be people who could testify about her past," Courtney realized, a chill running through her. "Making the scandal more difficult to contain if it breaks."

"All the more reason to neutralize Lockwood quickly," Farah said, setting down her teacup with determination. "We need to be methodical. While Rockwell investigates Lockwood's finances and potential indiscretions, we can use our own resources to prepare contingencies."

"What do you mean?" Courtney asked.

"Our investments," Farah explained, lowering her voice despite the privacy of the room. "The profits from our mills and shipping ventures. If needed, we could establish a substantial trust for Ava-Marie, ensuring her financial security regardless of societal reaction."

"That's thoughtful, but money alone won't shield her from scandal," Courtney said, her heart aching for the innocent child who had captured her heart as surely as her father had.

"No," Rockwell agreed. "But influence might. Between your family's connections, Farah's brother the duke, and my own standing, we could ensure that at least some doors remain open to her."

A fresh wave of tears threatened, but this time born of gratitude rather than despair. "Thank you," Courtney whispered. "Both of you. I came here feeling utterly alone in this, and now…"

"You're never alone," Farah said firmly, squeezing her hand. "Remember that tomorrow night when you face Lockwood. Behind you stands not just Lucien, but all of us who care for you both."

Rockwell rose, his expression resolute. "I should go immediately. There's much to arrange, and time is precious." He bowed to both ladies. "I'll send word as soon as I have anything useful."

As he moved toward the door, Courtney called after him. "Rockwell—what if we fail? What if Lockwood exposes Lucien's secret before we can stop him?"

He paused, turning back with unexpected gentleness in his usually sardonic eyes. "Then we face it together. Lucien survived losing his memory, building a life from nothing, discovering that life was built on deception, and returning to a family and fortune in ruins. He is stronger than even he believes, especially with you by his side."

After Rockwell departed, Courtney and Farah sat in silence for several moments, the gravity of their situation settling around them like a heavy cloak.

"I must ask you something," Courtney said finally. "Something that's been troubling me since I learned the truth." She met Farah's gaze directly. "Do you think Lucien could ever truly trust again? Trust me enough to love me as he once did?"

Farah considered the question carefully. "I believe," she said slowly, "that Lucien already trusts you more than anyone else in his new life. His failure to tell you about Ava-Marie wasn't about lack of trust in you specifically—it was fear of losing what you're rebuilding together."

"But—"

"Not many men in his position would risk such a revelation at all. Most would bury the secret forever, allowing their illegitimate children to believe a comfortable fiction rather than face potential scandal."

Courtney hadn't considered it from that perspective. "He did say that there was something he needed to tell me when we got back to London. Maybe he didn't want to ruin our time together in Dorset. It was very magical."

The realization soothed some of the hurt Courtney had been nursing. Perhaps Lucien's reluctance hadn't been about trusting her specifically but about trusting anyone with a truth that could destroy his daughter's future. Perhaps it had been less about their relationship and more about his own wounds, still raw from Ava's betrayal.

"Tomorrow night," she said with newfound resolve, "I will face Lockwood. I will buy us time. And when this is over, Lucien and I will face whatever comes—together."

Farah smiled, pride evident in her expression. "Lockwood has no idea what he's unleashed by threatening you and those you love. By the time we're finished with him, he'll wish he'd never conceived this scheme."

Courtney touched her engagement ring once more, drawing strength from its cool solidity. Lucien was far more damaged than she'd previously understood. She wished she'd known all of this when they were in Dorset. She could have told him it didn't matter a jot to her.

Before Lockwood's visit, she had worried whether Lucien could ever love her. Now, she understood that perhaps the more important question was whether she could love him enough— enough to fight for their future despite the obstacles, enough to help him heal his wounded trust, enough to embrace Ava-Marie as her own regardless of her birth.

The answer, she found, was unequivocally yes.

CHAPTER NINETEEN

L UCIEN SAT BY the fire in his study with a large brandy in hand, mentally exhausted. Wolfarth had taken him to the House of Lords today. It was as if he'd never sat in the house before and trying to learn the etiquette and rules drained him. He was staying in tonight and Courtney was supposed to have joined the family for dinner, but she'd cried off. A bad headache her note had said, probably due to tiredness. She needed time to recover from the journey home from Dorset. But still, something in her manner was off.

He missed her. He couldn't wait until they married, then she would be here with him all the time. He smiled as he remembered her laid out like the delectable feast she was, on his bed the night before they left Dorset. He'd finally thought the horror of the past five years were over and he was starting down a path that he should have walked before he was injured.

He had found a way to save his family and so far, no one had questioned his time in Ireland. He could finally begin to let his guard down. But he still had to tell Courtney. Did he? Wouldn't she be better off not knowing?

Or were his trust issues clouding his judgement?

She had spoken of trust. If they married and she found out later that he'd withheld this important information…would she be able to forgive him? He took another drink and admitted to himself that Courtney would never look down on his daughter. She had such a big heart, and he knew she already looked on Ava-

Marie as her soon-to-be daughter.

He sat gazing at the flames in the hearth. Tonight marked the first time in ages that he had a moment to himself to truly reflect on how much his life had transformed.

His daughter would have a life he'd never dreamed of giving her, and once he married and paid off the debts, he'd work his land and investments to ensure his family's legacy was in good shape for his sons. He hated how he needed to marry Courtney to achieve his goals, but he would work hard to provide her a life she loved. He would make her happy and never disappoint her.

Love. What a word. It held such trepidation but also such hope. He thought about Ava and what she'd done to him—to his family. The five years she had stolen from him. But he had to admit they were happy years. He'd been content. And he had Ava-Marie, the love of his life.

"I forgive you, Ava," he whispered into the silent room. He understood being desperate and that Ava grabbed the opportunity his injury presented. Wasn't he doing the same with Courtney? The fact she'd loved him and probably still did played in his favor.

He had deep feelings for Courtney, but he'd only known her for a few weeks. His body craved her. He could still remember her scent, her soft skin, her understated sensuality drew him. His possessive instincts rose at the idea of another man making love to her.

She's mine.

The grandfather clock in the hallway chimed ten as Lucien poured himself another brandy. The amber liquid caught the firelight as he swirled it in his glass, his mind still wrestling with his pending confession to Courtney. Tomorrow, he resolved. Tomorrow, he would tell her everything about Ava-Marie's birth.

A sharp knock at the front door echoed through the quiet house, followed by Phillips' muffled voice in conversation with a visitor. Lucien frowned. It was well past the hour for social calls, and he wasn't expecting anyone.

The study door opened without announcement, and Phillips

appeared, his usually impassive face betraying a hint of discomfort.

"My lord, there is a...woman who insists on seeing you immediately. A Mrs. Bellamy. I informed her of the late hour, but she claims the matter is most urgent."

"Mrs. Bellamy?" Lucien repeated, the name unfamiliar. "Did she state her business?"

"She said it concerns Baron Lockwood and Lady Courtney, my lord." Phillips lowered his voice. "She appears to be of...questionable character."

Lucien straightened, alarm flaring at the mention of Courtney's name. "Show her in."

Phillips hesitated only briefly before bowing and withdrawing. Moments later, an elegant woman swept into the study, her bearing refined despite the late hour. She was perhaps fifty years of age, with silver threading through dark hair that was still lustrous and expertly arranged. Her dress of deep burgundy silk was tasteful and well-made, speaking of prosperity rather than ostentation. Though time had softened her features, the bones of striking beauty remained evident in her high cheekbones and graceful neck. Her shrewd, intelligent eyes held the wisdom of a woman who had seen much of the world—and learned to navigate its darker corners with both dignity and pragmatism.

"Lord Furoe," she said, executing a curtsy that managed to be both practiced and inappropriate. "I appreciate you receiving me at this unconventional hour."

Lucien remained standing, making no move to offer her a seat. "You mentioned Baron Lockwood and Lady Courtney. Explain yourself."

Mrs. Bellamy gave a knowing smile. "Direct, aren't you? I heard you were different since returning from Ireland. I remember you as a young man. You visited my house often. You were very skilled at playing the game of social niceties." She glanced meaningfully at the chair opposite his. "This conversation might be better conducted sitting down. Shall we?"

After a moment's hesitation, Lucien gestured toward the chair. "Speak plainly, Mrs. Bellamy. Who are you, and what connection do you have to Baron Lockwood?"

She settled herself with grace, arranging her skirts before fixing him with a calculating stare. "I run a business—a rather substantial business. The baron, as have most of London's upper classes, has been a patron for many years."

"A brothel," Lucien stated flatly.

"I prefer 'house of pleasure'," she corrected, unruffled. "But yes. And in my line of work, information is as valuable as the services we provide." She leaned forward. "Baron Lockwood has been gathering information about you, my lord. About your time in Ireland."

Ice formed in Lucien's veins. "Go on."

"Through one of my girls, Kitty, he learned certain details about a woman named Ava." Mrs. Bellamy's eyes never left his face, watching for his reaction. "Kitty knew her in Dublin, before she relocated to Malahide with a gentleman suffering from memory loss."

Lucien's hands tightened on his glass. "And what exactly does Lockwood intend to do with this information?"

"He plans to ruin you," Mrs. Bellamy said bluntly. "Or rather, to blackmail Lady Courtney into breaking her engagement to you and marrying him instead."

The glass nearly shattered in Lucien's grip. "What?"

"He visited Lady Courtney yesterday morning, revealed what he knows about your…unconventional arrangement with Ava, and demanded she accept his proposal or watch as your daughter is branded illegitimate and your family name dragged through the mud."

Lucien set his glass down carefully, afraid he might crush it in his mounting rage. "That's impossible. Courtney would have told me immediately."

Mrs. Bellamy's laugh held no humor. "Would she? When Lockwood threatened to expose your secret the moment she warned you? When he made it clear that your sisters' prospects and your daughter's future would be destroyed if she didn't comply?" She shook her head. "No, my lord. Lady Courtney is protecting you, as women often must protect the men they love."

The realization hit him like a physical blow. Courtney's sudden headache, her canceled dinner engagement—she wasn't tired from travel. She could be buying time, trying to handle Lockwood's threats alone rather than risk him doing something foolish.

"Why are you telling me this?" Lucien demanded, suspicion cutting through his shock. "What's your stake in this affair?"

Mrs. Bellamy's expression hardened. "Lockwood promised me a percentage of Lady Courtney's dowry for the information my girl provided. A substantial sum that would have allowed me to retire from my current profession. Instead, through my contacts in Rotton Row, I've discovered he intends to cheat me out of my fair share."

"So, this is about money," Lucien said, disgust evident in his voice.

"Isn't everything?" she countered. "I've spent twenty years in a business where I'm scorned by the very men who seek my services. I've earned my retirement."

"And you expect me to pay you instead?"

Mrs. Bellamy shrugged. "I'm a businesswoman, my lord. I'm offering you valuable information in exchange for compensation."

Lucien crossed to the window, staring out at the darkened garden as he gathered his thoughts. "What exactly does Lockwood know? How detailed is his information?"

"He knows Ava worked in a brothel in Dublin before finding you injured after the rebellion," Mrs. Bellamy replied. "He knows she claimed to be your wife, when no such marriage record could be found. And therefore, your daughter would, by law, be illegitimate."

"And your…employee…is willing to publicly confirm these

details?"

"Kitty has no loyalty to Lockwood. She liked Ava and wishes to protect your daughter." Mrs. Bellamy smoothed her skirts. "She was fond of Ava, actually. Feels guilty about betraying her memory. But guilt doesn't put food on the table."

Lucien turned back to face her; his expression cold. "What's to stop me from simply denying everything? It would be my word against your girl's. An earl's son."

"Nothing," Mrs. Bellamy agreed readily. "Except Lockwood has been thorough. He's had men searching parish records throughout Ireland. There is no record of any marriage between you—under any name—and a woman named Ava. And several people in Malahide remember the 'widow Collins', who wasn't a widow until you supposedly married her."

The careful life he'd constructed since returning to England seemed to crumble around him. Everything he'd feared since discovering Ava's deception was coming to pass. His daughter would bear the shame of illegitimacy. His sisters would suffer for his mistakes. And Courtney—God, Courtney was facing Lockwood's threats alone, believing she was protecting him.

"What would you suggest I do?" he asked, his voice dangerously quiet.

Mrs. Bellamy's eyes glittered in the firelight. "Kill him."

Lucien stared at her, momentarily speechless.

"I'm perfectly serious," she continued, unperturbed by his shock. "Men like Lockwood don't simply go away. Even if you pay him once, he'll come back for more. You think he'll be satisfied with stealing your fiancée? Once he has Lady Courtney's dowry, he'll still hold your secret over your head."

"You're suggesting murder," Lucien said flatly.

"I'm suggesting a permanent solution," she corrected. "Men duel over less every day. Or accidents happen. A tumble downstairs, a runaway carriage, a midnight swim in the Thames."

Lucien shook his head, disgust welling within him. "I am not a murderer, Mrs. Bellamy."

"No? That's a shame," she remarked, watching him carefully. "Sometimes violence is the most direct path to justice."

"Is that what this is about for you? Justice?" Lucien's laugh was bitter. "Or merely revenge because Lockwood is cheating you of your blood money?"

Mrs. Bellamy rose, drawing herself up to her full height. "Call it what you will. I have my reasons. But consider this—Lockwood intends to meet Lady Courtney tomorrow night at Lady Fenchurch's ball. He expects her answer then. If she refuses him, he plans to spread his poison immediately. Your reputation, your daughter's future, your sisters' prospects—all destroyed before sunrise."

Lucien's mind raced. If what the woman said was true, he had less than twenty-four hours to counter Lockwood's scheme. "And your price for this information?"

"Two thousand pounds," Mrs. Bellamy said promptly. "A fair sum for information that could save your family from ruin."

"Two thousand—" Lucien broke off, incredulous. "That's extortion."

"That's business," she replied calmly. "Consider it an investment in your daughter's future."

Lucien moved to the desk, pulling out paper and ink. "I won't have that money until I marry. You must have heard my family is broke. I can provide you with a promissory note."

Mrs. Bellamy considered this, then nodded. "I can wait for the wedding. Unlike Lockwood, I won't be back for more. I'm rather proud of what Ava achieved and we working ladies must stick together."

As Mrs. Bellamy rose to leave, a cold determination settled in his chest. He would not kill Lockwood, no matter what this woman suggested. But he would stop him—immediately and permanently.

"One more thing," he said. "Where can I find Kitty? I may need to speak with her directly."

"You should call on your friend, the Duke of Blackstone. I

believe he's just set Kitty up in a house. She's not told anyone where that is. The duke does like his privacy. The girl has moved up, so don't ruin things for her."

Farah's brother? The man who was afraid of any scandal? The rigid and proper golden duke with a common prostitute? Lucien was astounded. He always thought the Duke of Blackstone was above such things, but he supposed all men had needs. He would call on the duke first thing in the morning. He had to find Kitty.

"One last thing, my lord. Lockwood is a snake—not a gentleman—so don't go thinking your society rules apply. If you get the chance, kill him."

"I'll manage. As you know, I haven't been a gentleman for the past five years," Lucien said curtly. "Is there anything else I should know about Lockwood's plans?"

Mrs. Bellamy paused at the door. "Only that he's desperate. His creditors are circling, and that makes him dangerous. Lady Courtney's dowry isn't merely desirable to him—it's necessary for his survival."

After she departed, Lucien stood motionless in the center of the study, the magnitude of the situation washing over him. Courtney was facing Lockwood's threats alone. The thought of her sacrificing herself, possibly agreeing to marry that snake to shield Ava-Marie from scandal, made him physically ill.

He should have told her the truth from the beginning. He'd been a coward, afraid of losing her respect, afraid she would walk away when she learned the full extent of his deception. Instead, his silence had left her vulnerable to Lockwood's manipulation.

Moving swiftly, Lucien crossed to his desk and pulled out fresh paper. He needed help, and quickly. He wrote a note for Blackwood, asking to call on him as early as convenient tomorrow.

As he wrote, his mind kept returning to Courtney. She must be terrified, believing she faced this threat alone. Yet she'd maintained her composure, even canceling their dinner engagement and going along with Lockwood's scheme.

Her strength humbled him. Her willingness to sacrifice herself for his family—for Ava-Marie—proved the depth of her character in ways words never could.

Something deep in his chest burst free and he almost dropped to his knees. Why was he fighting so hard? Why couldn't he just have loved this woman? Told her what he was afraid of. Half his hesitation in opening his heart was because everyone expected him to love her because of their past and he had fought that. But his fight was for nothing. Because she had been claiming pieces of his heart from the day he'd called upon her. It was as if his heart knew she was his, even if he couldn't remember.

Finishing his note to Blackstone, Lucien rang for Phillips. When the butler appeared, he handed him the sealed letter.

"Have this delivered to His Grace, Duke of Blackstone immediately, regardless of the hour. Then ready my horse. I'm going out."

Phillips looked startled. "At this hour, my lord? It's nearly midnight."

"This can't wait until morning," Lucien replied, his decision made. He would not let Courtney face this alone for another moment. "And Phillips—send word to prepare my pistols. I may have need of them."

As the butler hurried to comply, Lucien moved to the fireplace, staring into the dying embers. Mrs. Bellamy's suggestion of murder had repulsed him, but he couldn't deny the satisfaction he'd feel in putting a bullet through Lockwood if necessary. Not for revenge, but for protection—of Courtney, of Ava-Marie, of his family's future.

But first, he needed to see Courtney. To tell her he knew about Lockwood's threat. To promise her she wasn't alone in this fight. To finally confess the whole truth, not just about Ava-Marie's birth, but about his feelings for Courtney herself—feelings that had grown from cautious attraction into something deeper.

As he prepared to ride through the midnight streets to her

home, Lucien made himself a solemn vow: After tonight, there would be no more secrets between them. Whatever the cost, whatever the consequences, they would face them together.

And as for Lockwood—the baron would soon discover that threatening Lucien's family was the gravest mistake of his miserable life.

CHAPTER TWENTY

THE MIDNIGHT STREETS of London held a sinister quality Lucien barely noticed as he rode through them, his mind consumed with thoughts of Courtney. A fine mist had begun to fall, enshrouding the gas lamps in halos of diffused light and dampening his cloak, but he barely felt the chill. His heart pounded with a mixture of rage at Lockwood, fear for Courtney, and the burning need to see her—to explain everything. What was she thinking about him, about them? Did she hate him for not telling her? Had he lost her trust?

When he reached Lorne House, he circled to the garden side. Lauren had told him which window belonged to Courtney's bedchamber. A light still burned there, visible through the curtains—she was awake. Relief flooded through him, followed swiftly by determination.

Tethering his horse to a tree at the edge of the property, Lucien studied the ancient oak that grew beside the house, its branches stretching toward Courtney's window. Once, years ago, he might have climbed it with practiced ease. Tonight, he would have to relearn the skill quickly.

The damp bark made his hands slip as he hauled himself up, finding footholds in the gnarled trunk. His muscles strained with the effort, but adrenaline drove him ever upward. A branch cracked beneath his boot, making him freeze momentarily, listening for any sign he'd been detected. Hearing nothing, he continued his ascent until he reached the branch that extended nearest to her window.

Perched precariously, he leaned forward and tapped gently on the glass. No response. He tapped again, slightly louder, then pressed his face close to the pane, trying to see through the gap in the curtains.

Suddenly, the curtains parted, and there she was—her auburn hair loose around her shoulders, her amber eyes widening in shock as she recognized him. She hastily unlatched the window.

"Lucien?" she whispered, her voice a mixture of disbelief and alarm as she pushed the window open. "What on earth are you doing? You could break your neck!"

"I needed to see you," he said, his voice roughened by emotion. "Please, let me in."

She didn't hesitate, allowing him space to climb through the window. She stuck her head out and looked around before slamming the window sash closed.

He landed on her bedroom floor with less grace than he'd intended, then straightened, taking in her appearance. Her fine lawn night dress was almost transparent in the firelight, and with her hair tumbling loose and her face pale with worry, she was the most beautiful thing he'd ever seen.

"You shouldn't be here," she said, though she made no move to call for help. "If anyone discovers you—"

"I know about Lockwood," he interrupted, watching her face closely. "I know what he's threatening to do. What he's asking of you."

Her face drained of color. "How did you—"

"Mrs. Bellamy came to see me tonight. She owns the establishment where Lockwood learned about Ava."

Courtney sank onto the edge of her bed, her knees seemingly unable to support her. "Then you know everything," she whispered.

"Everything Lockwood knows," Lucien confirmed, moving to kneel before her. "But not everything I should have told you myself long ago." He took her hands in his, finding them cold and trembling. "Courtney, I am so sorry."

Her eyes searched his face. "You lied to me—be it by omission. I wish you could have trusted me!"

"I was going to tell you when we got back to London," he said, squeezing her hands. "I didn't want to ruin our time in Dorset. I was a coward."

"I did wonder if that was the case." A single tear traced down her cheek. "I wouldn't have judged you, Lucien. Surely you know that?"

"Deep down, I did," he admitted. "But I was so afraid of losing you. Of seeing disgust or disappointment in your eyes when you learned how thoroughly I'd been deceived. How I fathered a child with a woman who wasn't even truly my wife."

"Tell me now," she urged gently. "I want to hear it from you."

Lucien rose, unable to remain still. He paced the length of her bedroom, gathering his thoughts. "After I was injured in the rebellion, I woke with no memory of who I was. Ava told me I'd been injured in the crossfire. She hid the fact that I was an officer in the British army. She nursed me back to health, telling me we were husband and wife."

"But how did she explain the brothel?" Courtney asked, her voice soft with understanding rather than judgment.

"She told me that I had been the head groom looking after the stables and she worked in the kitchen. I had no reason to doubt her. It was the only work we could get. She created an entire fiction—that we were John and Ava Collins. When I recovered enough strength, she told me her father had died and had left us a small farm. So, she moved us to Malahide, to a small cottage far from anyone who might know differently."

He paused, looking out the window at the London night. "I believed her completely. Why wouldn't I? I had no memories to contradict her story. And she was kind to me, caring—loving. And she was very beautiful. I came to love her."

"It must have hurt when you discovered her lies."

He sighed and turned to face her. "It destroyed me, and I'm thankful she was dead when I learned the truth. I don't know what I would have done if she'd been still alive. I've found it hard to trust anyone ever since I learned how badly she deceived me."

"And Ava-Marie?" Courtney asked softly.

A smile touched his lips, despite the pain of the memories. "I was overjoyed when Ava told me she was with child. I'll never regret having her."

"She is a lovely little girl." Courtney hesitated. "And there is no doubting she's your daughter."

"Yes," Lucien said with absolute certainty. "She has my eyes, my stubborn chin. Ava may have lied about many things, but she never betrayed me that way. Ava-Marie is my flesh and blood."

Relief washed over Courtney's face. "I'm glad. I've grown to love her because she is a part of you."

The simple statement nearly undid him. He returned to kneel before her again, taking her hands. "It wasn't until Rockwell arrived and we decided to check the parish records that I realized her entire story had been fabrication. Even Caitria believed us married."

"That must have been devastating," Courtney whispered.

"It was," he admitted. "To discover that the life I'd built was founded on lies...that the mother of my child, a woman I'd loved had deceived me so thoroughly..." He shook his head. "She stole five years of my life where I could have been here, preventing my father's descent into a dark hole."

His voice broke slightly. "I never imagined this secret would put you in danger."

"Is that why you didn't tell me? You thought I couldn't handle the truth?"

"No," he said firmly. "I was afraid—terrified—that you would think less of me. That the man you were coming to care for again would be revealed as a fool who couldn't even recognize when he was being manipulated." He lowered his head. "I was ashamed."

"And why was that important?"

Courtney was implying he needed her for her money. "How can you lov—marry a man you don't respect?"

Courtney's hand came to rest on his cheek, gently lifting his face to meet her gaze. "Lucien, you were injured. You had no memory. How could anyone blame you for believing what you were told? For trusting the woman who cared for you. I love that about you. How you saw the good in people."

"Now I distrust everyone. Ava took that from me." The understanding in her eyes was almost too much to bear. "I should have told you before we became engaged. I almost did, that night in the library. But then you accepted my proposal, and you looked so happy… I couldn't bear to ruin that moment."

"And when we got back to London?"

"I was going to tell you this morning. I swear it." He released a shaky breath. "But now Lockwood has threatened everything. You, Ava-Marie, my sisters' futures… I don't know how to stop him. Maybe I should take the wind out of his sails and simply announce that I've now found out Ava and I were never married."

A flash of anger crossed Courtney's face. "No. We will find a way out of this mess. We have powerful friends. This is not your fault. It's Lockwood's. He's the one using this information to blackmail us."

"And you were planning to sacrifice yourself," Lucien said, his voice rough with emotion. "To marry that snake to protect my family. To protect Ava-Marie."

Her chin lifted slightly. "I would have done whatever was necessary. But I too had a plan of sorts."

"I beg your pardon?" he demanded, rising to his feet again. "Why would you make such a sacrifice for me? For a child born of another woman? For a man who couldn't even trust you with the truth?"

"Because I love you," she said simply, the words hanging in the air between them. "I never stopped loving you, Lucien. Not when I thought you were dead. Not when you returned with no memory of me. Not when I learned about Ava and Ava-Marie. Love isn't something you can simply turn off like a lamp."

Her words struck him like a physical blow. He had known, intellectually, that she had loved him before his disappearance. He had suspected she still harbored feelings for him now. But to hear her declare it so openly, so fearlessly, in the face of everything she'd learned...

"I don't deserve you," he whispered, his voice thick with emotion.

"That's not for you to decide," she countered, rising to stand before him. "I choose who to give my heart to. And I choose you, Lucien. The man you were, the man you are now—I choose all of you."

Something broke inside him then—a dam holding back emotions he'd kept tightly controlled since his return to England. Without conscious thought, he pulled her into his arms, burying his face in her hair.

"I can't lose you," he murmured against her temple. "Not to Lockwood. Not to anyone."

"You won't," she promised, her arms tightening around him. "Lockwood underestimated us both. I've already spoken with Rockwell and Farah. They're gathering information to use against him."

Lucien drew back, surprise evident on his face. "You went to Rockwell?"

She nodded. "I couldn't come to you. Lockwood said if I did, he'd reveal all. I suspect he has men watching this house and yours. I hope you weren't followed here. Yesterday, after Lockwood left, I knew I couldn't face this alone. Rockwell is contacting everyone who might have information about Lockwood's finances, his secrets—anything we could use to counter his threats."

"So, you weren't just surrendering to his demands," Lucien realized, relief washing through him.

"Of course not," she said firmly. "I was buying time. At Lady

Fenchurch's ball tomorrow night, I'm supposed to tell Lockwood I'll accept his proposal, but that I need a few days to break my engagement with you 'discreetly'."

A fierce pride filled Lucien's chest. "You're remarkable, do you know that?"

She smiled, though it didn't quite reach her eyes. "I would have done anything to protect Ava-Marie from scandal. She's an innocent in all this."

"You love her that much?" he asked, wonder in his voice.

"How could I not?" Courtney said simply. "She's so full of life, so curious and kind. She's a miniature you."

Lucien's heart swelled with an emotion too powerful to name. This woman—this extraordinary woman—had not only accepted his past, his mistakes, but had taken his daughter into her heart as well.

"I learned something else tonight," he said, his voice low and urgent. "Mrs. Bellamy told me about a woman named Kitty who knew Ava in Dublin. She's the one who told Lockwood about Ava's past. I intend to find her tomorrow."

"Is that wise?" Courtney asked, concern evident in her voice. "Lockwood could be watching you—watching us."

"It's necessary," Lucien insisted. "We need to understand exactly what Lockwood knows—and what he might not know. Kitty might be persuaded to help us, especially since Lockwood apparently intends to cheat her and Mrs. Bellamy of their 'share' of your dowry."

Courtney's face hardened. "He truly is despicable."

"Yes," Lucien agreed, his voice cold. "And he will pay for threatening you. For threatening my daughter."

"Please don't do anything stupid." She stepped closer, her hands coming to rest on his chest. "We will face him together," she said firmly. "No more secrets between us, no more lonely battles. Whatever comes, we face it as one."

The conviction in her voice, the strength in her gaze, over-whelmed him. For so long, he had carried his burdens alone—the loss of his memory, the discovery of Ava's deception, the despair of carrying his family's financial situation, the fear for his daughter's future. Now, here was Courtney, offering not just her love but her partnership, her unwavering support.

"What would I do without you?" he whispered again, his hand coming up to cradle her face. "But I am profoundly grateful for you."

"Lucien," she said softly, her amber eyes luminous in the lamplight, "I can't lose you again. When I thought you had died in Ireland, it nearly destroyed me. I won't let Lockwood or anyone else take you from me a second time."

The raw emotion in her voice stripped away his last defenses. He lowered his head and claimed her lips in a kiss that held all the words he couldn't yet say—his gratitude, his admiration, his growing feelings that might someday match the love she so freely offered.

She responded with equal fervor, her arms sliding around his neck, drawing him closer. What began as comfort quickly blazed into desire, the tension and fear of recent days finding release in passionate connection.

His hands tangled in her loose hair, while hers worked at the buttons of his coat, pushing it from his shoulders. They moved as if by mutual agreement toward her bed, shedding layers of clothing as they went.

"Stay with me tonight," she whispered against his lips. "I need to feel you close to me."

"Are you certain?" he asked, his voice rough with desire but his eyes searching hers for any hesitation.

"More certain than I've ever been," she replied, her fingers tracing the contours of his face. "We've lost so much time already, Lucien. I don't want to waste another moment."

Her nightdress fell to the floor, leaving her gloriously bare before him. The sight of her stole his breath—her creamy skin illuminated by the soft glow of the bedside lamp, her auburn hair cascading over her shoulders, her eyes dark with desire for him.

"You're beautiful," he murmured, running reverent hands down her sides. "So beautiful it hurts to look at you."

She smiled at that, her hands working at the fastenings of his shirt. "Then don't just look," she suggested, her voice a gentle tease despite the heat in her gaze.

They fell onto the bed together, hands exploring, lips seeking, bodies teaching each other anew. He worshipped every inch of her, marveling at her responsiveness, at the soft sounds she made when he found a particularly sensitive spot.

When he finally joined with her, it was with a sense of coming home—a belonging so profound, it caught in his throat. They moved together in perfect harmony, building toward a shared release that left them both trembling and breathless.

Afterward, as she lay in his arms, her head resting on his chest, he felt a peace he hadn't known since leaving Ireland. Whatever Lockwood planned, whatever challenges they might face, he was no longer alone. Courtney was his partner in this fight, his equal in every way. And most of all, he trusted her.

"I will stop him," Lucien promised, pressing a kiss to her temple. "*We* will stop him. And then we'll build the life we should have had before Ireland. Before Ava. Before everything."

She lifted her head to look at him, her eyes serious despite her smile. "Not before everything, Lucien. I wouldn't erase Ava-Marie from our story, not for anything."

His heart constricted with emotion. "Nor would I. She is the one pure gift to come from all of this."

"Then we'll build a new life," she said, settling back against his chest. "Not the one we planned before, but one that includes her, that honors all we've been through, all we've learned."

As sleep began to claim them both, Lucien held Courtney close, his mind still turning over plans for confronting Lockwood. But the desperation that had driven him through London's midnight streets had eased. In its place was a cool determination, strengthened by Courtney's love and his own newfound clarity.

Whatever happened tomorrow at Lady Fenchurch's ball, one

thing was certain: Baron Lockwood had made the gravest mistake of his life in threatening what Lucien held most dear. And he would soon discover just how formidable an opponent Lucien Furoe could be.

COURTNEY WOKE ALONE in the early dawn light. She rolled over and ran her hand over the bed where Lucien had slept. His sandalwood scent lingered on her sheets and on the pillows. She breathed in deeply and gave a contented sigh, almost like a purr.

They had agreed to a plan for the ball tonight. She would start an argument with Lucien and storm off. She would tell Lockwood the engagement was off, but that he still had to convince her father to allow the marriage. She would tell him it would not be easy, as Tarquin also would object. Her brother did not like Lockwood. That would buy them time.

She'd wanted to go with Lucien to talk with Kitty, but they couldn't risk being seen together. Still, Lucien agreed to take the Duke of Blackstone with him.

She stretched, loving the feel of her nakedness and remembering the pleasure from last night. She should ring for her lady's maid and organize a bath, but she wanted to luxuriate in bed with her memories and joy for a while longer.

On a low groan, she rose and pulled the bell for her maid.

Once dressed, she made her way to the drawing room, having asked Graves to send for her brother. She'd best inform Tarquin what was going on. He might even be able to help Lucien deal with Lockwood, too.

She'd just poured herself a cup of tea and taken a seat in the sun coming through the large terrace door windows, when Graves entered. "Your brother and your father are not at home at present, my lady. They are at Tattersalls."

"Of course. I forgot they were attending the horse auction

today. The minute my brother returns, can you ask him to please attend me?"

"As you wish. Also, Lady Ashley is below. Should I send her up?"

Rockwell's sister, Ashley, was here? That couldn't be a coincidence. "Of course, Graves. And bring some more tea."

Courtney set her teacup down as Ashley swept into the drawing room, her forest green walking dress immaculate despite the light drizzle outside. Ashley's usual composed demeanor seemed slightly rattled this morning, her cheeks flushed and her eyes bright with what Courtney recognized as curiosity mixed with scandal.

"My dear Courtney," Ashley said, hastily removing her gloves as Graves withdrew from the room. "I hope I'm not disturbing you at this early hour."

"Not at all," Courtney replied, gesturing for her friend to join her by the window. "I'm delighted for the company. Father and Julian are at Tattersalls for the horse auction today."

Ashley settled into the chair opposite, a knowing gleam in her eye. "I suspected as much. Most of the gentlemen seemed to be heading that direction when I was on my way here." She leaned forward. "But that's not why I've come at this unseemly hour."

Courtney poured her friend a cup of tea. "I gathered as much from your expression. You look like a cat that's found the cream."

"Oh, my dear, it's far more delicious than cream." Ashley accepted the cup with a conspiratorial smile. "I've just come from Farah's, where I learned the most astonishing piece of information that simply couldn't wait."

Courtney's heart skipped. "About Lockwood?" she asked, lowering her voice despite the empty house.

"No, though Rockwell is making progress there," Ashley assured her. "This is about your Lucien and his quest to find the mysterious Kitty."

"He's found her already?" Courtney set down her cup with a small clatter. "But it's barely nine in the morning. How could he possibly—"

"That's just it," Ashley interrupted, eyes dancing with mischief. "He didn't have to search very far. It seems your Kitty, the woman who knew Ava in Dublin, is none other than the Duke of Blackstone's mistress!"

Courtney laughed. "Mistresses are not unusual for men of his standing. He's still young, about nine and twenty, isn't he? Still sowing his wild oats. Except I've never known the duke to be wild about anything. He's so staid and proper."

"Exactly! That's why I think Blackstone having a mistress is very amusing," Ashley confirmed with obvious relish. "Our stern, proper, never-a-hair-out-of-place duke is keeping a former low-class lady of the night in a small but elegant house in Chelsea."

Courtney couldn't reconcile the image of the austere, imposing duke—known throughout society for his rigid adherence to propriety and his barely concealed disdain for scandal—with a man who would keep a former brothel worker as his mistress.

"There may be an innocent explanation," she protested. "He may be trying to help her leave the profession."

Ashley's laugh tinkled through the room. "The very same man who once gave Julian a twenty-minute lecture on the impropriety of loosening his cravat at White's after midnight, helping a lowly Irish prostitute. Not likely."

"You dislike him. Or are you protesting too much?" Courtney shook her head in disbelief.

"Rubbish," Ashley stuttered. "He's a hypocrite. The same duke who refused to attend the Smythsons' garden party because their daughter had been seen riding in an open carriage with her fiancé without a proper chaperone?" Ashley said, helping herself to a biscuit. "According to Rockwell, who seemed rather amused by the whole thing, Lucien called on His Grace at an ungodly hour this morning. After explaining the situation, the duke apparently went quite pale and admitted that Kitty has been under his protection since he met her at Cyprian's masked ball."

Courtney sat back. "Does Farah know? He was so strict with her."

"She does now," Ashley replied with a laugh. "You should have seen her face when Rockwell told us. I thought she might faint from the shock. She kept saying, 'My brother? My Raven?' as if there might be another Duke of Blackstone lurking about London."

Courtney couldn't help but join in her friend's laughter, the absurdity of the situation momentarily distracting her from her own troubles. "The man who sits in judgment of us all has been the greatest hypocrite in London."

"It does rather put his treatment of my family in a new light," Ashley remarked, her smile dimming slightly. "He's barely acknowledged my existence since my scandal broke three years ago. I really loathe the man."

Courtney reached across to squeeze her friend's hand. She couldn't say anything because Ashley had never shared the details of her scandal with the sisterhood. "How insufferable. To think, he's looked down his aristocratic nose at you all this time, while keeping a former brothel worker as his mistress."

"In a very nice house in Chelsea, no less," Ashley added with a rueful smile. "Apparently, he's quite devoted to her. Rockwell says the duke has been teaching her to read and has engaged tutors to instruct her in proper speech and deportment."

"Good heavens," Courtney murmured. "It sounds as if he's quite smitten."

"Besotted, according to Rockwell." Ashley's eyes twinkled. "Can you imagine the Duke of Blackstone in love? The man whose expression never changes, even during the most scandalous on-dits at Almack's?"

"The mind boggles," Courtney agreed, trying to picture the stern duke's face softening with affection. "Though I suppose it explains why he's refused every eligible young lady presented to him these past seasons."

"Including Lady Harriet Pembroke, and she's quite the diamond," Ashley noted. "Her father was furious when the duke showed not the slightest interest."

Courtney sipped her tea, contemplating this revelation. "I wonder what this Kitty is like, to have captured such a formidable heart."

"Rockwell says she's quite lovely—red-haired and vivacious—but more importantly, Lucien believes she'll help us. Apparently, Mrs. Bellamy told Lucien that she feels terribly guilty about revealing Ava's secret to Lockwood. She had no idea he intended to use the information for blackmail."

"Will she testify against him if necessary?" Courtney asked, hope rising in her chest.

"That's what Lucien and the duke have gone to determine." Ashley gave her a reassuring smile. "Kitty seems eager to make amends. And with the duke's support…"

"It seems almost too good to be true," Courtney murmured. "Of course, Blackstone may not want this information made public. It would tarnish his image."

Ashley nearly choked on her tea with laughter. "Can you imagine? The look on Lady Jersey's face alone would be worth the scandal of revealing the information."

"I loathe scandal, but after his treatment of you and Farah, he does need taking down a peg or two," Courtney added, warming to the jest. "Plus, it might distract him from our investment challenge. I really want Tiffany to beat him."

"Oh, he would definitely glower," Ashley agreed. "He has at least seven different varieties of glower that I've cataloged over the years. My favorite is the one where his left eyebrow barely rises while his mouth turns down precisely three millimeters at the corner."

Ashley demonstrated the expression, causing Courtney to dissolve into giggles.

"I received that exact glower when I had the audacity to suggest that his opinion on female education might be somewhat archaic," Courtney recalled, smiling at the memory. "I believe he told me that 'young ladies should concern themselves with accomplishments suited to their delicate constitutions.'"

"While teaching his mistress to read and hiring tutors for her," Ashley added wryly. "The hypocrisy is simply breathtaking."

"Perhaps there's hope for him yet," Courtney mused. "If he can care so deeply for someone society would deem unsuitable, maybe his rigid exterior hides a more compassionate heart than we've given him credit for."

"Or perhaps he simply fell in love despite himself," Ashley suggested. "The heart doesn't always follow the dictates of propriety, after all."

The observation sobered Courtney, reminding her of her own situation. "No, it certainly doesn't."

Ashley reached across to touch her hand. "How are you truly, Courtney? This terrible business with Lockwood—"

"I'm better now that Lucien knows everything," Courtney admitted. "We spoke last night. He came to me after Mrs. Bellamy revealed Lockwood's scheme."

"He came to you? At night?" Ashley's eyebrows rose suggestively. "How very...improper of him."

Courtney felt her cheeks warm. "Yes, well, desperate times call for desperate measures."

"And did these desperate measures include a reconciliation?" Ashley teased gently.

"We...reached an understanding," Courtney replied, unable to keep a small smile from her lips. "He told me everything about Ava, about his time in Ireland. No more secrets between us."

"I'm glad," Ashley said sincerely. "You deserve happiness, Courtney, after all you've endured these past years."

"If we can survive Lockwood's scheme," Courtney reminded her, glancing at the clock on the mantel. "Lucien and I have a plan for tonight's ball, but much depends on what he learns from Kitty today."

"Do you think Lockwood suspects anything?" Ashley asked, her expression growing serious.

"I'm not certain," Courtney admitted. "He seemed so confident when he issued his ultimatum. I can only hope he believes I'm too frightened to defy him."

"The man is a snake," Ashley declared with uncharacteristic vehemence. "To threaten you and that innocent child—"

A sudden crash of breaking glass interrupted her words. Both women whirled toward the terrace doors where three figures stood amid the shattered remains of the French doors—Baron Lockwood flanked by two rough-looking men Courtney had never seen before.

"Ladies," Lockwood drawled, brushing glass fragments from his immaculate coat sleeve. "I do apologize for the dramatic entrance, but I find myself requiring Lady Courtney's immediate company."

Courtney rose to her feet, her heart hammering against her ribs. "Baron Lockwood, have you lost your mind? Breaking into my father's home in broad daylight—"

"A necessary expediency," he interrupted, advancing into the room. His pale eyes held none of the false charm he'd displayed during their previous encounter—only cold calculation. "I've learned that Lord Furoe has been making inquiries this morning. Inquiries that suggest you may have betrayed our arrangement."

Ashley stepped between them, her chin lifted defiantly. "You will leave immediately, sir, or I shall scream the house down."

One of Lockwood's companions—a burly man with a scar bisecting his left eyebrow—smiled unpleasantly. "Scream all you like, my lady. The servants are otherwise engaged in the kitchen. A small fire broke out just minutes ago. Most unfortunate timing."

Ice slid down Courtney's spine as she realized the depth of Lockwood's planning. "What do you want?" she demanded, though she already knew the answer.

"A revised timeline," Lockwood replied smoothly. "Rather than waiting for you to break your engagement gracefully, we'll be departing for Gretna Green immediately. I've taken the liberty of arranging swift transportation."

"You're mad," Courtney breathed. "I shall never marry you voluntarily. I'll scream the church down."

Lockwood's smile didn't reach his eyes. "I'm afraid you've misunderstood, Lady Courtney. This is no longer a request." He nodded to his companions, who began advancing on either side of Ashley. "Your father will find his beloved daughter has eloped. Most shocking, but these things happen in the best families. Upon our return as husband and wife, I'm certain he'll find it in his heart to forgive the impetuosity of young love—and provide the agreed-upon dowry."

"I doubt that very much. You'll ruin my life for nothing."

He stepped toward her. "A father doesn't like seeing his daughter hurt, and unfortunate accidents can happen if money is not forthcoming."

"You'll never get away with this," Ashley hissed, backing up as the men approached. "Her father will have you hanged."

"Only if he catches me before we wed, so get a move on," Lockwood countered.

In a sudden movement, Ashley seized a heavy crystal vase from a nearby table and hurled it at the scarred man, catching him in the shoulder. "Run, Courtney!" she shouted.

Courtney bolted for the door, but the second man—younger, leaner, but no less menacing—intercepted her, grabbing her around the waist and lifting her off her feet. She screamed and struggled, kicking wildly as she was dragged back toward the broken terrace doors.

Ashley launched herself at Lockwood, her small fists pummeling his chest as she tried to impede his progress. The baron backhanded her across the face with shocking force, sending her crashing into a delicate rosewood table that splintered beneath her weight.

"Ashley!" Courtney cried, watching in horror as her friend crumpled to the floor, a thin line of blood appearing at her temple where she'd struck the edge of the broken table.

"Regrettable," Lockwood commented dispassionately. "But

she should have known better than to interfere."

"You monster," Courtney seethed, renewing her struggles as the man holding her tightened his grip painfully around her ribs. "You'll hang for this!"

"I think not," Lockwood replied calmly, producing a small cloth from his coat pocket. "Now, I'm afraid we must expedite our departure before someone investigates that little fire in the kitchen."

Before she could protest further, the cloth was pressed against her face, its sickly-sweet smell flooding her nostrils. Courtney held her breath, trying to twist away, but the man's grip was unyielding. Eventually, her lungs burning, she was forced to inhale, and immediately the room began to spin around her.

Her last conscious thought was of Lucien, of the promises they'd made to each other just hours ago. As darkness claimed her, she prayed he would find her before it was too late.

⊰⊱

ASHLEY REGAINED CONSCIOUSNESS to the sound of frantic voices and the acrid smell of smoke. Her head throbbed viciously, and when she tried to move, pain lanced through her skull, making her gasp.

"Lady Ashley! Oh, thank heavens!" Graves appeared in her blurred vision; his usually impassive face creased with worry. "Don't move, my lady. You're injured."

"Courtney," she managed, her voice a rasp. "Where is Lady Courtney?"

The butler's expression confirmed what she already knew. "She's…gone, my lady. There was a small fire in the kitchen—a distraction, we now realize. By the time we discovered it was deliberately set, it was too late."

Ashley struggled to sit up despite the butler's protests and the room's alarming tendency to tilt around her. Blood had dried on the side of her face, pulling at her skin uncomfortably.

"Baron Lockwood," she said, gripping Graves' arm for support. "He's taken her. We must find Lord Furoe and my brother immediately." Using the remains of the rosewood table to steady herself, she forced her legs to cooperate as she rose unsteadily to her feet. "And send someone for the Duke of Blackstone and Viscount Milburn. Tell them it's a matter of life and death."

She'd faced this exact situation several years ago and she knew the gravity of the situation. A woman's reputation was destroyed—her life irrevocably captured by circumstances. If Lockwood got her to Grena Green before they were found....

As servants scurried to obey her commands, Ashley sank onto a nearby chair, pressing a handkerchief to her bleeding temple. Courtney was gone, spirited away by a man whose cruelty she had witnessed firsthand. A man desperate enough to commit abduction in broad daylight.

"Please be safe," she whispered, watching as a footman raced toward the stables to send messengers to Lucien and the others. "Please hold on until we find you."

She refused to consider any other possibility. Not when Courtney had finally found happiness again after years of grief. Not when so much depended on her safe return.

CHAPTER TWENTY-ONE

LUCIEN RODE THROUGH the early morning mist, his mind racing with plans and strategies. The memories of his night with Courtney made every inch of his body heat and he was even more determined to ensure Lockwood didn't ruin anything for him—for them.

London was just beginning to stir, shops opening their shutters, servants sweeping doorsteps, and milk carts rattling over cobblestones. The heavy weight of responsibility and determination propelled him toward Blackstone House, where he hoped to find the first thread that might unravel Lockwood's schemes.

The Duke of Blackstone was not known for receiving callers at such an unseemly hour, but Lucien's situation left no room for social niceties. As he approached the imposing Mayfair mansion, he steeled himself for what would likely be a frosty reception.

To his surprise, the duke's butler informed him that His Grace was already awake and in his study. Lucien was shown in with minimal delay, finding the austere nobleman seated behind a massive mahogany desk, reviewing correspondence with a severe expression that seemed permanently etched onto his aristocratic features.

"Lord Furoe," Blackstone acknowledged without rising, his dark eyes betraying only mild curiosity at the unexpected visit. "What brings you to my door at this hour? I trust it must be a matter of some importance."

Lucien bowed slightly. "Your Grace, I apologize for the intrusion, but I find myself in need of your assistance with a rather delicate matter."

The duke set down his letter opener with precise movements. "Indeed? And what might that be?"

"I'm trying to locate a woman named Kitty," Lucien said directly, watching the duke's face closely. "I believe she once worked at Mrs. Bellamy's establishment and might have information crucial to my family's welfare."

The effect was instantaneous and remarkable. The duke's composed expression shattered like thin ice, his face draining of color as he abruptly rose from his chair. His hands, always steady and controlled, gripped the edge of his desk with such force that his knuckles whitened.

"What business could you possibly have with…" Blackstone caught himself, visibly struggling to regain his composure. "How did you know?" he continued stiffly, though the slight tremor in his voice betrayed him.

"Mrs. Bellamy came to see me."

Lucien had not expected such a visceral reaction from the notoriously controlled duke. The man before him was not merely affronted by the improper topic—he was personally affected. The realization dawned with startling clarity: the Duke of Blackstone, paragon of propriety and moral rectitude, harbored feelings for this woman.

"Forgive me, Your Grace," Lucien said carefully, "but this is not an attack on your character or an attempt to pry into your personal affairs. My interest in Kitty is purely because she knew my late wife Ava in Dublin. There are matters regarding my daughter's future that I believe she might help clarify."

Blackstone's shoulders relaxed marginally at the explanation, though wariness remained in his eyes. "Your late wife?"

"Yes," Lucien confirmed. "I've recently learned that Kitty and Ava were acquainted in Dublin before my time in Ireland. As you may know, my memory of that period remains fragmentary at best, and there are…" he hesitated, choosing his words carefully, "aspects of my time in Ireland that I need clarified."

The duke seemed to wage an internal battle, his aristocratic features contorting subtly as he weighed his options. After a long moment, he moved to a cabinet, withdrew a crystal decanter, and poured two glasses of brandy despite the early hour.

"Sit, Furoe," he commanded, handing Lucien a glass before taking the chair opposite rather than returning behind his desk. The gesture, less formal and more personal, marked a significant shift in their interaction.

"I presume returning to society's folds has not been easy," Blackstone remarked, studying the amber liquid in his glass.

"It has had its challenges," Lucien admitted, seeing no benefit in further deception. "Certain parties are threatening to share misinformation about my past that could harm my daughter and threaten Lady Courtney's reputation."

Blackstone's eyes sharpened. "Lockwood?"

Lucien sat forward in surprise. "How did you—"

"The man has been making discreet but determined inquiries about your time in Ireland for weeks," Blackstone explained with distaste. "He approached several of my acquaintances seeking information, though I didn't realize the extent of his investigation."

"Then you understand why I must speak with Kitty," Lucien pressed. "If she can tell us what Lockwood knows—and what he doesn't—that might neutralize his threats. You do understand how gossip takes flight until it is believed."

The duke drained his glass in one decisive swallow and set it down with uncharacteristic force. "Kitty is under my protection," he stated, the words carrying unmistakable weight.

"I mean her no harm," Lucien assured him quickly. "Quite the opposite. I believe she may have been manipulated by Lockwood, just as he's attempting to manipulate Lady Courtney and myself."

"She was," Blackstone confirmed, his voice hardening. "The man promised her a substantial sum for information about former…colleagues. She had no idea he intended to use it for blackmail."

The depth of the duke's knowledge confirmed Lucien's suspicion about his personal connection to Kitty. The notorious stickler for propriety, who had reportedly cut his own cousin for marrying an actress, was romantically involved with a former courtesan.

"I need to speak with her," Lucien said simply. "Today, if possible. Lockwood has demanded Lady Courtney's answer by tonight at Lady Fenchurch's ball."

Blackstone paced the length of his study, an uncharacteristic display of agitation from a man known for his rigid self-control. Finally, he turned to face Lucien.

"I will take you to her," he decided, his tone suggesting the concession cost him dearly. "But I will be present during your conversation."

"Of course," Lucien agreed readily. "I welcome your presence, Your Grace."

The duke rang for his valet and issued crisp instructions for his carriage to be prepared immediately. As they waited, an uncomfortable silence settled between them until Lucien decided to address the obvious.

"Your discretion in this matter is greatly appreciated," he said carefully. "As is your willingness to facilitate this meeting."

Blackstone's expression remained guarded, but something in his eyes softened fractionally. "We all have aspects of our lives that we prefer to keep private, Lord Furoe. I understand that better than most."

"Indeed," Lucien acknowledged, respecting the duke's need for oblique reference rather than direct acknowledgment of his relationship with Kitty. "Life rarely conforms to society's neat categories."

"No," Blackstone agreed quietly. "I'm beginning to understand it does not."

The carriage was brought around promptly, and both men

settled into the luxurious conveyance in silence. As they traveled through London's increasingly busy streets, Lucien observed the duke's growing tension. His gloved fingers tapped an irregular rhythm against his knee—the only outward sign of his discomfort.

"She resides in Chelsea," Blackstone said abruptly as the carriage turned westward. "In a small but comfortable house that I…arranged for her."

"I see," Lucien replied neutrally, careful not to betray any surprise or judgment.

"She has been pursuing an education," the duke continued, seemingly compelled to justify his arrangement. "Languages, literature, music. She has a remarkable aptitude for learning."

"That speaks well of her character," Lucien offered.

"She is…" Blackstone hesitated, searching for appropriate words, "…exceptional in many respects. Her circumstances before our acquaintance were not of her choosing. Her father's death left her without protection or resources."

The defensiveness in his tone revealed more than any direct confession could have. This was not merely a convenient arrangement between a wealthy nobleman and a beautiful woman—the Duke of Blackstone was in love with Kitty.

"We often have little control over the paths life forces us to walk," Lucien observed quietly, thinking of his own journey from amnesia-stricken farmer to reclaimed viscount. "True character reveals itself not in the absence of hardship, but in how one navigates it."

Blackstone studied him with new interest. "An unusually philosophical perspective for a peer of the realm."

"My time in Ireland altered many of my perspectives," Lucien replied with a wry smile. "Amnesia has a way of stripping away pretensions."

The carriage slowed as it entered a quiet, respectable neighborhood of Chelsea—not fashionable by aristocratic standards, but certainly genteel. They stopped before a modest brick house with gleaming windows and a well-tended front garden. Despite its modest size, the property spoke of comfort and care rather than ostentation.

"Wait here," Blackstone instructed the driver before turning to Lucien. "I should speak with her first, to explain the situation."

Lucien nodded his agreement, recognizing the protective instinct driving the duke's request. As they approached the door, both men noted the unusual silence. No servants appeared to take their hats and coats, and the house had an unsettling stillness about it.

"Something's wrong," Blackstone said sharply, his hand moving instinctively to the walking stick he carried—one Lucien now suspected might conceal a blade. The duke tried the door and found it unlocked, swinging open at his touch.

"Kitty?" Blackstone called, his customary reserve cracking as concern flooded his voice. "Are you here?"

The silence that answered chilled Lucien's blood. They moved swiftly through the entrance hall toward the drawing room, where a faint sound—a weak moan—drew them forward.

Blackstone's hand trembled as he turned the brass doorknob. The silence that greeted them was wrong—all wrong. In the months he'd been visiting, Kitty's house had always hummed with gentle activity: the soft scratch of her pen as she practiced her letters, the melodic Irish lilt of her voice as she read aloud, the whisper of silk as she moved through her daily routines.

"Kitty?" Blackstone called again, his voice cracking despite his efforts at control. "My darling, are you—"

The words died in his throat as they stepped into the drawing room.

The scene that greeted them would haunt Lucien for years to come, but for Blackstone, it shattered something fundamental in his soul. This room—their sanctuary, where he had taught her to read, where she had laughed at his stuffy pronunciations, where they had planned a future that society would never accept—lay in ruins.

The small writing desk where she practiced her letters had been overturned, ink spreading like black blood across scattered pages. Her careful penmanship—"I love you, Raven" written over and over in increasingly confident script—now trampled underfoot. The delicate porcelain tea service he'd given her lay shattered, the painted roses he'd chosen because they matched her complexion now broken fragments glinting in the morning light.

But it was the larger destruction that made both men's breath catch. The heavy bookshelf—the one filled with volumes he'd selected to expand her world—had been torn apart, as if someone had searched frantically behind each leather spine. Books lay scattered like wounded birds, their pages torn and crushed.

And in the center of this devastation, surrounded by the remnants of their stolen happiness, lay Kitty.

Her magnificent red hair—the hair he loved to watch catch firelight during their quiet evenings—spread around her head like spilled wine. The morning dress he'd bought her just last week, a soft blue that brought out her eyes, was now stained with an expanding circle of crimson that seemed to pulse with each beat of his own racing heart.

"No." The word escaped Blackstone as barely more than breath. Then, louder, raw with anguish: "No, no, NO!"

He was across the room before Lucien could stop him, falling to his knees so hard the impact echoed through the house. His hands hovered over her still form, desperate to touch, to comfort, to heal, but terrified that his touch might somehow make this nightmare real.

"Kitty, my darling girl, what have they done to you?" His voice broke completely now, the Duke of Blackstone's legendary composure cracking like ice in spring. "I'm here now. I'm here."

Her eyelids fluttered—barely perceptible, but enough to send hope surging through him. He gathered her carefully into his arms, and the warm wetness that immediately soaked through his waistcoat made his stomach lurch.

"Don't try to speak," he whispered, though every word seemed to cost him. "I'll get help. The physician, he'll—"

"Raven." Her voice was a whisper, blood frothing at the corner of her lips. But her green eyes—those eyes that had looked at him with such love, such trust—focused on his face with what remained of her strength. "You came back to me."

"Always," he promised fiercely, his own tears falling onto her upturned face. "I told you I'd always come back."

Lucien knelt beside them, his own hands shaking as he pressed his handkerchief against the wound in her abdomen. But even as he applied pressure, he knew with sickening certainty that it was far too late. The blade had found its mark with deadly precision.

"Who did this?" Blackstone asked, his voice deadly quiet now, though his hands remained infinitely gentle as they stroked her hair. "Tell me who hurt you, my love."

"Lock…" she gasped, her bloodstained fingers clutching weakly at his waistcoat. Each word seemed to tear from her throat. "Lockwood. Wanted me to…lie. About…your marriage."

The name hit Lucien like a physical blow, but he forced himself to lean closer. "What did he want you to say?"

Her eyes found his, and in them he saw not just pain, but a fierce determination that reminded him suddenly, heartbreakingly, of Courtney. "Told him…you were…properly married. Wouldn't…wouldn't let him…"

She coughed, and more blood painted her lips crimson. Blackstone made a sound like a wounded animal, his aristocratic features contorting with grief.

"Why?" he whispered. "Why would you lie for a stranger?"

A ghost of her old smile touched her bloodless lips. "Not…stranger. Your friend's…daughter. Innocent…little girl. Deserves…better than…my life."

The simple words, spoken with her dying breath in defense of a child she'd never met, broke something in both men. Here was a woman who had been forced into a life society scorned, who had clawed her way out through her own courage and Blackstone's love, and she was spending her final moments protecting another innocent.

"The physician," Blackstone said desperately, looking up at Lucien. "We need—"

"Raven." Kitty's voice was growing fainter, her grip on his coat weakening. "Cold...so cold..."

Without hesitation, he shrugged out of his jacket and wrapped it around her, as if the finest wool could shield her from death itself. "I'm here, my darling. You're not alone."

"Don't...leave me," she pleaded, her voice suddenly very young, very frightened.

"Never," he vowed, pressing his lips to her forehead. "I'll never leave you. Not in this life or the next."

Her breathing grew more labored, each inhalation a visible struggle. "I...love..."

The words never came. Her body went limp in his arms, her eyes staring sightlessly at the ceiling where they had once traced patterns in the plaster while planning their impossible future.

For a long moment, the only sound in the ruined room was Blackstone's ragged breathing. Then, with infinite tenderness, he closed her eyes and arranged her limbs as if she were merely sleeping.

When he finally looked up at Lucien, his face was a mask of such cold fury that it made Lucien instinctively step back.

"Lockwood will die for this," the duke said with absolute certainty. Not a threat—a promise written in stone. "Slowly, if I have any say in the matter."

Lucien rose to his feet, his own rage coalescing into something focused and deadly. "We need to find Courtney," he said urgently. "If he's desperate enough to murder Kitty in her own home, he might—And there is Mrs. Bellamy too."

The unfinished thought hung between them, too terrible to voice.

Blackstone removed his coat and covered her with it, the

gesture achingly intimate. Then he rose to his full height, every inch the aristocrat once more, but with something new and dangerous in his bearing.

"We will find Lady Courtney," he stated with deadly calm. "And then we will hunt Lockwood like the animal he is."

"You realize what this means," Lucien said, watching the duke carefully. "To avenge her, to get justice—"

"I don't give a damn about my reputation," Blackstone cut him off savagely. "Let the world know I loved her. Let them whisper and stare. It changes nothing." His gaze dropped to Kitty's covered form, grief momentarily breaking through his rage. "She died trying to protect your daughter's future. I swear on everything I hold sacred; Lockwood will pay for what he's done."

Lucien extended his hand, a gesture of solidarity that transcended their different stations. "We'll make him pay. Together."

Blackstone clasped his hand firmly; the pact sealed between them without further words. They would find Lockwood, and they would ensure he never harmed another woman. Whatever it cost them, whatever society might think—some debts could only be paid in blood.

As they strode from the house to organize a proper team to care for Kitty's body and begin their hunt for Lockwood, Lucien's thoughts turned to Courtney. He prayed she was still safe, still protected by the belief that she would meet Lockwood that evening at Lady Fenchurch's ball.

But something in his gut told him their carefully laid plans had gone terribly awry. Lockwood had changed the rules of the game, escalating from blackmail to murder. And Courtney was now in far graver danger than any of them had imagined.

THE MEN ARRIVED at the Marquess of Lorne's town home to find it in chaos. Rockwell, Farah and Wolf and Tiffany were there hovering around Lady Ashley who was being attended to by a physician.

Lucien's blood turned to ice as he took in the scene before him—the shattered French doors, furniture overturned, blood on the carpet where Ashley sat with a physician tending to her head wound. His eyes swept the room frantically, searching for any sign of Courtney, though he already knew with sickening certainty that she wasn't there.

"Where is she?" he demanded, his voice cutting through the murmur of concerned voices.

Ashley looked up from the physician's ministrations, her face pale but her eyes blazing with fury. "Lockwood took her," she said, her voice hoarse but steady. "He came through the terrace doors with two men. Said something about Gretna Green."

The words hit Lucien like physical blows. Gretna Green. The bastard intended to force a marriage, to compromise Courtney so thoroughly that her father would have no choice but to accept the union or see his daughter ruined forever.

Blackstone stepped forward, his aristocratic composure barely concealing the murderous rage that had been building since they'd found Kitty's body. "When did this happen?"

"Perhaps an hour ago," Ashley replied, wincing as the physician cleaned her wound. "They created a distraction—set a small fire in the kitchen to draw away the servants. It was all planned, methodical."

Lucien's hands clenched into fists at his sides. While he'd been discovering Kitty's murder, Courtney had been fighting for her life, facing Lockwood's violence alone. The thought of that monster laying hands on her, of what he might be doing to her even now…

"Was she hurt during her abduction?" Wolf asked, though the question was barely necessary given Ashley's obvious injuries.

"She fought," Ashley said with grim satisfaction. "Kicked and screamed until they used some sort of cloth—chloroform, I suspect. The last thing I saw was them carrying her unconscious through the garden."

"That's not good. She can hardly try to escape or leave clues if she's rendered senseless," Wolf said.

Unconscious. Lucien closed his eyes briefly, imagining Courtney's terror in those final moments before the drug took hold. She would have known exactly what Lockwood intended, would have understood that everything they'd planned, everything they'd hoped for, was crumbling around her.

"We have to go after them," he said, his voice rough with barely controlled emotion. "Every moment we delay gives him more distance."

Rockwell stepped forward, his usual languid demeanor replaced by sharp focus. "Which route would he take? The Great North Road is the most direct path to Scotland, but also the most obvious."

"He's desperate, not stupid," Farah interjected, her face tight with worry. "He might take a less traveled route to avoid pursuit."

Lucien forced himself to think tactically, though every instinct screamed at him to simply mount his horse and ride hellbent in pursuit. "He has money troubles, creditors closing in. He can't afford a leisurely journey with multiple stops. He'll want speed over subtlety."

"The Great North Road, then," Blackstone said decisively. "But we should send men to cover all routes, just in case. He'll have at least an hour's head start, possibly more if he had horses waiting outside London. We will have an advantage in that we will be on horseback and Lockwood will be traveling by carriage."

"Can Courtney slow him down?" Tiffany asked, voicing the question that tormented Lucien. "If she regains consciousness…"

"She'll try," Lucien said with absolute certainty. "But Lockwood has already proven he's willing to use violence. If she resists…" He couldn't finish the thought. The image of Kitty's broken body was burned into his memory, a terrible reminder of what Lockwood was capable of when crossed.

Farah moved to Ashley's side, taking her friend's hand. "Did he say anything else? Any indication of his plans beyond Gretna Green?"

Ashley shook her head, then immediately regretted the movement, pressing a hand to her temple. "Only that her father would accept the marriage once it was done. That accidents could happen to her father if the dowry wasn't forthcoming." Her voice hardened. "He threatened Courtney and as we know, Lord Lorne will do anything for her safe return."

The casual mention of threatening Courtney's father sent fresh rage coursing through Lucien's veins. Not content with abduction and forced marriage, Lockwood was prepared to use violence against her family as well.

"We need horses," Lucien said, already moving toward the door. "The fastest in London. And weapons."

"Wait," Rockwell called after him. "Charging off half-cocked won't help Courtney. We need a plan."

Lucien whirled around, his control finally cracking. "While we're planning, he's dragging her further from London! He could be doing anything to her—" His voice broke slightly on the words.

Blackstone placed a firm hand on his shoulder. "I understand your urgency," he said quietly, the grief for Kitty lending weight to his words. "But Rockwell is right. We have one chance to get this right. If we fail, if Lockwood reaches Scotland…"

He didn't need to finish. They all understood the implications. Once married, even by force, Courtney would be trapped by law and society's strictures. Her reputation would be destroyed, her freedom forfeit.

"Three hours," Wolf said grimly. "That's how long it typically takes for chloroform to fully wear off. If she's unconscious in a moving carriage…"

"She'll be violently ill when she wakes," Tiffany finished, her face pale. "Disoriented, weakened."

The clinical discussion of Courtney's suffering made Lucien want to put his fist through the nearest wall. Instead, he forced himself to focus on what could be controlled.

"Lockwood has two men with him," he said, his military training reasserting itself. "That's three against however many we can muster. But they'll be encumbered by Courtney, especially if she's fighting them."

"Four of us," Rockwell said immediately. "Wolf, Blackstone, you and myself."

"Five," came a weak voice from the settle. Ashley was attempting to rise despite the physician's protests. "I'm going with you."

"Absolutely not," Lucien said firmly. "You're injured, and—"

"And I watched him take her," Ashley snapped, her eyes flashing. "I failed to protect her. I won't compound that failure by sitting here uselessly while she's in danger."

The guilt in her voice was unmistakable, and Lucien felt a stab of sympathy. But he couldn't allow sentiment to cloud his judgment.

"You'll slow us down," he said bluntly. "And if there's fighting…"

"There will be fighting," Blackstone said with cold certainty. "Lockwood won't surrender peacefully. Not after what he's done."

The duke's tone suggested he was looking forward to the confrontation, and Lucien found himself sharing that anticipation. The thought of finally having Lockwood within reach, of being able to exact payment for Kitty's murder and Courtney's abduction…

"I'll organize fresh horses at the coaching inns," Farah said, her practical nature asserting itself. "Send word ahead so you don't lose time changing mounts."

"And I'll contact the magistrate. They might be able to stop him until we can catch up," Wolf added. "Make sure they understand the urgency when Lockwood is apprehended."

When, not if. Lucien appreciated his friend's confidence, even as his own doubts gnawed at him. They were making assumptions about Lockwood's route, his timing, his intentions. What if they were wrong? What if even now Courtney was being subjected to horrors he couldn't bear to contemplate?

Rockwell said, "Graves has already sent a missive to her father and brother at Tattersalls. I've asked for Fane, Axton, and Julian to aid us too." He turned to Lucien and added, "We have the numbers on our side. Plus, we will be on horseback and he's in a carriage. We will be faster. We will catch him."

The thought of her alone, terrified, possibly hurt, made his chest tighten with an emotion he'd been trying to deny for weeks. It wasn't just desire or companionship or even deep affection that drove his desperation to find her.

He loved her.

The realization hit him with startling clarity, cutting through his fear and rage to settle in his chest with warm certainty. Not the remembered love of their youth, but something new and fierce and entirely his own. The love of a man who had been through hell and found someone willing to share the journey back.

And he might lose her forever because he'd been too much of a coward to simply tell the truth from the beginning.

If he'd just announced to society that he'd been deceived in Ireland, that his marriage had been a fiction, that Ava-Marie was illegitimate—yes, there would have been scandal, whispers, social ostracism. His sisters' prospects would have suffered. His own standing would have been damaged.

But Courtney would be safe.

Instead, his need to protect his family's reputation had trapped him again, just as it had five years ago when he'd felt obligated to buy his colors and serve in Ireland. Once again, the weight of the Furoe name and legacy had led to disaster.

"I should have told the truth from the beginning," he said

suddenly, his voice raw with self-recrimination. "About Ireland, about Ava-Marie. None of this would have happened if I'd simply been honest."

"Lockwood would have simply found something else to use," Rockwell said firmly. "The man's a monster, Lucien. This isn't your fault."

"Isn't it?" Lucien laughed bitterly. "I've spent my entire life being shaped by what's expected of a Furoe. Five years ago, I felt duty-bound to serve in Ireland because our family has always sent sons to war, quite forgetting I was an only son and therefore it was an idiotic thing to do. Now I've hidden the truth about my time there because I couldn't bear to bring more shame on the family name. And in both cases, the people I care about have paid the price."

Blackstone's expression was grim but understanding. "The burden of legacy," he said quietly. "I know it well. But you cannot let guilt paralyze you now. Lady Courtney needs you focused on the present, not the past."

The duke was right, of course. Self-recrimination was a luxury he couldn't afford while Courtney's life hung in the balance. But the knowledge that his choices—his cowardice—had led to this moment would haunt him regardless of the outcome.

"Twenty minutes," Wolf said, checking his pocket watch. "That's how long it will take to ready horses and supplies. We can be on the road within the half hour."

It felt like an eternity. Twenty minutes during which Lockwood could travel another several miles, during which Courtney could... Lucien cut off that line of thinking before it could fully form.

"She'll slow him down," Ashley said suddenly, as if reading his thoughts. "Courtney's stronger than she appears. Smarter too. If she can find ways to delay their progress..."

"She will," Lucien said with fierce conviction. "She'll fight him every step of the way."

And God help Lockwood if he hurt her while she did. Because when Lucien caught up with them—and he would catch up with them—there would be a reckoning that would make Kitty's murder look merciful by comparison.

The thought should have disturbed him, this cold anticipation of violence. Instead, it steadied him, gave him purpose beyond the gnawing fear for Courtney's safety.

Lockwood had made the gravest mistake of his miserable life when he'd threatened what Lucien held most dear. And before this day was over, he would understand exactly how grave that mistake had been.

CHAPTER TWENTY-TWO

CONSCIOUSNESS RETURNED TO Courtney like waves lapping at a distant shore—first the rhythmic jolting that seemed to shake her very bones, then the musty smell of worn leather and unwashed bodies, and finally the nauseating roll of her stomach that threatened to empty itself at any moment. Her head pounded with each bump and sway of what she quickly realized was a moving carriage, and her mouth felt as dry as parchment.

She kept her breathing steady and her eyes closed, feigning continued unconsciousness while her mind raced to assess her situation. The chloroform had left her feeling weak and disoriented, but anger was already beginning to burn through the fog in her thoughts. Lockwood. The bastard had actually done it—kidnapped her in broad daylight from her own father's house.

Through her closed eyelids, she could sense the dim light filtering through what must be drawn carriage blinds. The vehicle was moving at considerable speed, the springs creaking with each rut in the road. She could hear at least two male voices, though the noise of wheels and hooves made it difficult to distinguish words.

Carefully, she tested her bonds without moving visibly. Her hands were tied behind her back with rough rope that chafed against her wrists. Her ankles were similarly bound, though not as tightly—perhaps they'd been more concerned with speed than thoroughness. The ropes were tight enough to restrict movement but not so tight as to cut off circulation entirely. A small mercy, though she suspected it had more to do with Lockwood's need to present her as relatively unharmed for their forced marriage.

She was wearing her morning dress of pale yellow muslin, though she could feel tears in the fabric and suspected her appearance was far from that of the composed lady she'd been when Lockwood had smashed through the terrace doors. How he was going to explain that to anybody, she had no idea. Perhaps she could use that as evidence she'd been abducted.

Ashley. Fear clenched her stomach as she remembered her friend's brave attempt to help her, the sickening sound of Lockwood's hand striking her face. Was Ashley alive? Badly hurt? The uncertainty was almost worse than her own predicament.

She forced herself to concentrate on the present. The carriage was well-sprung and moving fast, which suggested they were on a major road—likely the Great North Road toward Scotland. Gretna Green, where marriages could be performed without banns or parental consent. Where Lockwood intended to force her into a union that would give him legal claim to her dowry and her person.

Over her dead body.

The thought gave her a grim satisfaction. She would not go quietly to her ruin. If Lockwood thought a bit of chloroform and some rope would turn her into a compliant victim, he was about to discover his error.

But first, she needed information. How many men were with them? What were their plans? How far had they traveled? She strained to listen to the conversation taking place in the carriage.

"—should reach the Swan and Crown by nightfall if we keep this pace," one voice was saying. She didn't recognize it—presumably one of Lockwood's hired thugs.

"Good," came Lockwood's cultured tones, though she detected an edge of strain beneath his usual smoothness. "We'll change horses there and push through the night. I want to be in Scotland as soon as possible."

"Driving at night could be dangerous. If a horse stumbles in a rut at night, the carriage could go over."

"It's a risk I'm willing to take. They won't be far behind me." She could hear fear in his voice. And so he should fear. Tarquin would want blood and Lucien—hell, he'd want to kill him.

Lucien. She knew he would come for her, and so did Lockwood, but it also meant he was pushing hard—perhaps too hard. Tired horses and exhausted men made mistakes.

"What about the girl?" asked a third voice, rougher than the others. "She's been out a long time. That stuff you used…"

"She'll wake when she wakes," Lockwood replied dismissively. "And when she does, she'll find herself in circumstances that require…cooperation."

The casual cruelty in his tone made Courtney's skin crawl, but she forced herself to remain limp and unresponsive. Information was power, and the more she could learn while they believed her unconscious, the better her chances of escape.

"Speaking of cooperation," the first voice continued, "you sure that Irish whore won't be talking? Looked pretty lively when we left."

Courtney's blood turned to ice. Irish whore. They had to be talking about Kitty—the woman who had known Ava in Dublin, whose testimony Lockwood had been trying to secure.

"Kitty won't be talking to anyone," Lockwood said with satisfaction that made Courtney's stomach lurch. "I made certain of that before we left."

"Dead certain?" the rough voice pressed.

"Quite dead," Lockwood confirmed, and Courtney had to bite the inside of her cheek to keep from gasping aloud. "The knife went in clean between the ribs. She'll be found eventually, but there is no evidence we were even there."

Murder. The word echoed in Courtney's mind with horrible clarity. Lockwood hadn't just threatened and blackmailed—he'd actually killed someone. A woman whose only crime had been knowing Ava years ago in Dublin.

"What about the old madam?" the first voice asked. "She

know too much too?"

"Mrs. Bellamy has also been permanently silenced," Lockwood replied coldly. "Unfortunate, but necessary. She was becoming greedy. She double crossed me by going to Furoe. My men had her followed. Better to eliminate the complication entirely."

Two murders. Courtney felt bile rise in her throat as the full scope of Lockwood's desperation became clear. He'd killed two women to protect his scheme, which meant he had absolutely nothing left to lose. A man who had already committed murder wouldn't hesitate to kill again if she proved too troublesome.

"Anyone see you at the brothel?" the rough voice continued.

"No one who matters," Lockwood said dismissively. "Mrs. Bellamy's establishment isn't the sort of place where respectable witnesses congregate. A few whores and drunkards, perhaps, but who would believe them? And who would care enough to investigate?"

The casual way he dismissed the lives of people he considered beneath his notice made Courtney's hands clench involuntarily. She forced herself to relax, to maintain the illusion of unconsciousness while her mind raced.

Lucien would care. When he discovered what had happened—and he would discover it—his rage would be terrible to behold. She'd seen glimpses of the harder man he'd become during his years in Ireland, the steel beneath the gentleman's polish. Lockwood had no idea what he'd unleashed.

But Lucien would also blame himself. She knew him well enough to understand that he would see this as the consequence of his own choices, his own secrets. The knowledge that Lockwood's victims had died because of information about his past would torment him.

She had to survive this. Not just for herself, but for Lucien, for Ava-Marie, for the life they were trying to build together. She couldn't give a toss if society knew he was never married. They had each other, and their true friends, and that would be enough.

She had to find a way to escape or at least delay their journey long enough for rescue to arrive.

The carriage hit a particularly deep rut, jarring her against the seat and making her stomach rebel violently. She couldn't quite suppress a small groan, and immediately felt all attention focus on her.

"Ah," Lockwood's voice held satisfied amusement. "Sleeping Beauty awakens. How are you feeling, my dear? I do apologize for the dramatic departure, but you left me little choice."

Courtney opened her eyes slowly, blinking as if disoriented, though her mind was razor-sharp with purpose. She let herself appear weak, confused—exactly what Lockwood would expect from a gently bred lady who'd been drugged and kidnapped.

"Where…" she managed, her voice convincingly hoarse. "What have you done?"

"Merely expedited our engagement, darling," Lockwood said with false cheer. "I decided waiting until tonight's ball was unnecessarily theatrical. This way is so much more…efficient."

Courtney struggled against her bonds as if only now discovering them, letting real fear show in her eyes while her mind catalogued every detail of her surroundings. Two men sat across from her—the scarred brute from her drawing room and a younger, leaner man with cold eyes and quick hands. Both were armed, she noted, with pistols visible beneath their coats.

Lockwood himself sat beside her, impeccably dressed despite their hurried departure, his pale eyes holding a mixture of triumph and calculation that made her skin crawl. He was watching her with the focused attention of a predator with cornered prey.

"You're insane," she said, putting genuine conviction behind the words. "My father will never consent to this marriage."

Lockwood's smile was cold and confident. "I think you overestimate your father's principles, my dear. Once we're wed, once you're thoroughly compromised, and with child, and I keep you hidden with the threat of harm hanging over you, he'll find it expedient to accept the situation and pay me."

The awful thing was, he might be right. Her father was a good man, and he'd do anything to protect his daughter. "There is nowhere in England you can hide me that Lucien and my brother won't find. They'll never stop looking."

"Who said I'd hide you in England. Perhaps the Americas," Lockwood continued conversationally, "I've heard the lands are so vast, you'd never be found."

She briefly closed her eyes as the fear built. She had to escape this hell. Lost in her thoughts, she barely heard him say, "Your virtue is quite safe with me during our journey. I have no desire to sample damaged goods. Once we're properly wed, of course, things will be different."

The threat was delivered with such casual cruelty that Courtney had to fight not to show her revulsion. Instead, she forced tears to her eyes—not difficult, given her circumstances—and let her voice break convincingly.

"Please," she whispered. "Let me go home. I swear I won't tell anyone what happened. We can pretend this never occurred."

"Sweet child," Lockwood said, reaching out to stroke her cheek with one gloved finger. She flinched away instinctively, which seemed to amuse him. "But that would defeat the entire purpose, wouldn't it? I need your dowry, you see. My creditors have become most insistent."

"I'll give you money," she said desperately, though part of her recoiled at the idea of rewarding his crimes. "Whatever you need. I have investments. My allowance, my jewels—"

"A few hundred pounds?" Lockwood laughed. "My dear girl, I need thousands. Tens of thousands. Only marriage to you can provide that kind of security."

"My investments amount to almost five-thousands pounds. My father doesn't know of them. Tiffany has been investing for me—"

"Tiffany? What rubbish. A woman? Stop lying. Your dowry is worth considerably more, and come to think of it, if what you say is true, you're worth even more to me."

The casual way he discussed her reduction to a financial asset made Courtney's anger flare, but she forced herself to maintain the appearance of a terrified, helpless victim. Let him underestimate her. Let him think her weak and compliant. When the moment came to act, surprise would be her greatest weapon.

"My father won't pay," she said, injecting a note of defiance into her voice. "Even if you force me to marry you, he'll find a way to withhold my dowry."

For the first time, genuine uncertainty flickered across Lockwood's features. "He'll pay," he said, but she heard the forced confidence in his tone. "Men like your father always pay in the end. The alternative is simply too costly."

"And if he doesn't?" she pressed, sensing weakness. "What then? You'll have a wife with no fortune and creditors still demanding payment. How does that solve your problems?"

The scarred man leaned forward with interest. "She's got a point, gov'nor. What if her family cuts her off complete-like?"

"They won't," Lockwood snapped, but Courtney could see the worry in his eyes now. "The scandal would destroy them. They'll pay to avoid that."

But doubt had been planted, and Courtney could see it taking root. Lockwood's entire plan depended on her family's willingness to buy their way out of scandal. If they chose defiance instead…

"My brother's a politician," she said quietly, pressing her advantage. "He understands that scandals can be weathered, but paying blackmail only invites more demands. And my father…he's proud, stubborn. He might decide that my ruin is preferable to rewarding criminal behavior."

She was lying, of course. Her family would move heaven and earth to protect her, would pay any price to secure her safety. But Lockwood didn't know that, and uncertainty was eating at his confidence like acid.

The carriage began to slow, and through the drawn blinds,

Courtney could see the amber glow of an inn's windows. The first coaching stop, where fresh horses would be waiting. Where there might be opportunities for escape, or at least delay.

Where people might notice a well-dressed young lady who appeared to be traveling against her will.

"Remember," Lockwood said quietly, his hand moving meaningfully toward the pistol beneath his coat, "you are my wife, traveling to visit my parents. Any attempt to draw attention or cry for help will result in…unpleasant consequences. Not just for you, but for any Good Samaritans who might try to intervene."

The threat was clear, and Courtney nodded reluctantly. She wouldn't risk innocent lives by crying out, but that didn't mean she was helpless. There were other ways to leave signs, other methods of delay.

As the carriage rolled to a stop in the inn's courtyard, Courtney began planning her first move in what she was determined would be a very long and difficult journey to Scotland.

Lockwood might have won this round, but the game was far from over.

The Swan and Crown Inn bustled with evening activity as their carriage rolled into the torch-lit courtyard. Courtney could hear the clatter of hooves, the shouts of ostlers, and the general commotion of a busy coaching inn. Through the gap in the blinds, she glimpsed other travelers—merchants, gentlemen, a family with young children—all going about their business, blissfully unaware that a kidnapping victim sat mere yards away.

"Remember what I told you," Lockwood murmured as the carriage lurched to a stop. "One word out of place, and innocent people will suffer for your foolishness."

The scarred man—whom she'd heard called Briggs—climbed down first, his eyes scanning the courtyard for potential threats. The younger man, Murphy, followed, positioning himself near the carriage door. Both kept their hands near their weapons, she noted.

Lockwood stepped down with his usual theatrical flourish,

every inch the gentleman traveler. Only Courtney could see the tension in his shoulders, the way his gaze darted nervously between the other patrons.

"Your turn, my dear," he said, extending his hand with mock gallantry. "Do try not to draw attention to yourself."

Briggs had loosened the ropes around her ankles before they'd stopped—she could walk, though not easily with her hands still bound behind her back. Lockwood had draped his coat over her shoulders to hide the restraints, and to any casual observer, she might appear to be a lady being helped down from her carriage by an attentive fiancé.

Courtney stepped carefully onto the mounting block; her legs unsteady after hours of inactivity. The fresh air was a blessing after the close confines of the carriage, and she breathed deeply, trying to clear the last of the chloroform from her system.

"We'll go inside. One word and someone gets hurt," Lockwood said, his hand gripping her elbow with bruising force. "We'll take some refreshment while they change the horses."

They moved across the courtyard in a tight group, Briggs leading the way while Murphy brought up the rear. Courtney's mind raced as she took in her surroundings. The inn was larger than she'd expected, with multiple buildings arranged around the central courtyard. Stables to the left, the main inn straight ahead, and what looked like additional lodgings to the right. Plenty of places to hide, if she could just find an opportunity.

"How long to change out the horses?" Lockwood asked the head ostler, a burly man with graying hair and capable hands.

"Not long. Not that busy tonight."

Lockwood nodded curtly. "See that it's quick. We have pressing business in the north."

As they approached the inn's side entrance, Courtney stumbled deliberately, crying out as if her ankle had turned. "I can't walk hobbled like this. I've hurt my ankle. Besides, someone will notice," she hissed. Lockwood caught her arm roughly, and she used the moment of distraction to scan the area more thoroughly.

The stables were busy with activity—ostlers unhitching tired horses, leading fresh teams from their stalls, hauling feed and water. Most importantly, she noticed a large pile of fresh straw near the stable entrance, tall enough to provide concealment for someone willing to burrow into it.

"Careful, darling," Lockwood said loudly for the benefit of nearby travelers. "The courtyard stones can be treacherous in this light." But he removed the ropes, and his hand tightened on her arm.

"Forgive me," Courtney replied, playing the part of a tired wife. "I'm simply so excited about our journey, I'm not watching where I step."

The performance seemed to satisfy the few people who'd noticed her stumble. A middle-aged woman in traveling dress even smiled sympathetically.

Inside the inn, they were shown to a private parlor—Lockwood's doing, no doubt, to avoid curious eyes. The room was small but comfortable, with a fire crackling in the grate and a table set for a simple meal. Under other circumstances, it might have been quite pleasant.

"Some ale and bread," Lockwood told the serving girl who appeared at the door. "And be quick about it. We don't have long."

Briggs positioned himself by the door while Murphy took up station by the single window. Courtney was pushed into a chair near the fire, Lockwood's coat still draped over her shoulders to hide her bound hands.

"Comfortable?" Lockwood asked with false solicitude as he took the seat opposite her. "I do hope you're not too fatigued. We have a long night ahead of us."

"Where are we?" she asked, though she suspected she knew the answer.

"About forty miles north of London," he replied, checking his pocket watch. "Making excellent time, actually."

The serving girl returned with a tray of simple fare—dark

bread, hard cheese, and pewter mugs of ale. Courtney's stomach rumbled despite her circumstances; she'd eaten nothing since breakfast, and the chloroform had left her feeling hollow and weak.

"You must eat something," Lockwood said, cutting a piece of bread and holding it out to her. "Can't have you fainting at the altar."

The casual way he spoke of their forced wedding made her skin crawl, but she accepted the bread gratefully. She refused to let the fact he was hand feeding her put her off eating. She needed strength for whatever opportunity might present itself.

As she ate, she continued to study the room and its occupants. Murphy kept glancing toward the courtyard, clearly nervous about potential pursuit. Briggs seemed more relaxed, but his hand never strayed far from his pistol. And Lockwood... There was something brittle about his confidence now, a crack in his composure that hadn't been there in London.

His bravado was waning. He probably knew Lucien would be fast approaching.

"Horses are ready, gov'nor," came a call from the courtyard.

Lockwood stood immediately, his relief evident. "Excellent. Come, my dear. Time to continue our romantic journey."

They moved back through the inn's common area, past travelers settling in for the night or preparing for their own departures. Courtney found herself cataloguing faces, hoping desperately that someone might remember them if questioned later.

In the courtyard, the carriage with fresh horses awaited with four horses rather than two. Clearly, Lockwood was serious about making up time.

As they approached the carriage, Courtney made her decision. The stable was perhaps thirty yards away, the straw pile clearly visible in the flickering torchlight. If she could break free for just a few seconds...

"I need a moment," she said suddenly, stopping dead in her

tracks. "Private business."

Lockwood's eyes narrowed suspiciously. "What sort of business?"

Courtney felt heat rise in her cheeks, though this time it was genuine embarrassment rather than performance. "The sort that requires…privacy. Surely you understand."

For a moment, she thought he might refuse. Then he gestured impatiently toward a small building that clearly served as the inn's necessary. "Briggs will escort you. And be quick about it."

The scarred man moved to her side, his grip firm on her arm as they walked toward the small structure. Murphy remained by the carriage while Lockwood supervised the loading of their luggage.

Once she'd relieved herself, she looked around. This was her chance. Her only chance.

On the way back to the conveyance, Courtney pretended to stumble again, this time falling heavily against Briggs. The man cursed and loosened his grip to steady himself, and in that instant, she broke free.

She ran.

Not toward the inn's entrance where people might help—Lockwood's threats against innocent bystanders were too real to ignore. Instead, she bolted toward the back of the stables, her skirts hampering her stride but adrenaline lending her speed.

"Bloody hell!" Briggs shouted behind her. "She's running!"

Courtney saw a hole in the back stable wall and crawled through it just as shouts erupted behind her. Without hesitation, she dove into the pile of fresh straw, burrowing deep into its scratchy embrace. The sweet smell of hay filled her nostrils as she pulled armfuls of the stuff over herself, trying to become invisible.

She heard the men reach the corner of the stable. "Where did she go?" Lockwood's voice, sharp with fury. "It's so hard to see in the dark. Grab some lanterns," he bellowed.

"She might have run for the woods just beyond the house up

there," Briggs replied, breathing heavily from his pursuit.

"Then find her, you fool! She can't have gone far with her hands bound."

Footsteps pounded past her hiding place as the men spread out to search. Courtney pressed herself deeper into the straw, trying to control her breathing despite the way her heart hammered against her ribs.

"Women. Flighty aren't they. What did you do?" He laughed. "Probably ran off into the fields," one of the ostlers suggested. "Seen it before with nervous young ladies. They come to their senses quick enough when they realize they're alone in the dark."

"The fields," Lockwood mused. "Yes, that makes sense. She'd want to get as far from here as possible."

More footsteps, moving away from the stables and toward the open countryside beyond the inn. Courtney allowed herself a small smile of satisfaction. Every minute they spent searching for her in the wrong place was a minute closer to potential rescue.

She'd hidden for perhaps twenty minutes, forcing herself to breathe slowly despite the way her heart hammered against her ribs. The sweet scent of hay filled her nostrils, and every rustle made her freeze, certain discovery was imminent.

Through the gaps in her makeshift shelter, she could hear Lockwood's increasingly frustrated shouts growing more distant. Good. Let them search the fields and woods while she hid in plain sight.

But hiding wouldn't get her back to London. Wouldn't get her back to Lucien.

Courtney's mind raced as she assessed her situation with the cold logic her brother had taught her during their childhood war games. Assets: she was free, unguarded, and her captors were searching in the wrong direction. Liabilities: her hands were still bound, she was miles from help, and once they realized their error, they would search more systematically.

She needed transportation. A horse would be fastest, but the ostlers were still about their business, and a lady attempting to steal a mount would certainly be noticed and stopped. Unless…

The sound of approaching hoofbeats made her burrow deeper into the straw. Through a gap, she watched a well-dressed gentleman dismount from a fine bay gelding. The man was clearly a patron of the inn—his clothes spoke of quality, his manner suggested someone accustomed to good service.

More importantly, he left his horse saddled.

"See to it that he's watered and ready," the gentleman instructed one of the ostlers, tossing a coin that glinted in the torchlight. "I'll not be long. Just enough time for a proper meal and perhaps a bottle of that excellent burgundy you keep in your private stores."

The ostler grinned and pocketed the coin. "Aye, sir. An hour or two then?"

"At least," the gentleman confirmed, already striding toward the inn's welcoming lights. "No rush at all."

Courtney's pulse quickened. An hour. More than enough time to put significant distance between herself and her captors, assuming she could manage to mount with her hands bound.

She waited, counting slowly to one hundred, then two hundred, until she was certain the gentleman was well settled inside. The bay stood patiently near the mounting block, occasionally stamping or tossing his head, but showing none of the nervous energy that would make him difficult to manage.

Carefully, she began to extricate herself from the straw pile, moving with the patience her brother Julian had drilled into her during their childhood games of hide-and-seek. Every movement was deliberate, calculated to minimize noise.

A piece of straw caught in her hair made her freeze as it scratched against the pile. In the distance, she could hear Lockwood's voice, closer now than it had been moments before.

"She can't have gone far," he was saying, and the fury in his tone made her blood run cold. "The stupid chit has her hands bound. She's probably cowering behind some tree, waiting for rescue that will never come." He made his way into the darkness behind the barn."

If only he knew how wrong he was.

Courtney emerged from the straw pile like a ghost, her yellow dress now thoroughly stained with dirt and bits of hay. The bay turned his head toward her, ears pricked with curiosity but showing no alarm. Good—a calm temperament would be essential for what she was about to attempt.

Moving as quietly as possible, she approached the horse, speaking in the soft, low tones her father had taught her years ago. "Easy, boy. We're going to help each other, aren't we?"

The bay snorted softly but didn't shy away as she led him toward the mounting block. With her hands bound behind her back, conventional mounting was impossible, but years of unconventional riding lessons with Lucien had taught her alternative methods.

Using the mounting block for leverage, she managed to get her left foot into the stirrup. The angle was awkward, painful, making her shoulder scream in protest as she twisted to accommodate her bound hands. For a terrifying moment, she thought she might not have the strength, that she would fall and alert everyone to her presence.

Then she thought of Lucien—of his face when he discovered she was gone, of the self-recrimination that would consume him, of Ava-Marie losing another mother figure to violence. The images gave her strength she didn't know she possessed.

With a combination of momentum, desperation, and pure determination, she hauled herself into the saddle. The bay danced nervously beneath her, sensing her tension, but she managed to get herself seated securely.

Now for the most dangerous part. Taking the reins in her teeth—an undignified but necessary expedient—she managed to work them around until she could grasp them awkwardly behind her back. Not ideal, but workable.

"Good boy," she whispered, patting the bay's neck with her bound hands. "Now let's see how fast you can run. I hope you're not too tired."

She dug her heels into the horse's sides, and he responded immediately, leaping forward with an eagerness that suggested he was as ready to leave this place as she was. They burst from behind the stables at a full gallop, hooves striking sparks from the cobblestones.

Shouts erupted from every direction as stable hands and patrons scattered from the path of the charging horse. She heard Lockwood's voice rise above the commotion, finally realizing that his quarry had outmaneuvered him completely.

"Stop her! She's stolen a horse! Twenty pounds to the man who brings her back!"

But Courtney was already through the inn's gates, the bay's powerful stride eating up the ground as they raced back down the Great North Road toward London—toward Lucien—toward safety.

The wind whipped her hair free of its remaining pins, and tears streamed from her eyes at the exhilarating speed of their flight. Behind her, she could hear the frantic sounds of men scrambling to mount pursuit, but she had precious minutes of lead time.

More importantly, she was riding toward help, while they would have to follow her route exactly. Every moment they spent organizing pursuit was another moment closer to potential rescue.

Hold on, she told herself as the bay's hooves drummed against the packed earth of the road. *Hold on and ride like your life depends on it.*

Because it did. And for the first time since Lockwood had smashed through her father's terrace doors, Lady Courtney Montague felt truly, gloriously alive.

CHAPTER TWENTY-THREE

LUCIEN WAS TIRED. He'd not really slept the night before, spending pleasurable hours in Courtney's bed, but the tension strumming through him kept his eyes from closing.

The thunder of eight horses' hooves against the packed earth of the Great North Road had become a rhythm in Lucien's blood—relentless, desperate, driving him forward through the moonlit night. Thank God it was a full moon on a clear night, or they'd see nothing.

His horse's flanks were lathered with sweat, but the animal seemed to sense his rider's urgency and maintained its punishing pace without complaint.

Beside him, the Duke of Blackstone rode with the grim determination of a man who had already lost everything that mattered. Behind them, Rockwell, Wolf, Julian, Tarquin, Fane, and Axton formed a formidable hunting party that would have intimidated any sensible criminal.

But Lockwood had proven himself far from sensible.

They had been riding hard for hours, stopping only to change horses at coaching inns where they learned that a carriage matching Lockwood's description had indeed passed through. Each confirmation drove Lucien harder—they were on the right track, but were they gaining ground?

Now, as the first pale light of dawn began to creep across the horizon, Lucien's eyes swept the road ahead with desperate intensity. Every shadow might conceal danger. Every bend in the road could bring them face to face with their quarry.

"There!" Julian's sharp cry cut through the morning air. "On the right side of the road!"

Lucien's heart stopped as he saw what had caught Julian's attention—a dark shape crumpled in the tall grass beside the road, partially hidden by the shadow of an ancient oak. Even from a distance, he could see the pale yellow of what looked like a woman's dress.

Was it her? Please let it be her and God let her be alive! "Courtney!" The name tore from his throat as he urged his horse forward, the others thundering behind him.

He was off his mount before the animal had fully stopped, his boots hitting the ground at a run. The sight that greeted him made his chest constrict with a mixture of relief and terror.

Courtney lay motionless on her side, her yellow morning dress torn and stained with grass and dirt. Her auburn hair had come completely free of its pins and spread around her like a halo, with bits of leaves and twigs caught in the tangled strands. Her hands were still bound behind her back with rope that had chafed her wrists raw, and there was a livid bruise forming along her left temple.

But she was breathing. Her chest rose and fell with reassuring regularity, and as Lucien dropped to his knees beside her, her eyelids fluttered.

"Courtney," he said softly, his hands hovering over her as he tried to assess her injuries without moving her. "Can you hear me, love?"

Her eyes opened slowly, unfocused and confused. When her gaze found his face, she blinked several times as if trying to make sense of what she was seeing.

"Lucien?" Her voice was barely a whisper, slurred with confusion. "You're…you're here. I knew you'd come for me. You must find my horse. He must be frightened…he saved me…"

"What horse, darling?" he asked gently, even as Julian worked to cut the ropes binding her wrists. The relief of finding her alive was so overwhelming he could barely think straight.

"The bay," she said, her words still not quite connecting properly. "I took the gelding from the inn. Not my horse. Fast horse. Very fast. But the rabbit…" She trailed off, her eyes losing focus again.

Lucien exchanged a sharp glance with Rockwell. She had escaped. Somehow, his brave, brilliant Courtney had gotten away from Lockwood and been trying to reach them.

"She's not making sense," Tarquin said grimly, kneeling on her other side. "Head injury, most likely. When did you fall, Court? How long have you been here?"

Courtney tried to sit up, but Lucien gently pressed her back down. "The rabbit ran right in front of us," she said, her voice stronger but still disoriented. "Scared him. The horse shied and I…my hands were tied, I couldn't…" She looked at her freed wrists in bewilderment. "They were tied. I couldn't hold on."

"A rabbit spooked your horse," Rockwell said, understanding dawning in his voice. "You were thrown."

"The straw," Courtney continued, her narrative jumping erratically. "I hid in the straw pile. They looked in the fields. Wrong direction." A small, triumphant smile crossed her bruised face. "I fooled them."

"Yes, you did," Lucien said, his throat tight with emotion and pride. His brave, clever Courtney had not only escaped her captors but had managed to steal a horse and ride toward help. "You magnificent, brilliant woman."

Julian had produced a flask and was helping her take small sips. "How long ago did you escape, Court? Do you know where Lockwood is now?"

"Behind me," she said, some clarity returning to her eyes as the water helped clear her head. "They'll be searching for me. They'll be so angry…" Fear flickered across her face. "Ashley. Is Ashley—?"

"She's alive," Blackstone assured her, his voice gentler than Lucien had ever heard it. "Injured, but alive. She's the one who told us you'd been taken."

Tears of relief filled Courtney's eyes. "I tried to run sooner, but he said he'd hurt innocent people if I called for help. He killed Kitty. And Mrs. Bellamy. I heard him talking with his men—"

"We know," Lucien said softly, brushing dirt and leaves from her hair. "We found Kitty. I'm so sorry."

The grief that flashed across Blackstone's face was quickly buried beneath cold fury, but Courtney saw it. "Your Grace, I'm sorry."

"She was a good woman," Blackstone said simply, his hands clenched into fists at his sides.

Axton, who had been examining the ground nearby, called out softly, "There's a bay horse about fifty yards that way, standing calm as you please near those trees. Probably wondering where his rider went. I'll go fetch him."

"That's him," Courtney said with more clarity. "Good horse. Saved my life until the rabbit…"

Fane, who had been scanning the road behind them, suddenly straightened in his saddle. "We have company," he announced grimly. "Three riders, coming fast from the north."

Lucien's head snapped up, his hand instinctively moving to the pistol at his side. In the distance, he could see dust rising from the road—Lockwood and his men, having apparently realized their quarry had doubled back.

"Can you ride?" he asked Courtney urgently, helping her sit up properly. "We need to get you away from here."

She struggled to focus, her head obviously still spinning from her fall. "I think so. But slowly. Everything's…tilting."

"No time for slowly," Wolf said tersely, watching the approaching riders. "They'll be in pistol range in minutes."

"Julian, Tarquin, get your sister to safety," Lucien commanded, his voice taking on the authoritative tone of his military training. "The rest of us will handle Lockwood."

"No." Courtney's hand shot out to grasp his coat, her grip surprisingly strong despite her injuries. "He's killed two people,

Lucien. He has nothing left to lose. If you confront him here—"

"We outnumber him eight to three," he said to reassure her, and she nodded, letting go of his coat and falling back exhausted in his arms.

"He won't get the chance to hurt anyone else," Blackstone said with deadly calm, checking the priming on his pistol. "Some debts can only be paid in blood."

The approaching riders were close enough now that individual figures could be distinguished. Lockwood in the lead, his face twisted with rage, flanked by his two surviving thugs. All three had pistols drawn. The three men reined in their horses upon seeing the force facing them. The silence lengthened as they sat staring until a shot rang out next to Lucien's head.

The duke fired upon Lockwood, his intent clear. "I'm coming for you, Lockwood. Kitty told me it was you who shot her and you will pay," he yelled, and before the men could stop him, the duke mounted and charged toward the three villains. Axton, Fane, and Wolf quickly followed.

The Duke of Blackstone's war cry echoed across the dawn landscape as he spurred his horse into a thunderous charge, his aristocratic composure finally shattered by grief and rage. Behind him, Axton, Fane, Wolf, and the Montague brothers followed in hot pursuit, leaving Lucien holding Courtney while Rockwell moved to secure the bay horse that had carried her to freedom.

"Your Grace, wait!" Fane shouted, but Blackstone was beyond hearing, beyond reason. The man who had spent his entire life bound by rigid propriety and social expectations had been transformed by love and loss into something primal and dangerous.

Lockwood's eyes widened as he saw the charging nobleman bearing down on him, pistol raised. The baron yanked his horse's reins hard to the left, trying to wheel away from the duke's direct assault, as he took aim and fired on the duke. But Blackstone anticipated the move, and the bullet whizzed harmlessly by. Years of hunting had honed his instincts, and he adjusted his aim with deadly precision and fired again.

The crack of the duke's pistol split the morning air.

Lockwood jerked backward, a crimson bloom spreading across his immaculate waistcoat. His own weapon discharged harmlessly into the air as his nerveless fingers lost their grip. For a moment that seemed suspended in time, he swayed in his saddle, his pale eyes wide with shock and the dawning realization that his schemes had finally caught up with him.

"That was for Kitty," Blackstone said coldly, his voice carrying clearly across the distance between them.

Lockwood's mouth opened as if to speak, but only blood emerged. He toppled from his horse, hitting the ground with a dull thud that spoke of finality. The man who had terrorized Courtney, murdered two innocent women, and torn apart so many lives lay motionless in the dust of the Great North Road.

His two remaining companions—Briggs and Murphy—found themselves suddenly facing five armed gentlemen with no escape route. Briggs, the scarred veteran, raised his hands slowly, his street-smart instincts telling him that resistance would only lead to a quick death. Murphy, younger and more impulsive, swung his pistol toward the duke, but Wolf was faster.

"I wouldn't," Wolf said conversationally, his own weapon trained on Murphy's chest. "You're outnumbered and outclassed. Surrender now, and you might live to see trial."

"We ain't done nothing," Briggs protested, though his eyes darted nervously between the mounted gentlemen surrounding him. "Just following orders, we were."

"Orders to kidnap a lady?" Tarquin's voice was ice-cold with controlled fury. "Orders to help commit murder?"

"We didn't kill nobody," Murphy said quickly, his youth making him eager to distance himself from the more serious charges. "That was all Lockwood. He paid us to grab the lady, nothing more."

Fane dismounted smoothly, keeping his pistol trained on the two men. "Axton, help me search them for weapons. We'll need rope to secure them properly."

As the younger men worked to disarm and bind Lockwood's thugs, Julian examined the baron's body with professional thoroughness. "He's dead," he announced grimly. "Shot through the heart. The duke's aim was true."

Blackstone sat motionless on his horse, staring down at Lockwood's corpse with an expression that mixed satisfaction with profound emptiness. The woman he'd loved had been avenged, but vengeance, he was discovering, was a hollow comfort when measured against loss.

"Your Grace," Wolf said gently, approaching the duke's horse. "We need to decide how to handle this. There will be questions, investigations—"

"Let them come," Blackstone replied flatly. "I killed him in self-defense. He shot at me as I tried to apprehend him for the kidnapping of Lady Courtney and for Kitty's murder. I'll answer for my actions to any magistrate in England."

"It won't come to that," Tarquin interjected with the smooth confidence of a seasoned politician. "Lockwood was a known criminal who had just committed kidnapping and murder. Any reasonable magistrate will see this as justifiable killing in the course of preventing further crimes."

Meanwhile, Briggs and Murphy found themselves bound hand and foot, their weapons confiscated and their immediate future looking decidedly grim. Briggs, with the pragmatism of a career criminal, had begun calculating the benefits of cooperation.

"Look, gents," he said, his voice taking on a wheedling tone. "We're just hired muscle, right? Lockwood paid us to do a job, but we ain't murderers. We can tell you everything—where he was planning to take the lady, who else might've been involved, that kind of thing…"

"You helped kidnap her," Julian said coldly. "You're accessories to attempted rape and forced marriage. That's enough to see you transported, if not hanged."

Murphy, younger and more emotional, began to panic. "It wasn't supposed to go like this! He said it was just a business arrangement, that the lady would understand once they were married. He never said nothing about killing nobody!"

"But you knew she was unwilling," Axton pointed out, checking the ropes binding the prisoners. "You heard her screaming, saw her fighting. That didn't give you pause?"

"We needed the money," Briggs said simply, though shame flickered in his eyes. "Times are hard for men like us. We don't get to be choosy about our work."

Fane studied the two bound men with the calculating gaze of someone well-versed in London's criminal underworld. "What did Lockwood tell you about his plans after Scotland? Surely, he had contingencies in case the lady's family refused to pay?"

Briggs and Murphy exchanged nervous glances. Finally, Briggs spoke. "He talked about taking her abroad if things went bad. Said there were places a man could disappear with a woman and never be found."

The casual mention of what amounted to permanent abduction made Tarquin's jaw clench with renewed anger. "Where? What places?"

"The Americas. He had contacts, he said. Men who'd help for the right price." Murphy's voice shook as he realized how completely he'd been drawn into Lockwood's web of criminality.

Wolf began searching through Lockwood's saddlebags while the others secured the prisoners. Among the baron's effects, he found several items of interest: a substantial amount of gold coins, documents that appeared to be forged travel papers, and most damning of all, a blood-stained knife wrapped in cloth.

"Gentlemen," Wolf called, holding up the wrapped blade. "I believe we've found the weapon used on Kitty."

Blackstone's face went utterly white at the sight, his hands tightening on his reins until his knuckles stood out starkly. "That bastard," he whispered. "He carried her blood with him like a trophy."

"Which makes this even more clearly a case of justified killing," Tarquin observed with grim satisfaction. "Lockwood was armed and dangerous, with physical evidence of recent murder on his person."

As the immediate crisis settled into the more mundane business of dealing with prisoners and evidence, the group's attention turned to the more pressing matter of Courtney's condition. She remained conscious but clearly struggling with the effects of her head injury and the trauma of her ordeal.

Rockwell had managed to calm the bay horse, and now he approached Lucien with practiced efficiency. "We need to get her back to London and try to contain this scandal. The longer we stay here, the more questions we'll face from local authorities."

"Can she ride?" Lucien asked, his voice tight with concern as he studied Courtney's pale face.

"With support," Rockwell replied. "I'll help you mount, and you can hold her. My horse is the steadiest of the lot—he won't spook or bolt. I'll ride this bay."

Courtney stirred in Lucien's arms, her amber eyes focusing on his face with obvious effort. "I can ride," she said, though her voice was still somewhat slurred. "I won't slow you down."

"You could never slow me down," Lucien replied fiercely. "You're the strongest, bravest woman I've ever known. What you did today—escaping from them, stealing that horse, riding toward help—it was extraordinary."

A weak smile crossed her lips. "I had good motivation. I knew you'd come for me."

"Always," he promised, pressing a gentle kiss to her forehead. "I'll always come for you."

Rockwell brought his horse alongside where Lucien knelt with Courtney. The animal stood patient and steady, well-trained and responsive to its master's commands. "Up you go," Rockwell said, offering his hands to help Lucien mount while still supporting Courtney.

The process was awkward and careful, with Lucien settling

into the saddle before Rockwell carefully lifted Courtney up to him. She gasped softly at the movement, her head obviously still paining her, but she managed to lean back against Lucien's chest with evident relief.

"There," Lucien murmured against her hair. "I've got you. You're safe now."

Meanwhile, the practical business of dealing with their prisoners continued. Fane and Axton had fashioned a travois from broken branches and their own cloaks to transport Lockwood's body—they couldn't simply leave it by the roadside, and they would need it as evidence of what had transpired.

"What about these two?" Julian asked, nodding toward Briggs and Murphy, who sat bound and miserable in the morning sun.

"We take them to the nearest magistrate," Tarquin replied. "Let them answer for their crimes properly. Their testimony about Lockwood's plans and methods might be valuable in closing this case completely."

Blackstone, who had remained silent through most of these arrangements, finally spoke. "I'll escort the prisoners myself. I want to ensure they reach the authorities safely."

"Your Grace," Wolf said carefully, "are you certain that's wise? You've just killed a man, however justified it might have been. Perhaps it would be better—think of the scandal."

"For once, scandal be damned," Blackstone said, cutting him off. "I'll protect Courtney's name from any scandal. This will only be about Kitty's murder. There is no need for anyone to find out about Lady Courtney's abduction."

"Thank you, your grace," Lucien said.

"You shot him because he shot at you, Blackstone," Fane assured him. "What you did was completely justified. But the social ramifications…"

"Thank you," the duke replied with quiet vehemence. "I won't forget your support."

The raw grief in his voice made even the hardened criminals shift uncomfortably. Here was a man who had lost everything that mattered to him and found that revenge provided no real comfort.

As they prepared to separate, the main group heading back to London with Courtney, while others dealt with prisoners and evidence, Rockwell approached Blackstone one final time. "The word of a duke won't be disputed. You should do all the talking with the magistrate."

With final arrangements made, the group began to disperse. Fane and Axton took charge of the prisoners, while Julian and Tarquin flanked Lucien and Courtney for the ride back to London. Wolf remained with Blackstone to help manage Lockwood's body and coordinate with the local magistrate.

As Rockwell's steady horse began the long journey south, Courtney settled more comfortably against Lucien's chest. The rhythmic motion of the horse's gait seemed to ease her discomfort somewhat, and color was slowly returning to her pale cheeks.

"It's over," Lucien said quietly, his arms tightening protectively around her. "He can't hurt you anymore. He can't hurt anyone anymore."

"I know," she replied, her voice growing stronger as they put distance between themselves and the scene of Lockwood's death. "Your—our—secret is safe." He pressed a kiss to her forehead and wondered what price they all might have paid, and that perhaps secrets were dangerous. He had some thinking to do.

She was quiet for several minutes, watching the countryside roll past as they rode. Finally, she spoke again. "When I was hiding in that straw pile, when I thought I might never see you again, I realized something important."

"What's that?"

"I don't care what society thinks about Ava-Marie's birth. I don't care if they whisper about your time in Ireland or question our marriage. All that matters is that we're together, that we're building a life based on truth and love." She turned her head to look up at him. "You don't have to carry those secrets anymore, Lucien. We're stronger than whatever scandal they might create."

Relief flooded through him—relief so profound it left him momentarily speechless. He had been dreading the eventual revelation of Ava-Marie's illegitimacy, had been planning strategies to manage the social fallout. But Courtney was right. Their love, their family, was stronger than society's judgment.

"You took the words out of my mouth. I love you," he said suddenly, the words emerging with startling clarity and conviction. "Not because I'm supposed to, not because we were engaged before, but because of who you are now. Because of your courage, your compassion, your incredible strength. I love you, Courtney Montague, and I want to spend the rest of my life proving myself worthy of that love."

Tears filled her eyes, but they were tears of joy rather than sorrow. "I love you too," she whispered. "The man you are now, the father you've become, the partner you're choosing to be. We're going to be so happy together, Lucien. All of us—you, me, and Ava-Marie and our children."

Before them, London's spires were beginning to appear on the horizon, promising safety, healing, and the beginning of their new life together. The ordeal was finally over, and their future stretched ahead bright with possibility.

As they rode toward home, Lucien found himself thinking not of the past or its secrets, but of tomorrow and all the tomorrows to come. Whatever challenges lay ahead, they would face them together—honestly, bravely, and with love as their foundation.

With Courtney in his arms, a vision of his future—a vision of a *happy* future—filled him, and Lucien finally felt as if he were home. He knew exactly who he was and where he fit in this world. And he knew the woman who fitted with him was safely in his arms. He'd never let her go again.

EPILOGUE

Six weeks after Baron Lockwood's death on the Great North Road, London society had found new scandals to occupy its attention. The official account—that the baron had been killed while resisting arrest for the killing of two women—had been accepted without question. The Duke of Blackstone's word carried sufficient weight that no magistrate dared question his account of self-defense, and the transportation sentences handed down to Briggs and Murphy had closed the matter definitively.

What society didn't know, and never would, was the detail that a small gathering in the Earl of Danvers' library had sworn to keep secret—the truth about Ava-Marie's birth.

Lucien stood by the window, watching his daughter play in the garden with Lauren while the adults conducted their serious business inside. The decision had been unanimous—the secret would remain within the family circle for now, but if it ever came to light, they would face it together rather than allow anyone to use it as a weapon against them.

"It's decided then," the Marquess of Lorne said, his authoritative voice bringing the meeting to a close. "The truth remains among us, but we won't live in fear of its discovery. If it comes out, we weather the storm together."

Tarquin nodded his agreement. "Better to control the narrative ourselves than let others twist it against us."

Farah, seated beside Rockwell on the settee, spoke up. "Ava-Marie deserves to know the truth when she's old enough to understand it. But that's years away yet."

"She'll know," Lucien assured them, his voice firm. "But she'll also know that her legitimacy in the eyes of society matters far less than her legitimacy in the eyes of those who love her."

The meeting dispersed with embraces and promises of continued support. As the families prepared to leave, Courtney approached Lucien at the window, slipping her hand into his.

"Tomorrow," she said softly, "we'll be married."

He turned to face her, marveling as he did each day at the miracle of her presence in his life once again. "Tomorrow, you'll become my wife in truth, not just in my heart."

"I've been yours in truth for so many years," she replied, reaching up to straighten his cravat. "Tomorrow is simply making it official."

Their wedding at Westminster Abbey the following morning was a magnificent affair that drew half of London society. Courtney walked down the aisle on her father's arm, radiant in ivory silk and her grandmother's pearls, while Lucien waited at the altar with Ava-Marie beside him as a flower girl, her dark curls crowned with a wreath of roses.

The archbishop's voice echoed through the ancient stones as he pronounced them husband and wife, and when Lucien kissed his bride, the assembled guests erupted in applause that seemed to shake the very rafters.

But it was the reception that evening at Blackstone House that would be remembered long after the wedding itself had faded from memory.

The Duke of Blackstone had insisted on hosting the wedding ball, claiming it was his honor for his friend. What he hadn't admitted was that the elaborate celebration was also his way of trying to forget he'd lost Kitty. A woman who he shouldn't have loved, but had.

Blackstone House glittered like a jewel in the London night, every window blazing with candlelight, the gardens transformed into a fairy wonderland with thousands of paper lanterns strung between the trees. The ballroom overflowed with the cream of society, all eager to celebrate the romantic conclusion to what many considered the most dramatic courtship of the season. A wedding that should have occurred five years ago.

Lucien and Courtney moved through their first dance as husband and wife with perfect synchronization, lost in each other's eyes despite the hundreds of guests watching their every move.

"No regrets?" Lucien murmured as he spun her through a turn.

"Only that we lost so much time," she replied, her amber eyes sparkling with happiness. "But we have the rest of our lives to make up for it."

Ava-Marie, resplendent in a miniature version of her new stepmother's gown, watched from the sidelines with barely contained excitement. Neither of them cared that it really wasn't appropriate for Ava-Marie to be there. Society had best get used to Lucien's ways.

When the dance ended, she rushed forward to claim her turn with her father, causing the assembled guests to "aww" collectively as Lucien swept his daughter into his arms for an impromptu waltz.

As the evening progressed, the Duke of Blackstone made his way steadily through what appeared to be several bottles of his finest brandy. His grief for Kitty, carefully hidden behind aristocratic composure during the day, seemed to manifest itself in increasingly reckless drinking as the night wore on.

Lady Ashley Ware noticed his condition when she stepped onto the terrace for a breath of fresh air, needing respite from the crowded ballroom and the pitying looks that still followed her wherever she went in society. Her own scandal from three years past had never quite been forgotten, and events like this reminded her acutely of her diminished status.

She'd never seen His Grace drunk. Had never seen him with a hair out of place or showing any weakness. Perhaps he was human after all. When she heard His Grace stumble and curse, followed by a loud crash, she knew she should simply get one of the stuffy duke's servants, but Courtney had told her of Kitty's death. Being a kind person, she realized the duke was hurting. That was why the normally composed and correct man was drunk. She decided to help him.

Moving further into the garden, she found the duke slumped on a stone bench in a secluded corner, his usually immaculate appearance disheveled, his dark hair falling across his forehead. In the moonlight, he looked younger somehow, more vulnerable than she'd ever seen him.

"Your Grace?" she approached cautiously, concerned despite their history of mutual dislike. Due to her scandal, the duke considered her a bad influence on his sister Farah. Before her marriage to Rockwell, Farah had never been allowed to enter their house, for example. And he'd barely acknowledged her presence if they were in the same room. "Are you quite well?"

He looked up at her with eyes that held a grief so profound it took her breath away. "Lady Ashley," he said, his voice slurred but still recognizably aristocratic. "Come to witness the mighty fall?"

"I came for air," she replied honestly, studying his face with growing concern. "But I can see you're…unwell. Perhaps I should call for someone—"

"No." The word came out sharper than he'd intended, and he visibly struggled to moderate his tone. "No one else. They've all seen enough of my…weakness."

Ashley had intended only to check on the duke's welfare—a simple act of kindness from one wounded soul to another. But as she sat beside him on the stone bench, listening to his raw confession of grief, something fundamental shifted between them.

"Everything is about her," Blackstone whispered, his usual aristocratic reserve stripped away by brandy and anguish. "Every breath, every heartbeat, every waking moment. She's gone, and

I... I don't know how to exist without her."

The naked pain in his voice struck something deep in Ashley's chest. For three years, she had been defined by her scandal, reduced to a cautionary tale whispered about in drawing rooms. But here was the Duke of Blackstone—the man who had cut her dead at countless social events, who had looked through her as if she were invisible—revealing himself to be as broken as she was.

"I'm sorry," she said softly, her anger at his past treatment of her dissolving in the face of his genuine anguish. "I know what it's like to lose someone you love."

"Do you?" He turned to look at her properly for the first time, taking in her face in the moonlight. Without his usual mask of aristocratic disdain, he looked younger, more vulnerable. "I'd forgotten...your scandal. A love affair gone wrong."

The familiar sting of that assumption—that she had been some naive girl seduced and abandoned—rose in her throat. But tonight, with grief hanging between them like morning mist, the old defensive anger seemed pointless.

"It wasn't quite what everyone believes," she said carefully. "But the consequences were...severe."

His jaw tightened with unexpected anger on her behalf. "Society is cruel to women who dare to feel, to want, to love. You deserved better than their judgment."

"Did I?" Ashley's laugh held three years of accumulated bitterness. "I've been a cautionary tale for so long, I've almost forgotten what it felt like to be anything else."

"You were nineteen," he said, leaning closer. In the moonlight, his dark eyes held something she'd never seen before—compassion, understanding, recognition of shared pain. "Nineteen and caught up in circumstances beyond your control. What crime is that?"

The gentleness in his voice, so at odds with the cold disapproval she'd grown accustomed to from him, cracked something inside her chest. When he reached out to touch her cheek, she didn't pull away.

"You're not alone," he said quietly. "You don't have to carry this burden alone anymore."

Three years of careful composure of maintaining dignity in the face of whispers and snubs, suddenly crumbled. The tears came without warning, great gulping sobs that she tried desperately to muffle against his shoulder as his arms came around her.

"Shh," he murmured, his voice infinitely gentle. "Let it out. You're safe here."

Safe. When was the last time anyone had made her feel safe? When was the last time someone had held her without judgment, without calculation of what association with her might cost them?

When he tilted her face up to his, his thumb brushing away her tears, Ashley saw her own loneliness reflected in his eyes. Two people who had been surviving rather than living, finding unexpected solace in each other's pain.

The kiss, when it came, was born of desperation rather than passion—two drowning souls reaching for something, anything, to anchor them to hope. His lips were warm against hers, tasting of brandy and grief, and she kissed him back with equal fervor, pouring three years of isolation and loneliness into that single moment of connection.

Time seemed suspended in the moonlit garden. The distant sounds of celebration faded away, leaving only the whisper of wind through the trees and the thundering of her own heartbeat. This was madness—kissing the Duke of Blackstone, the man who had been her harshest judge, in a garden where anyone might see them.

But for these stolen moments, Ashley allowed herself to forget consequences, to forget propriety, to forget everything except the warmth of his embrace and the desperate comfort they offered each other.

It was the shocked gasp that brought reality crashing back.

"Good God!"

They sprang apart as if burned, Ashley's hands flying to her disheveled hair while Blackstone struggled to straighten his cravat. Lord Pemberton stood at the entrance to their secluded alcove, his wife and two other society matrons gaping behind him like carrion birds who had discovered a particularly choice piece of scandal.

The Duke of Blackstone, disheveled and clearly intoxicated, caught in a passionate embrace with the notorious Lady Ashley Ware. In a garden. At the most prominent wedding of the season. With witnesses.

Ashley felt the blood drain from her face as the full magnitude of her situation crashed over her. This wasn't merely another scandal—this was complete and utter ruin. No amount of careful behavior, no years of quiet dignity, could overcome being caught in such a compromising position.

"I…we…" she stammered, her mind reeling as she tried to find words that might somehow salvage this disaster.

But Blackstone had already risen to his feet, his aristocratic composure sliding back into place despite his obvious intoxication. When he offered her his arm with perfect propriety, as if they hadn't just been discovered in the most compromising circumstances imaginable, Ashley could only stare at him in bewilderment.

"Lord Pemberton," he said with icy politeness. "Lady Pemberton. I trust you're enjoying the wedding festivities."

The casual tone, as if nothing untoward had occurred, seemed to momentarily nonplus their audience. But Ashley could see the gleeful calculation in Lady Pemberton's eyes, could practically hear the scandal being refined into its most damaging form.

By tomorrow morning, all of London would know. By tomorrow evening, she would be completely ostracized, and the Duke of Blackstone's reputation would suffer considerably by association.

As Blackstone escorted her back toward the ballroom, Ashley's mind raced through her limited options. She could flee

London entirely, perhaps to Scotland or Ireland, where her notoriety hadn't yet penetrated. She could throw herself on her brother's mercy and hope he would find some remote corner of one of his estates where she could live in quiet exile.

Or she could face the scandal head-on and brazen it out, though she doubted even her courage was equal to that task.

What she hadn't expected was Blackstone's calm pronouncement when Wolf appeared at their side.

"Lord Wolfarth," the duke said without preamble, "I've come to request your sister's hand in marriage."

The silence that followed was absolute. Never in a crowded ballroom had the absence of sound been so complete, so thunderous. Ashley felt the world tilt around her as she realized what he had just done.

Marriage. To the Duke of Blackstone. The man who had spent three years treating her as if she were invisible, who had judged her harshly for circumstances he didn't understand. And now, because of a moment of shared grief and desperate comfort, he was offering to tie himself to her forever.

"I beg your pardon?" she managed to whisper.

"We are to marry," Blackstone repeated, his dark eyes meeting hers with steady resolve. "Why don't we make our way to my study to discuss the arrangements?"

As he guided her through the gaping crowd, Ashley's mind reeled with the implications. This wasn't love—it was honor, duty, the aristocratic response to a compromising situation. But it was also salvation for them both, a way to transform scandal into respectability through the alchemy of marriage.

The question was whether she could bear a lifetime tied to a man who saw her as an obligation rather than a choice, married to someone whose heart lay buried with a red-haired Irish woman in an unmarked grave.

Soon, they were all seated in his study with the door firmly closed.

"I can't believe this," Wolf said harshly, finding his voice at last. "How did you let this happen, Blackstone. You compromised my sister, and now you're doing what honor demands."

"Honor has very little to do with it," the duke replied coolly. "I'm offering marriage because it's what Lady Ashley deserves—protection, position, and the respect of my name."

Ashley sank into a chair, overwhelmed by the sudden turn her life had taken. Marriage to the Duke of Blackstone—the man she'd spent three years viewing as the embodiment of everything judgmental and cruel about society.

"I don't understand," she said faintly. "Last night, you were grieving another woman. Tonight, you were drunk, not thinking clearly. Surely in the morning—"

"The morning won't change anything," Blackstone interrupted. "A second scandal will destroy you and Lady Ivy."

Wolf stepped forward, his protective instincts overriding his confusion. "My sister doesn't need your pity, Your Grace."

"It's not pity," Blackstone said firmly. "It's the honorable thing to do and you know it."

Ashley looked up at him, searching his face for any sign of the tenderness she'd glimpsed in the garden. What she saw instead was resolve, determination, and something that might have been hope.

"A marriage of convenience?" she said quietly.

"Yes," he agreed honestly.

Wolf looked between them, his anger gradually giving way to understanding. "You're serious about this."

"Completely serious," Blackstone confirmed. "Lady Ashley will have the protection of my name, title and money. She will have my homes to manage and have a life of luxury."

"And if I refuse?" Ashley asked, though she already knew the answer.

Wolf's expression grew grim. "You don't have that luxury, Ashley. If you don't marry him, you'll be completely ostracized. No invitations, no social standing, no prospects whatsoever. And think of Ivy. She'll be ruined too."

"Your brother is correct," Blackstone said gently. "I'm afraid I've left you with very little choice. But I promise you this—as my wife, you'll be treated with every courtesy and respect. You'll want for nothing, and no one will dare to slight you again."

Ashley closed her eyes, feeling the walls of her carefully constructed life crumbling around her. Three years of exile had been difficult enough, but at least she'd retained some small measure of independence. Marriage to the duke would mean trading that independence for security and status, binding herself to a man who saw her as an obligation rather than a choice.

But what alternative did she have? Ivy—she had to protect her younger sister who was already tarnished by association.

"Very well," she said finally, opening her eyes to meet his steady gaze. "I accept your proposal, Your Grace."

Something flickered across Blackstone's features—relief, perhaps, or satisfaction. "Thank you," he said simply. "I promise you won't regret this decision."

"Won't I?" Ashley rose from her chair, gathering what remained of her dignity around her like armor. "I will hold you to those words, your Grace."

As Wolf and Ashley took their leave, with Wolf promising to call again later to discuss the arrangements, Ashley wanted to crawl into her bed and cry.

"You could do worse," her brother said finally, his voice gentler than it had been. "He's wealthy, titled, and despite everything, he has a reputation for treating women with respect."

"He's also in love with a dead woman," Ashley replied quietly. "Marriage lasts a lifetime." How lonely would she be?

"You'll have your children," Wolf suggested. "And society to rule over."

Her stomach clenched. Children—oh my god, she'd have to share his bed. An unexpected wave of heat washed over her. Why was that thought not terrifying?

Ashley turned to look out the window of the carriage; she'd stopped dreaming of a happy ever after when her first scandal broke. She'd had dreams of spinsterhood and being the best aunt she could be. Those dreams seemed very far away now. Never had she foreseen marrying—let alone the Duke of Blackstone.

"I suppose it doesn't matter what I want," she said softly. "This is my life now. Duchess of Blackstone, wife to a man who sees me as a duty to be discharged rather than a woman to be loved."

Wolf placed a gentle hand on her shoulder. "Love can grow, Ashley. Sometimes the strongest marriages are built on respect and understanding rather than passion."

"Can they?" She leaned into her brother's comfort, drawing strength from his steady presence. "I suppose I'll find out, won't I?"

THE END

About the Author

USA Today bestselling author, Bronwen Evans grew up loving books. She writes both historical sexy romances for the modern woman who likes intelligent, spirited heroines, and compassionate alpha heroes. Evans is a three-time winner of the RomCon Readers' Crown and has been nominated for an *RT* Reviewers' Choice Award. She lives in Hawkes Bay, New Zealand with her dogs Brandy and Duke.

You can keep up with Bronwen's news by visiting her website
www.bronwenevans.com
and get a FREE book by signing up to her newsletter
https://bit.ly/3eqYJx0
Or Amazon: amazon.com/stores/Bronwen-
Evans/author/B004LKXYLC
Or Facebook: bronwenevansauthor
Or Goodreads: bronwenevans
Or Bookbub: bookbub.com/authors/bronwen-evans